M000205103

THE WILDFIRE GIRL

BOOKS BY CAROLYN ARNOLD

DETECTIVE AMANDA STEELE SERIES

The Little Grave

Stolen Daughters

The Silent Witness

Black Orchid Girls

Her Frozen Cry

Last Seen Alive

Her Final Breath

Taken Girls

Her Last Words

BRANDON FISHER FBI SERIES

Eleven

Silent Graves

The Defenseless

Blue Baby

Violated

Remnants

On the Count of Three

Past Deeds

One More Kill

DETECTIVE MADISON KNIGHT SERIES

Ties That Bind

Justified

Sacrifice

Found Innocent

Just Cause

Deadly Impulse

In the Line of Duty

Power Struggle

Shades of Justice

What We Bury

Girl on the Run

Her Dark Grave

Murder at the Lake

Life Sentence

Sara and Sean Cozy Mystery series

Bowled Over Americano

Wedding Bells Brew Murder

Matthew Connor Adventure series

City of Gold

The Secret of the Lost Pharaoh

The Legend of Gasparilla and His Treasure

Standalone

Assassination of a Dignitary

Pearls of Deception

Midlife Psychic

CAROLYN ARNOLD

THE WILDFIRE GIRL

bookouture

Published by Bookouture in 2024

An imprint of Storyfire Ltd.
Carmelite House
50 Victoria Embankment
London EC4Y 0DZ

www.bookouture.com

Copyright © Carolyn Arnold, 2024

Carolyn Arnold has asserted her right to be identified
as the author of this work.

All rights reserved. No part of this publication may be reproduced, stored in any
retrieval system, or transmitted, in any form or by any means, electronic,
mechanical, photocopying, recording or otherwise, without the prior written
permission of the publishers.

ISBN: 978-1-83790-936-0
eBook ISBN: 978-1-83790-935-3

This book is a work of fiction. Names, characters, businesses, organizations,
places and events other than those clearly in the public domain, are either the
product of the author's imagination or are used fictitiously. Any resemblance to
actual persons, living or dead, events or locales is entirely coincidental.

Dedicated to Max(imus) the Beagle,
a sweet fur baby who will always be loved and remembered.
Thank you for being such a great Entertain and Inspire Agent!

PROLOGUE

Her head spun, even lying down with her eyes shut. But that made no sense. She'd only had one glass of wine after dinner. He must have found out her plans to leave and drugged her drink.

She tried to move, but her arms and legs were weighed down to the bed.

Smoke and the smell of something burning teased her lungs and had her throat closing in on itself.

Slowly, she was able to wriggle her fingers and toes and open her eyes. They burned in the acrid air, and she couldn't make out much. The only light in the room was dampened moonlight that had fought its way around the curtains. Yet, there was a shadow in the corner of the room. Was it him, sitting there, smoking a cigarette, and taking delight in her terror?

"Why are you doing this?" she called out.

Her petition was met with no response, and as her eyes adjusted to the darkness, she realized her mistake. She was alone. But smoke was billowing under and around the door. The crackling of the flames gave off a vibrational hum as it consumed all in its path. It wouldn't be long before the door itself was devoured by flame. She had to get out of here!

She struggled to get up, her arms and legs finally cooperating, and searched for her cell phone on the nightstand. It wasn't there, though she could have sworn that's where she'd set it before going to bed.

She tried the landline, but there was no dial tone. She followed the cord and found it wasn't plugged in. The jack had been cut off.

He's trying to kill me! Shit! Shit! Shit!

She stumbled to the window and tried to pry it open, but it was sealed shut. She screamed, not that anyone would hear her cries for help. The nearest house was a distance away. Looking down, she contemplated smashing the glass and jumping, but a second-story fall was likely to break bones. At worst, her neck.

A loud boom. She spun around. A beam had sliced through the ceiling and taken out the door. Now there was nothing to stand between her and the hungry flames as they roared and their heat suffocated.

It was either jump out the window or chance going through the fire.

She elbowed the old leaded glass and punched out a hole. But large pointed shards still stuck out from the corners of the frame like rays of sunshine. She pulled off her shirt and wrapped it around her hand, working to pry out the glass. The exertion made it even harder to catch a solid breath.

A coughing fit seized her. All the while, if she didn't work faster, she was certain to die. She looked over her shoulder, hypnotized by the angry flames parading toward her. They ate everything in their path, moving quickly and without mercy.

She had to jump to give herself a chance of surviving. But her vision started to swim. Eventually, her body collapsed, and she slumped against the wall. Her consciousness floated. Only when a searing agony engulfed her body did she jolt awake. Powerless to fight against it, the flames were consuming her flesh. She tried to scream, but the sound stuck in her throat. She sent up a silent prayer that if this was her time she'd go quickly, and he'd pay for what he'd done to her.

ONE

The stench of charred human flesh clung heavily in the morning air. Similar in sweetness to barbecued pork but with a rancid edge. Detective Amanda Steele recognized the smell the second she got out of the department car and started walking toward the crime scene with her partner, Trent Stenson.

It had been nearly three years since they worked a case involving the murders of young women burned alive in fires. But it was offered up on fresh and instant recall. Just like then, strobing lights of police cruisers marked the scene.

The van from the Chief Medical Examiner's Office was already in the parking lot as was the vehicle from Crime Scene. Both came from Manassas, and it was a rare thing when both beat Amanda and Trent to a scene.

The odor intensified the closer she got, but only a very small part of her recoiled. She was a veteran cop at thirty-nine and a generational one. Her father had been the police chief for Prince William County PD, the department for which she now proudly wore the badge.

The body had been found in an alley behind Patriot Plaza in Woodbridge, a few blocks from Central where the

PWCPD's Homicide Unit was stationed. The passage accessed Ingrid Street on one end and a parking lot on the other. That space accommodated parking for customers of the strip mall and a neighboring grocery store.

Officer Wyatt, with notepad and pen in hand, was talking with a man in front of the plaza. He was likely recording everything the civilian was telling him. Amanda would surmise he was the one who had found the body. His arms were awkwardly flailing about, and his face was mostly pale except for his flushed cheeks.

Amanda and Trent would follow up with him after they looked at the scene. They approached the alley from the parking lot. Officer Leo Brandt was posted there, and he dipped his head silently to them in greeting. His job was to ensure no one got past him unless authorized to do so. Just by its nature, an outdoor crime scene was vulnerable to contamination, and precautions were taken where they could be. One of these was reducing foot traffic. Weather also posed a threat and could wash away vital evidence. Thankfully, Mother Nature was on their side today with no rain in the forecast, though that could change. It was May. Warm, balmy, and promising of summer one minute, and chilly and wet the next. So far today, there was a cool breeze, as if spring was getting in one last hoorah before summer arrived next month.

Amanda looked past Officer Brandt toward a green dumpster. Next to it were the medical examiner, his assistant, and two crime scene investigators. She recognized all of them. Hans Rideout, the ME, his assistant, Liam Baker, and CSIs Emma Blair and Isabelle Donnelly. In the murder business, it wasn't long before a bond grew between the regulars. Their presence offered comfort and soothing amid the hostile landscape of a crime scene.

The foursome stood on the other side of the dumpster,

likely where the remains were. The body couldn't be seen from this vantage point.

"Want to bring us up to speed?" Trent said to Leo.

"Sure, no problem. Dispatch sent out units after a nine-one-one call came in at six thirty this morning reporting that burned human remains were found behind the plaza."

Sergeant Malone had called Amanda after seven, which was just over an hour before she was due to start her shift. But with other detectives in the unit working active cases, it left her and Trent. It had been tough leaving her boyfriend, Logan, before breakfast, and even harder not being able to say goodbye to Zoe, her eight-year-old daughter, before she headed out. But duty called.

"He the caller?" Trent butted his head toward Officer Wyatt and the man he was talking with.

"That's right. His name's Benjamin Weaver, and he manages Modern Cellular."

The plaza housed four storefronts, but only three units were currently occupied. Along with the cell phone company, there was a sandwich shop and a nail salon.

"Six thirty seems early for the manager to be showing up," she said. "I'd think they'd open closer to nine, nine thirty?"

"Ten, but apparently, the store is in the middle of a makeover. Paint, shelving, inventory. And it's all running behind schedule. The owner requested Mr. Weaver come in early to get a start on things."

"Manager and reno man?" Trent said. "Rather impressive."

"Maybe? But Weaver didn't sound too thrilled about it. Guess the shop's still open for business too, even as it's undergoing all that."

The manager must be under immense pressure to balance everything, but business owners often failed their employees by expecting more for less. It was a phrase that Amanda despised. Now, while Weaver's presence at the store made sense, it wasn't clear what brought him to the alley. She'd guess the smell, but investigations didn't stand on assumptions. "Why was Weaver back here?"

"That horrid stench."

"I figured but had to ask."

"Well, he came back to investigate that and got the surprise of his life. Just a heads-up. It's not a pleasant sight."

"I can't imagine it would be." It didn't even need to be said. Burned bodies weren't for the faint of heart or queasy of stomach. "Did you run a background on Weaver?"

"Of course." Stated in a nonchalant, almost cheery nature. "No criminal record."

She nodded, not suspecting Weaver at this juncture, but asking was due diligence. "All right, we're off to check things out for ourselves."

Leo waved Amanda and Trent past.

She took shallow breaths as she walked toward Rideout, but another smell hit her above charred flesh. "Gasoline," she said to Trent over her shoulder.

"I smell it too."

Amanda braced herself and rounded the dumpster. But nothing could have prepared her for what she saw.

TWO

Amanda stared at the remains of what had once been a living, breathing person. All that remained was a burned-out husk, mostly sucked dry by flames. The remaining flesh appeared mummified, and the jaw was gaped open as if captured in a scream.

"As you can see, we've got ourselves a crispy critter." Rideout's morgue humor effectively spun a violent death into a moment of levity without coming across as disrespectful of the dead.

Amanda's gaze caught a melted mass of red plastic next to the body.

"We suspect that's what's left of a jerry can," Rideout said, noticing what had grabbed her attention.

"Trent and I were saying we smell gasoline."

"I'd say it's safe to conclude the vic was doused with it."

"While they were alive or were they already dead?" Trent asked, but his voice held an air of hesitancy, like he wasn't quite sure he wanted the answer.

"That I can't tell you until I get the remains back to the morgue and run tests."

"Okay, but if the person was burned alive," Trent began, "I'd think they would have tried to run for help or rolled on the ground. Any evidence of that?"

"No, but that's not entirely telling. Evidence of that could have been destroyed or very hard to determine. Such as in the case he rolled where he'd come to rest."

"He?" Amanda latched on to the fact the ME noted a gender. It might be a generic umbrella, but she suspected it was more than that.

"That's right. I'm confident enough to conclude the victim was a man, and I'd say he was over forty."

"How can you tell all that from *that*?" Trent gestured toward the remains.

"Age, I estimate based on the fact he has silver tooth fillings. Dentists stopped using amalgam in the early nineties on patients under nineteen."

"Now they use a white filling," Trent inserted.

Rideout nodded. "So running with the assumption he was an adult when he needed fillings, he's most likely to be close to fifty or older. As for determining his gender, I ascertained that from the facial structure and overall size. There's also a man's gold wedding band on his ring finger." Rideout added a smile to his latter statement, releasing any illusion he had some magical superpower.

Amanda's heart pinched at the thought the victim was married. Presumably he'd have left behind a spouse, possibly children. She'd been there. The one left behind when her husband and six-year-old daughter had died. It was just two months shy of nine years ago now, but it had been sudden. Even though Amanda was blessed with Logan and Zoe, who she'd adopted a few years ago, they would never take her original family's place. They did help heal her and make her feel whole again though.

"Any wallet or cell phone?" It was likely a long shot, but in the least his loved ones deserved to know what had happened.

Rideout shook his head. "Given the delicate condition of the remains, I'll take care of that once I have him back at the morgue."

It was the ME's fallback position, but Amanda knew better than to argue once Rideout had made up his mind. Not having the victim's ID at the onset was a setback from an investigative standpoint. It stripped them of a suspect pool, leaving them to theorize motives based solely on material evidence before them. "Keep us posted. I assume you'll be working on him right away?"

Rideout gestured toward Liam, his assistant, who managed his schedule.

Liam pecked into a tablet, then said, "There is another autopsy on the docket before this one, so it will be this afternoon for Crispy Critter. I'll text with a time as the day moves along."

The assistant didn't have the same panache as the medical examiner. To hear *Crispy Critter* from his lips soured Amanda's gut. She hoped that wasn't how Liam was entering the autopsy into the calendar.

"Yep. Don't worry. Until then, we'll keep him on ice." Rideout smiled at his joke, not seeming to have noticed his protégé's floundering attempt at morgue humor.

Amanda glanced at Trent to get his reaction and found him staring at the remains. Was it just the grotesqueness of the scene or something more? Rideout spoke before she could question her partner about what seemed to have him spellbound.

"Now, I realize you normally ask for time of death and cause, but it's too early to provide you with either. Once I know, you will."

"Thanks," she said distractedly and watched now as Rideout and Liam skillfully placed the man's remains into a black bag and loaded it onto a wheeled gurney. Rideout gave a salute as they left the alley.

Amanda turned to Trent to find he was now staring into space. "Are you all right over there?" She raised her eyebrows.

"Ah, yeah, I'm fine."

"That wasn't exactly easy to see." She showed empathy, wondering if it would draw him out to share what was obviously bothering him.

"Crispy Critter. Jeez." CSI Emma Blair was shaking her head. "Just slightly insensitive."

"You know Rideout," Amanda said.

"He's one thing, but Liam? That kid should stop trying to emulate his mentor's humor."

That kid was in his late twenties, but Amanda smiled at Blair. There had been a time when they hadn't gotten along. But it had come out in the last couple of years that Blair had an affair with Amanda's father almost three decades ago. Their union had resulted in a secret pregnancy and given Amanda a half-brother, Spencer. He was now twenty-seven years old and a firefighter with the Dumfries Triangle Volunteer Fire Department.

"Any early finds you want to share with us?" Trent asked Blair, his question marking an end to the idle chitchat.

"Just that this alley sees a lot of action."

"Foot traffic?" he countered.

"Ah, sure, but I was referring to another kind of action."

"Are you being serious?" Amanda swallowed her disgust. It wasn't the most concealed area in town. Just from where she stood, she could see Ingrid Street and the vacant lot directly across.

"I kid you *not*. I've found used condoms, and Isabelle and I get the distinct *pleasure* of collecting them. After all, one never knows what might matter to the case."

"Yuck." Amanda had been curious what CSI Donnelly was picking up next to the building. One mystery solved.

"Just one of the lovely perks of the job. There's some drug paraphernalia too." Blair bent down and scraped the flattened red goo off the pavement. From there, Amanda knew she'd put it into an evidence bag and process it.

In addition to collecting condoms, they'd likely have to dumpster dive too. If it was between getting her hands dirty and handling the families, Amanda would choose the latter, no matter how tough that could get.

"You ready to catch up with the manager, Benjamin Weaver, and see what he might have to tell us?" Trent asked.

"That sounds like the logical next step to me." She was about to ask him if he was okay, the memory of him staring at the body fresh on her mind, but he was already well on his way to the end of the alley.

THREE

Amanda caught up to Trent, bypassing Officer Brandt. "Wait up," she said as she touched Trent's wrist.

He stopped walking immediately and turned around. She shouldn't have made physical contact. They had a volatile chemistry if that's what their mutual attraction could be labeled. But considering she was already in a committed relationship, it was even more dangerous. Incendiary. She cleared her throat and retracted her hand.

"What's up?" He had tossed out the question nonchalantly, as if he hadn't noticed the sparks still flying between them.

"Uh, back there, you couldn't seem to take your eyes off the body. You okay?"

"Yeah, I'm fine. I was just thinking about something, and I'll share if it ends up mattering."

She gave it a few seconds, seeing resolve in his eyes. Pressing him wouldn't do any good. "All right, when you're ready. If it ends up mattering," she said, reusing his exact words.

"Yep." He took a step, but she didn't follow. She didn't dare reach out to stop him either.

"Trent, just before we talk to Weaver, can we brainstorm

some of our early thoughts?" She wasn't meaning to push him into the territory from a moment ago, but she was interested to know if he had anything to offer yet.

"Sure." He pivoted back. "I'll even start. We can safely rule out an accident." His tone was serious, but the corners of his mouth twitched. Levity was essential to maintaining sanity at crime scenes, but they were in view of Weaver. She couldn't imagine two detectives laughing it up in the aftermath of what was likely a brutal murder reflecting well on the PWCPD.

"Very funny."

"It's just we don't have a lot to discuss yet, do we?"

"Not a lot, but I'd wager the victim was likely targeted. Whoever did this was prepared. They came with the gasoline in the jerry can."

"I'll play along... That would suggest it wasn't an opportunistic killing. Unless the killer is a real psychopath, and anyone would have done. Blair did point out the alley had a lot of traffic."

"Huh. Which brings us to something else. Why did the killer choose this spot? Sure, it's a safe bet the types who have sex and shoot drugs back there aren't looking to get involved with the police. But, still, they are potential witnesses."

"Obviously at this point, we can't assume what the killer was thinking. But could it be they were looking to make a statement of some sort?" Trent shrugged. "Possibly a vigilante who is out to rid the city of filth."

"I sure hope not." That theory would mean more victims. "Let's flip this another way. We don't even know if the victim was alive when he was doused or not. Maybe the fire was just a means of hiding the true cause of death. It would also destroy forensic evidence and potentially hide the vic's identity."

"It's all plausible. But either way, it's a drastic measure. Could the fire serve multiple purposes? The ones you mentioned and going back to what I had said, that it was a message? A warning? Are we looking at organized crime?"

"Like the mafia?" Her partner's suggestions could be fanciful sometimes.

"I was thinking more along the lines of a gang."

"They typically stick to guns, but we'll wait on cause of death." She was back to thinking the fire would hide forensic evidence, but if there was a bullet to find, Rideout would get it. "Running with the victim being targeted... How did the killer know where to find him? Did both he and the victim come here regularly? Though we could be wrong to assume the killer is a man. We might also be overcomplicating things. The victim was married. If he came here to hook up for sex or score drugs, what's to say his wife didn't find out?"

"And then she came here and took him out. Well, if that's the case, I hope I never run into her. Talk about a woman scorned. She sets her cheating spouse on fire..." Trent whistled. "And I know we're assuming the fire killed him. But while that's a scary thought, we're being premature speculating motive, don't you think? We don't even know who Crispy Critter is."

"Yeah, don't do that either." She smiled at him. "All right, let's talk with Weaver." She assumed the lead.

Wyatt excused himself from the manager of Modern Cellular and met with them a few feet away. "His name's Benjamin Weaver, clean record, and he's being fully cooperative."

"We got his name from Officer Brandt and his background update. Also why he's here and how he came to find the body," Amanda said.

"Then there's probably not much more I can tell you. The guy is suffering from what he saw, though. I'd suggest finding him a place to sit. It might make him more comfortable."

Wyatt must have had some reason he hadn't wanted to let Weaver sit in his car. "Noted, and thanks."

"You're very welcome."

Amanda and Trent joined Benjamin Weaver. "Detective Steele, and this is Detective Stenson. You're Benjamin Weaver?"

"Uh-huh."

"We understand that you've been giving your statement to Officer Wyatt, but we have a few questions of our own," she said. "Would you be more comfortable if we spoke in the store?"

"Ah, sure." He gestured toward Modern Cellular but stayed put, as if seeking permission to head in that direction.

"Certainly. Maybe we could find a place to sit down too," she said kindly.

"We can go back into the office." Benjamin entered the store first, and passed the door to her, and she to Trent. Half of the store was operational, while the other was in the midst of renos. The entire place smelled strongly of fresh paint.

He took them past the checkout counter and a restroom, down a short hallway, and through a doorway into a functional office. "Sorry, I don't have somewhere for you to sit." Benjamin dropped into the swivel chair behind the desk. His eyes carried a haunted look.

From what Amanda was seeing, she highly doubted the manager had anything to do with putting that body in the alley. "That's fine." She didn't prefer to stand over someone, but it was what it was. "Officer Wyatt may have mentioned this to you, but the Prince William County PD offers Victim Services. These are trained counselors whose job is to help those affected by crime. Their assistance is free of charge." Amanda reached into the left pocket of her suit jacket and pulled a card with the direct number to that unit.

Benjamin took it from her without hesitation. "Thank you."

"You are very welcome. No one should have to see what you did," she began.

"You can say that again. I don't think I'll ever forget it. If

only I had known what that smell was... I'd never have... *have...*"
He covered his mouth, gagged, and his eyes grew large and
round. He shot up from his chair and out the door, likely
headed to that restroom they'd passed. She heard the door shut,
but gratefully nothing more from there.

"Guy's not gonna recover at this rate," Trent said.

"It's still rather fresh, but he won't be eating barbecued
meat for a while."

Trent winced. "Keep talking like that and I might be joining
Weaver in the restroom."

They didn't say any more while they waited for the
manager to return.

"Sorry about that." Benjamin's complexion was pale, and
sweat was beaded on his forehead.

"There's nothing to apologize for," Trent assured him.

"What can I help you with? I told that officer everything,
which isn't even much." Benjamin rooted in the top drawer of
his desk and came out with a tub of gum. He kindly offered
them a piece, but they both declined. He popped one in his
mouth.

"Is there anything you can tell us about the business that
takes place in that back alleyway?" Amanda asked.

"Business?"

"There's indication that it's used for hookups and shooting
up," she said.

"Hookups? No, it's more than that."

"Indulge us." Trent pulled out his notepad and clicked his
pen. He often volleyed between old-school notetaking and a
tablet. The latter typically came out for more formal interviews,
not ones on scene.

Benjamin let his gaze dance back and forth between them.
"You really don't know? Wow, okay. Well, I like to mind my
own business. There's less trouble that way, but I'm quite sure
hookers sometimes conduct their business back there."

Amanda was aware the neighborhood was shady but hadn't expected this. "So they offer sexual services right there? Essentially out in the open?"

Trent looked over at her and raised his eyebrows as if her surprise surprised him. Though she supposed he had reason. Prostitutes and their 'clientele' weren't exactly known for morals or discretion.

"Yeah," Benjamin dragged out.

"Have you ever called the police about this?" Amanda asked.

"As I said, I like to mind my own business."

"Right, you did say that. How do you even know this goes on back there? I'd think Modern Cellular is closed long before those types would come out."

"We close at nine, but word gets around, and I can see evidence of what goes on back there. The needles and used condoms. Heck, some of the girls linger around earlier in the evening. It's no guess what they are up to. You can tell by the way they look. Most of them are strung out and dressed in tight and revealing clothing. Do you think the dead guy was one of their johns?"

The back of Amanda's neck tightened. "We never said the victim was a man." She might have been too quick to dismiss him. She doubted a layman's eye could tell gender.

Benjamin stopped chewing his gum. "My mistake. I just assumed. That... that *thing* barely looked human."

"Well, I assure you they were human remains, Mr. Weaver." She felt defensive on behalf of the dead man, despite the fact Benjamin had a point. The body looked more alien than human.

"Do any cameras cover the back of the store?" Trent asked, his pen poised over a page in his book.

"No, but not for lack of trying. The plaza management

company refuses the investment despite store owners petitioning for full surveillance."

Some companies adhered to strict budgets, but security
cameras in this neighborhood felt necessary. The fact they
hadn't installed them didn't settle well. Even more, when
factoring in the illegal dealings going on behind the plaza.
"We'll need their name."

"Dunbar Management Group." Benjamin provided their
phone number from memory.

Trent quickly scribbled in his book. "And who do you deal
with there?"

"Elwood Harris."

Trent wrote that down, while she gave her card to
Benjamin.

"Call me if you think of anything," she said. "Including if
you see any sex workers, drug dealers, or their clientele lurking
around." The ask might be a stretch. First, Benjamin would
need to be willing to violate his own code and involve himself in
other people's business. Second, would any of the prostitutes or
drug dealers admit to seeing something *and* be willing to talk to
the police?

FOUR

Amanda stepped outside, taking shallow breaths due to the smell. Meanwhile, the stress bearing on her shoulders wished she'd inhale and exhale deeply. But the pressure was there at the onset of every murder investigation. Her internal compulsion to find the answers and obtain closure for loved ones. She didn't have the luxury of dwelling on the hopes and dreams of the deceased, or she'd quickly go insane. Rather, she let her drive for justice fuel her forward, while not considering that sometimes the system failed and justice wasn't served.

Trent stepped up next to her, tucked his notebook and pen away, exchanging it for his phone. "We need to contact Dunbar and see why they've never put cameras in."

"I'm onboard with that."

Trent already had his phone at his ear and was asking for Elwood Harris. He started tapping a foot. A few seconds later, "Mr. Harris?" Trent went on to identify himself and the reason for his call, while keeping it vague. A crime had been committed behind Patriot Plaza, and he was inquiring why video surveillance hadn't been installed. "Uh-huh... okay... Thank you." He pocketed his phone.

"And...?"

"Lack of funds, or so he told me. He didn't even seem fazed at the mention of a crime being committed back there. Not sure if I had said murder, it would have gotten his attention either. Guy seemed indifferent."

"And what do we take from that? He knows what's going on and doesn't care?"

"That's where I'd go."

"Huh. But why? Does he or the company benefit somehow?"

"Not sure we have any reason to go there. I think they're just cheap."

"Seriously, how much can cameras and security cost?"

"According to Harris, more than the Dunbar Management Group can afford."

"Still not entirely buying that, but it is what it is." She appreciated that businesses needed to be profitable to keep their doors open, but surveillance protected the larger investment—the property. "But now what?"

Trent hitched his shoulders and looked around. "The grocery store could have cameras aimed this way. It's worth checking out anyway."

They walked to the building, searching along the roofline. There were cameras, but none appeared to cover any part of the alley. A quick chat with the store's manager confirmed that.

"Well, cameras are out," she said. "All we do know is we've got a married John Doe. That means there's likely a spouse out there somewhere wondering where their husband is." She removed gender, not wanting to leap to the conclusion he'd been wedded to a woman.

"And we're no closer to giving them answers."

She shook her head. "No time of death to work from either, though I'd suspect the victim was killed late last night or in the wee hours of this morning."

"Ripe time for druggies and sex workers."

"Yeah, but it's too bad they'd adhere to the code of the street. Mind your own."

"Precisely. And snitches get stiches."

She laughed.

Trent was smiling. "It's not likely anyone's going to talk to us."

"Not likely but not impossible. We'd have to find a good reason to make them talk."

"Good luck with that."

"Before we need to worry about that, we'd need to find an eyewitness. But there needs to be something we can do right now." She hated feeling this helpless so soon in an investigation. Cases often did tilt from feast to famine though. Sometimes you had the victim's ID and a slew of possible motives and suspects right from the hop. Then there were times like this when the answers took far more effort to find these things out. She paced a few steps. "We considered our victim was targeted..." She was determined there was something actionable in that.

"And a regular in the alley, making it easy for the killer to find him."

"Right. But how did the vic normally get to the alley? Did he walk, take the bus, a car service or... drive himself?" Her eyes widened. "There could be a vehicle out there for us to find. If so, we'll get our vic's ID."

"Good idea."

There weren't any unaccounted-for vehicles in the lot, just their department car, police cruisers, the Crime Scene van, and an old Mazda in front of Modern Cellular, which likely belonged to Benjamin Weaver.

"I'm thinking if the victim did drive here, he probably didn't park far away," she said. "You up for a walk?"

"You know it. I say we try Ingrid Street. It's located just to the other side of the alleyway and might make the most sense."

"Let's go." She started off in that direction, appreciating the slightly cooler temperature and the clear blue sky. No fear of breaking a sweat or catching a chill.

They cut across the front of the plaza to reach Ingrid Street. Unfortunately, the corner where the plaza was nestled didn't have traffic lights. It was a four-way stop, so no CCTV to avail them.

Ingrid was a residential street and houses lined both sides, except for the vacant lot directly across from the alleyway. Parking was allowed on the street during the day, but not overnight. Given the earlier hour, she took the sight of a navy-blue SUV at the curb as a good sign.

It was parked five houses down from the plaza, just before the road rolled up a small hill. She pointed at the vehicle and picked up her speed. She looked over her shoulder when Trent didn't seem to be keeping up. "Stone in your shoe?" she teased.

"I'm coming." Curt and moody. Clearly something was weighing on his mind.

They reached the vehicle, a Buick Encore GX, and Trent rubbed his jaw and grimaced.

"Talk to me," she told him.

Trent didn't, but he stood there raking his hand through his hair, staring at the ground, then the sky. His jaw was clenched, and his eyes a storm.

She stood in front of him, resisting the urge to place her hands on his shoulders. "I think it's time you start talking. What's going on in that head of yours?"

"I know the owner of this SUV." Spoken coolly while refusing eye contact.

Amanda took a few beats to absorb what he'd told her. "You're sure?"

His cold stare met her gaze. "It belongs to my aunt's husband, Don Lambert."

That explained his mood. He hated the man, but there was

something she needed to point out. "A lot of people own this type of vehicle."

"Not *this* one. It's his. I know the plate." He crossed his arms and was shaking his head.

His reaction triggered her to recall how fixated he'd been on the body, but what if it wasn't that? "You already had a hunch, didn't you? You weren't staring at the remains. It was the wedding band. You recognized it."

He wasn't looking at her now, and he didn't deny it.

"Why didn't you—" She snapped her mouth shut, letting rage wash over her. "If you suspected this, you should have said something right away."

"No, I shouldn't have," Trent snapped back. "I wasn't certain. Sure, the ring looked familiar, but it's not like it was the only one made."

"No," she pushed out. "That's not why you held back. There's more here. Start talking, Trent."

"What more do you want from me, Amanda?" His blue eyes were riddled with pain when he met her green ones and pierced right through them. She received his message.

"Oh..." She closed her mouth. If her hunch was right, he was questioning whether his aunt was the killer. "You think your aunt might have done this?"

"I don't want you thinking that." Trent turned away, and her stomach clenched.

His aunt was in an abusive marriage that led to her estrangement from Trent and the rest of his family. She could have finally had enough and struck back. Trent had to see that, but she had been in a similar state of denial when someone close to her was guilty of murder. This didn't change the facts though. Or what they needed to do next.

FIVE

Trent's head was spinning. His dear, sixty-seven-year-old aunt Gertrude would never harm a fly, let alone be capable of cold-blooded murder. But she could have finally had enough. It was possible Don had finally pushed her to her breaking point. Not that he wanted to accept it. Though if she had... Well, his conscience absolved her of wrongdoing. Lord knew Don deserved the most painful exit from this world as possible. A small, dark part of Trent even hoped the fire had been the cause of death and that he had suffered.

Don had preyed on his aunt, a widow, playing on the fact he was four years younger than her, and exuded false charm. It didn't take long for him to isolate her from family and friends and start using his fists to break what was left of her spirit. And to make matters even worse, he died wearing *that* ring!

"If the dead man is Don, you may need to step back from this case." Amanda's voice penetrated his thoughts. An unwelcome intrusion, as was her suggestion.

"Not going to happen, Amanda." He was quaking with rage at her hypocrisy. She had investigated the murder of the man responsible for making her a widow.

"I can understand why you—"

Trent shook his head. He wasn't going to be bullied into submission. If anything, his aunt needed him more than ever. To be assured her family was still there for her. "I'm not recusing myself," he said, his voice surprisingly level and calm. "I'll clear it past Malone myself, if I have to."

"Be prepared for just that. He'll probably ask for your alibi to start, so make sure you have one."

"Are you being serious right now?"

"He asked for mine when Chad Palmer was killed."

How could he forget that? Logan Hunter had been her alibi, and seeking his statement was how their relationship had gotten started. Essentially, also why Amanda was with Logan and not him. Though he was doing his best to reconcile himself to the fact that they'd never be a couple. It was easier these days because he had a girlfriend he'd been seeing for several months. "Okay, but telling me to be ready with an alibi implies I'd know the time of death. Which I don't. So, you think I killed Don?"

"Never meant that."

"Then you're suggesting I take a backseat until we have TOD?"

"It might not be a bad idea."

"Not doing it. But if it helps, I'll say it. I didn't kill the guy. Have I thought about it? Hell yeah, more times than I can count."

"You might do best to keep that to yourself."

"I've got nothing to hide. If I was going to kill him, it would have been long before now. I haven't seen my aunt since I last tried to get her to see reason last October."

"Okay, that's good."

"Uh-huh. And we figured he was probably killed late last night or the wee hours of this morning. If so, I was at home, in bed."

"Alone?"

He swallowed roughly, his Adam's apple bulging out. He hated how awkward it made him feel whenever Amanda treaded into his romantic life. He didn't need to apologize or explain. "I had company."

"Ah. We might need to speak to her."

She responded like the news washed right over her, though why should that surprise him? And why should she care? She had Logan. "If Malone insists on that, I'll give him her name and number."

"Just don't be surprised if he asks."

"I got the message the first time, and appreciate it's coming from someone who knows."

Her facial expression was devoid of emotion. "I need to ask again. Is there any part of you that thinks your aunt might have done this?"

"She's not a killer." He spoke with more confidence than he had any right to feel. They were estranged, but he clung to the memory of the aunt he had known. A woman with a kind heart. It was possible Don had destroyed that part of her. Trent had witnessed the dysfunctional marriage chip away at her piece by piece in the beginning. She went from being a family cheer-leader and social butterfly to a wallflower, and then one day she'd disappeared altogether. All this was made sadder by the fact that her late husband had treated her like a queen, like all women deserved. Trent had attempted reconciliation several times and was shot down for his troubles. He eventually accepted her answer. It was that or lose his sanity. But blood ran deep and thick, and if she needed him, he'd forgive the past and be there for her.

"I can appreciate you want to believe that, trust me. But what if Don pushed her too far? He employed a hooker. Your aunt found out and—"

"Just stop," he snapped.

"You can't just shoot down what I'm saying because you don't like it. It is possible she finally had enough."

"Let's just agree to disagree. Besides, why would she kill him for cheating and not retaliate when he was beating her in their home?"

"Are you sure you want me to answer that?"

A bitter feeling swirled in his gut. "Why not?"

"To start, killing him behind the plaza would shift suspicion from her. It opens the possibility of other suspects. She'd also have the advantage of blindsiding him to get the upper hand."

"I can't keep repeating what I've already said."

"She would never have done this," Amanda said. "But you'd be surprised by how little we know about what's going on in the minds of our loved ones. Take it from someone who knows."

He almost hated that she'd walked this path before him and had earned the right to preach from her soapbox. After all, someone close to her had killed a man. Trent let out a deep breath. "Regardless of Malone's decision, I need to be the one to tell her, to talk to her."

"I get that." She put a hand on his shoulder, and he stepped back out of reach.

"Let's just get it all over with." She had to stop touching him. Didn't she realize how unfair it was for her to do so, even if it was seemingly innocent? He wasn't secretive about his feelings for her, and it was just as plain that she had her own for him. They had their slips. Once before Logan, and another time this past December. After Logan. A kiss, but not *just* a kiss. It was loaded with hunger and promise. But it wasn't leading anywhere and needed to be shut down. She'd told him that clearly several times. She wasn't willing to sacrifice her relationship with Logan for a chance with him. And he got it. Sometimes. She had Zoe to consider too. Not that this made it any easier. Some days it was hard just sharing the same space with

Amanda. But when that distance closed and they came into physical contact, he lost his sanity.

She pulled out her phone. "Before we go talk to your aunt, I'd like to clear this situation past Malone. You are absolutely certain this SUV belongs to Don?"

"We can run the plates back in the department car if you want, but I am confident. A possibly faster way would be to call Rideout about the ring. He should be back at the morgue by now."

"And ask what?" Her brow wrinkled.

"There should be an inscription on the back that reads, 'My heart belongs to Tom.'" Rage burned hot at verbalizing his realization. That shit Don died wearing his uncle's ring.

"Who is— *Oh*."

"Yep. Tom was my aunt's first husband."

"And Don was wearing his ring," Amanda said slowly as if treading sacred ground.

Trent formed his hands into fists at his side. "Let's not dwell on it," he seethed.

She nodded. Her cheeks were flushed, and an understanding seemed to pass between them. She looked as disgusted by that revelation as him. Just as long as she didn't read his other treacherous thoughts. The ones that championed the person who took Don out of this world.

SIX

Amanda empathized. Trent would be suffering inner turmoil. A struggle between his commitment to the badge and his personal connection. As he'd pointed out, she'd been there. It was why she'd recommend Trent remove himself from the case if the victim was Don Lambert. But this was for two reasons. One, he'd be saved the drama, and two, this would reduce the likelihood of jeopardizing the integrity of the case. Not that she doubted his intentions, but when emotions came into play, things became a lot less clear. And she'd witnessed him lose his temper on the job during a case further from home. But like now, it had involved an abusive husband. Trent's opinion of such men wasn't a secret, just as he hadn't withheld his hate for Don. Heck, a moment ago, he had confessed to wishing him dead in the past. Did she really think Trent killed Don? No. But if Trent was going to stay on the investigation, he'd need to keep an open mind, even when it came to his aunt. Amanda needed the freedom to speculate and examine theories without fearing she'd tread on his toes. Could he remain impartial if the evidence ended up pointing at his aunt?

But before she was going to call Malone, she wanted to

verify the victim was, indeed, Don Lambert. She tried Rideout, thinking if he could verify the inscription quickly, it would save the time it would take going back to the department car and running the plate. Besides, Trent was confident this license was Don's. She struck out with Rideout, as he was tied up with another autopsy, but got Liam on the phone. Now she was on hold waiting for the verdict.

Liam returned, cutting out the hold music. "Sorry, that took a bit, Amanda." He went on to tell her what he found out while panting like he ran around to get the answer.

She listened to Liam's response as Trent stood watching her. "Thank you," she told Liam and hung up.

"So? It's him, isn't it?" Trent said.

"The inscription was on the ring." She wasn't daring enough to repeat it so as not to hurt Trent.

"Well, I've got something else too." He waved for her to follow him to the front of the Buick and pointed to a piece of paper stuck under a wiper.

"A parking ticket"—she leaned in and read the details—"that was issued at three AM."

"We already discussed the murder likely happened late last night or early this morning..."

"It's possible whoever issued this ticket saw the fire, even the killer without necessarily knowing that."

"I'd say this is our strongest lead so far. Except, you'd think the parking enforcement officer would call in the fire. Maybe it was already out? That would tell us that Don was dead at the time of the ticket."

"Like you said, this person is a strong lead."

Trent nodded. "In the least, we could ask them if they smelled anything unique in the air at three AM."

Unique wasn't the precise word, but it got his point across. "It could help narrow down time of death. If they smelled something then Don was already dead by the time of the ticket. But now that we know the vic's ID, do you have any idea what might have brought Don to the alley? Was he into drugs or paying for sex?"

"Nothing would surprise me when it comes to that guy."

Again, it fired through Amanda's mind how Trent's aunt would have felt if she found out her husband was employing prostitutes. Even more humiliating was the fact he may have taken part in these lewd acts in an alley, behind a plaza, no less. If Amanda were in the woman's shoes, livid wouldn't be a strong enough word. Had the aunt taken her revenge as a scorned wife? Though, Amanda's thinking was getting ahead of any evidence. They didn't have proof that Don had hooked up with prostitutes.

"I see it in your eyes, Amanda," Trent said, cutting through her thoughts. "My aunt didn't do this."

Amanda appreciated his loyalty, but it lacked a solid foundation. He had fallen out of touch with his aunt, the woman essentially a stranger for the last several years. And just wishing for something not to be true didn't make it so. But she'd let him cling to his belief. For now. Even if it was that point right there that troubled her. She shouldn't feel the need to tiptoe during an investigation. All aspects should be open to exploration. "What can you tell me about Don, aside from how he treated your aunt?" She was trying to get an idea of what might motivate other people to kill him.

"He was a heavy drinker. He might have gone to the alley to score drugs."

"You don't see sex workers being a lure for him?" She suspected he might not want to admit that because if Don was sleeping around it would present more motive for his aunt.

"Could be. Like I said, nothing about the guy would surprise me."

She had expected he might insert a defense for his aunt again. The fact he hadn't hopefully signaled he was striving to be openminded. "We'll see if we can get someone to talk to us later today. One of the girls or drug dealers might recognize Don, or even better we might uncover an eyewitness willing to talk."

"Worth a shot assuming the police activity doesn't scare them off for a bit."

"All right, so I'm just going to make a quick call to Malone, bring him up to speed. While I'm doing that, you want to contact Parking Enforcement and see if you can get the name of the officer who issued that ticket?" She nudged her head toward Trent's hand, as he now held on to it.

"You bet."

They stepped away from each other to put some space between them while they made their calls.

Malone answered hers on the second ring and listened as she laid out the situation. His response seemed a bit slow coming but eventually, he said, "Huh, well it's a little messy and it isn't."

She hadn't expected that. "Sir?"

"To start, there's no worries on my part that Trent was involved with the murder at all. I can't see how that would really fall into question. Aside from his character, you just told me that he hasn't seen her in quite some time. Logic would dictate if he was going to kill Lambert, it would have been long before now."

Malone had stressed a solid point. Trent had moved on about seven months ago when his last-ditch effort to help her had failed. When she'd turned him away, he gave Amanda every impression, he'd received closure. She had also worked with Trent long enough to see his dedication to the badge. *Even if he has lost his temper before...* The treacherous thought creeped in. Or was it *that* treacherous? It was actually further proof of Trent's innocence. He'd lashed out in the heat of the moment. He hadn't acted from pent-up rage hours, days, or months later.

Malone continued. "On the other hand, his aunt may have killed her husband. That presents potential for conflict of interest. Do you trust, if it came down to it, that Trent could arrest her?"

It was the same question she'd been bouncing around herself. But the same answer came to her every time. "He would."

"Then, I say Trent stays on the case."

Despite his reasoning, Amanda was surprised by Malone's fast clearance.

"Amanda, you heard what I said?" Malone prompted. "Do you have reason to disagree with my decision? If so, let me hear it now."

"No, I'm in agreement."

"Good. He's probably the best to speak with his aunt. She's likely to open up to him."

Amanda wasn't so sure about that. There was a broken bridge over the water of hurt feelings. It didn't mean things couldn't be repaired between them, but their history could make things difficult. But there was only one way to find out. "I'll let Trent know he's cleared to work the case."

A few beats of silence on Malone's end, then, "Is anything pointing at the aunt yet?"

"Nothing near solid, just hypotheticals."

"The spouse is always the first suspect?"

"That, but we believe that Lambert was targeted and that would indicate he was a regular in the alley."

"I'm not following the implication."

She informed him about the illicit business being transacted behind Patriot Plaza.

"Huh. It doesn't sound like he kept good company, so it's hard to say what caught up to him. Could be an angry sex worker or a drug deal gone bad. The possibilities are endless at this point."

"Agreed, though I steer away from your last option. A dealer would be more likely to shoot Don. Whoever killed Don came prepared with a jerry can of gasoline. With that said, you can count on us to explore all the angles."

"I wouldn't expect less. And don't let the aunt's culpability weigh on you too much. We can't be sure of her innocence yet obviously, but in domestic cases typically if the victim murders her abuser, it's done in the heat of the moment in self-defense."

"Which means at home," she added. "Trent made the same argument."

"All right. Well, it seems you have it under control, but again, I do appreciate the heads-up. Now, if things change though, if you see indication Trent is handling this case with bias, I want you to report back to me immediately."

"Will do."

Malone hung up, leaving Amanda holding on to her phone. She had this sour feeling in her stomach. If it came down to it, would she turn on Trent, her partner and friend?

SEVEN

Trent got through to Parking Enforcement and was told Cole Dorsey had left the ticket. Dorsey had worked the nightshift and got off at 7 AM. It was just after eleven, so he'd likely be sleeping now. Trent finagled his home address from the office manager though, and once Amanda got off the phone with Malone he'd suggest they stop by later today to question him.

Amanda was coming over to him as he was putting his phone away. His heart pinched just thinking that she was going to tell him he was benched. Thankfully, it turned out he had no reason to worry. He was approved to continue working the case. And while that was a victory, he wished he could say his lofty goal was to find justice for Don Lambert. In truth, his priority was to protect his aunt from taking the fall for his murder. It was possibly a warped mentality, but he could justify his thinking. While the job advocated for the victim, his aunt was one in her own right. And had been for years. But with all that considered, *if* she had killed Don, Trent would do the right thing. Above all, he held pride in the badge he wore.

"So, what did you find out?" she asked, and he filled her in on Dorsey.

They decided the next logical stop was his aunt's, but they checked in with CSIs Blair and Donnelly first. They told them the victim's ID and where they could find his Buick Encore GX on Ingrid Street.

As Trent drove to his aunt's house, his nerves kicked up, the closer they got. The last time he'd seen his aunt was last October and the occasion hadn't exactly made for a great memory. She'd been especially cruel when she sent him away. The only good that came from it was he'd received closure. He was then finally able to accept that he had tried everything to help her, and it was her decision whether she'd avail herself of that. And now, he was going back. The only thing helping his anxiety was he'd be there on official business not personal. But how would she react to seeing him on her doorstep? And how would he feel upon seeing her?

Trent parked in his aunt's driveway. The house looked the same but it somehow *felt* different. It had to be the past influencing his perception. After all, this was where she'd banished him from her life for good. He took a few steadying breaths and coached himself, *Just focus on the job.* He'd repeat the mantra as often as it took for it to hold sway.

"Are you hanging in okay?" Amanda asked from the passenger seat.

He looked over at her but couldn't meet her eye. "Yep. Just doing my job." He got out of the car, heart pounding, as he walked to the front door. He held his breath when he pressed the doorbell.

Inside, footsteps padded toward them. When the door opened, his aunt Gertrude was there, a scowl on her face. But Trent also noticed her bruised cheekbone, and the turtleneck she wore. He suspected there were more bruises underneath the collar as it was far too warm to justify the sweater. Maybe she *had* been pushed to her breaking point.

She flailed an arm in the air. "I told you that I don't want to see you anymore, and I meant it."

The verbal venom stung, even if he'd expected this reaction. It left him speechless, and she slammed the door shut in his face. But just before that happened, he'd noticed the hand she'd used. It was wrapped with a white bandage, and the sight churned the acids in his stomach. *Wrapped like one would a burn...* Though the thought could be no more than his imagination at work. Any number of reasons could explain the bandaged hand.

He banged on the door.

The door swung open. "Just leave me alone." When she tried to close it again, he wedged his foot between the door and its frame, his boot taking the brunt of the impact. His aunt looked down. "Have you lost your mind? Remove your foot this instant."

"No. You're going to listen to me." He'd never spoken this forcefully to his aunt in his life.

She cocked her head. "And why would I do that?"

"Don is dead." It was merciless to spit it out the way he had, but her cruel reaction to the sight of him had him barely holding his emotions together.

"No. He can't be. You must be mistaken." She rubbed her arms and was shaking her head. "You're trying to trick me so you can force yourself into our lives. Well, we don't need you interfering."

Her continued rejection hurt him to his core, but a part of him empathized. Don would have fostered her paranoia. "His remains were found this morning behind Patriot Plaza. He had been set on fire." He strove for a kind and gentle delivery, but the words that tumbled from his lips were far less tact and more cold, hard truth.

His aunt lost her balance and reached for the doorframe.

He rushed to keep her upright, but she batted him away. "You lie. Shame on you!"

His cheeks flamed at the rebuff. Why he bothered trying to show her love was beyond him. In black and white terms, the way she treated him didn't deserve his goodwill. But reality was less defined and more shades of gray. The woman before him wasn't his aunt. It was who she'd been manipulated to become. He'd choose to remember his aunt from before while also remembering he was here on business. "I assure you. He *is* dead."

"No. I just saw him last night."

"That may be, but he's dead now," Trent volleyed back, firm and aiming for detached. *Here on business...*

"Trent is telling you the truth," Amanda put in.

His aunt leveled her gaze at Amanda, as if seeing her for the first time. "And who are you?"

"Detective Amanda Steele, your nephew's partner."

"Hmph. Gertrude. But I can't believe this... about Don."

"It's the truth," Trent muttered under his breath, watching his professionalism melt away again.

His aunt narrowed her eyes as if weighing what she'd been told. "Okay," she eventually relented, backed up, and led them to the living room.

She dropped onto the couch, and Trent and Amanda each sat on a chair.

"You said that you saw Don last night," Amanda began. "What time was that?"

Trent appreciated that she had started the questioning. He was still processing his aunt's initial reaction to seeing him. It was hard to ignore how her contorted facial expression hit his bloodstream as poison, and her words struck his heart like a bullet. He was still finding his balance.

"Just before nine. That's when I go to bed every night," she deadpanned. Her initially charged denial to the news about Don had dampened. Shock might be taking the edge off, but regardless she had yet to shed one tear or show any grief. If she were anyone else but his aunt, he'd likely find that suspicious. Same too, for her bandaged hand. But just because it was injured, it didn't mean she'd burned it when lighting Don on fire. Don himself could have inflicted the wound whether it be a cut or burn under the wrapping.

Trent considered how to bridge the gulf between the personal and professional. Asking how she'd hurt her hand could open past scars. And as long as she was talking, broaching the topic of her hand could wait for now. "Well, he obviously left the house at some point. Any idea where he might have gone? What time he left?"

"I just told you I was asleep."

One simple sentence, but it came as a slap to the face and got his back up. "You must be a very sound sleeper. You are telling me you didn't hear him close the door or hear his vehicle start up in the driveway?"

"All I know is he was gone when I woke up. I'm not sure if he even came to bed. He could have and then left. I wouldn't know." She stiffened, body language defensive, and Trent was left to wonder why.

He also didn't care for his aunt's attitude. It was like she was purposefully being difficult. Had she killed him and her perceived barriers were erected to deflect guilt? It was very possible, and she'd have plenty of motive. There was the abuse, but the breaking point could have been discovering Don paid for sex. The latter was simply hypothetical though. Regardless, he could hardly blame her if she couldn't take him anymore and saw her way out. *Except for the fact that murder is against the law...* It was almost sad he had to remind himself of that, but the victim was Don. Trent's personal feelings for the man butted against and challenged his ethical code.

"You seem to take the idea of that in stride," Amanda said. "Did Don make a habit of going out at night, possibly staying out until morning?"

"He would sometimes, yes," his aunt replied.

Trent cleared his throat. "Where did he go?"

"Wouldn't know. It's not my place to ask."

Trent's hackles rose at *not my place*. As Don's wife, she had every right to know where her husband was galivanting about. "Did he ever have any reason to be around Patriot Plaza?"

"I don't know," she dragged out.

He had a feeling she knew more than she was saying though, and that thought had him getting angry. He was also pissed off that she was being so coy and dismissive. "You do realize the spouse is the prime suspect in murder cases? That unless you can give us something to work with—"

"Huh. I tell you to butt out of my life, and now you want to lock me up? Is that it?" She held out her wrists, and he flinched. The hits from her kept coming.

"Is that a confession?" Amanda edged in.

His aunt pinched her lips together and wrinkles shot out around her mouth. "No, it's *not* a confession," she hissed. "And why would I kill Don?"

Trent sat back, took several deep breaths, and petitioned Amanda to field that question. He was tapped out, with no desire and not enough courage to touch such a volatile question.

"We understand that you had quite a rocky marriage," Amanda said. "That your husband was known to be abusive."

She glared at Trent. "What he told you no doubt."

"He didn't need to. The bruising on your cheeks tells me that your husband may have taken liberties," Amanda said gently, as if she were tiptoeing on shards of glass.

"I could have fallen."

"We all know that's unlikely," Trent pushed out.

"I still wouldn't kill him."

Rage was swarming Trent's system and affecting his vision and his thinking. Even after showing his aunt compassion, she tossed back a flippant remark. "How did you hurt your hand?" He pointed it out, and she tucked it against her stomach and covered it with her other hand.

"None of your business."

Trent clenched his jaw. "You sure you didn't burn it when you lit Don on fire?"

"I. Never. Killed. That. Man."

"Then you shouldn't have a problem telling us what happened to your hand," he fired back, finally attaining cop mode.

"It..." She snapped her mouth shut and avoided eye contact. "I'm not saying any more. I have rights."

Was she being shady to protect her pride or guilt? The former had his heart aching for his aunt. Victims of abuse so often blame themselves while battling with humiliation. The only thing comforting Trent in this moment was the recollection of Don's dead, burned-out husk. But that flitted away at the memory of the gold wedding band on his finger. "Why was Don wearing Uncle Tom's ring?" His anger, his hurt, had tears springing to his eyes. He'd transitioned from cop back to nephew in a flash. Maybe he wasn't cut out to handle this case.

"It's no longer of use to Tom, so I gave it to Don."

Trent shook his head, recoiling at how dismissive she was about Tom being gone. She and his uncle Tom had a love affair of a lifetime. "Are you sure about that? Don didn't take it for himself?"

Finally, one little crack in his aunt's tough exterior opened with an eye twitch. But it wasn't a surprise she'd still be grieving a man who had loved and treated her kindly until his last breath. If anything, one could expect more appreciation after living with a man from hell.

"Despite what you think, Don wasn't a horrible man." Her mouth and chin quivered as she said this, the physical tells belying her words.

Trent being here and talking about Tom must have been churning up the past and how her life had fallen apart after his death. Now that Don was gone, hopefully his aunt could finally begin to heal. Her power should reawaken with her self-esteem. Then she'd finally realize she deserved better than men like Don. But physical abuse didn't stop with flesh and blood. It was also a mind game the victim was rigged to lose. Gaslighting cemented by an iron fist. The victims are told enough that the violence is their fault, they begin to believe that it is. And since most are isolated, they're left without a support network to bolster them. Without a sounding board, the victims start to excuse the way they are being treated. "You deserve a man who treats you like Tom did." Trent gingerly put that out there, hoping to fan a spark within her, but she grimaced.

"You're naive, Trent. You're just a child."

Despite her words, her tone had softened. Was he making progress at chipping through her hardened exterior? "I *was* a child, but I've long since grown up."

"I'll always see you as a little boy."

He swallowed the lump in his throat. "I need you to think hard before you answer my next question, Aunt Gertrude." He realized his faux paus instantly, how he made this personal. He cleared his throat, returned to cop mode. "You're sure you don't have any idea where Don might have gone the nights he went out? Was it a regular thing? If so, what nights?"

"I'm not his keeper."

Just when he thought she might be lowering her defenses, they were back up. She was frustrating the hell out of him. If only he could completely turn off all empathy for his aunt and deny her influence over his emotions. And how could his aunt continue to defend Don even when he was no longer a threat? Was it purely habit? "Yet I bet Don was yours. He controlled every inch of your life. He cut you off from your family and friends. You've never been a stupid woman. Lost maybe, sure, but not stupid."

His aunt remained quiet for a few beats, then said, "I'm not saying he was a saint. Lord knows he wasn't, but he was just a man."

"That doesn't justify what he did to you."

Gertrude waved her uninjured hand in dismissal, but her earlier words sank in. *He was just a man...* This was a textbook defense for an unfaithful husband.

"Was Don cheating on you?" He tensed, realizing this would provide his aunt with more motive to kill Don.

She hitched her shoulders. "There might have been other women..."

Trent passed a side-glance at Amanda and subtly shook his head. Despite his aunt's treatment of him, he was still ready to defend her. As far as he saw it, one of Don's lovers could have tracked him down and murdered him, just as easily as his aunt. "Their names?"

"I couldn't tell you."

He should have known better than to expect otherwise. But the news that romantic entanglements existed shifted some of the spotlight from his aunt. Only *some*. She had knowledge of Don's affairs and his habit of going out at night. Potential motive. And she was being evasive, refusing to tell them how she'd hurt her hand to start. She also had her own vehicle, a red Kia, and could have taken it to the plaza last night. To top off all this, she didn't have a verifiable alibi. "We're going to need to continue our conversation at Central." He gestured for his aunt to get up.

"Are you really arresting me, Trent?" Her voice was strangled.

"Not yet, but you need to start talking to us."

Leading his aunt out of the house and into the back of the department car was a surreal moment. His aunt could be a killer. But until that was a proven fact, he was resolved to stand by her. Even if it was painful to breathe the same air.

EIGHT

Amanda was proud of how Trent had handled things with his aunt. He had moments where his composure slipped, but he was fast to get it back. Gertrude certainly hadn't made it easy for him to strike and keep an emotional balance. She was callous with her words, and Amanda wanted to step in more than she had. While she saw the woman's projection as a barrier to protect her heart, there could be more at play. She could be trying to hide her guilt.

She and Trent set Gertrude up in an interview room at Central and set off to talk with Malone.

He was in his office with the door open, and he waved for Amanda and Trent to enter when they shadowed the threshold.

"You obviously have something to share, but I'm going first," Malone said. "I heard from the uniform division. A canvassing officer, working Ingrid Street, may have gotten us a lead. The house right where Lambert parked his SUV has a doorbell cam. The homeowner has asked everything go by the book, so it will take a bit to gather appropriate paperwork, serve it, and collect the footage, but I'll keep you posted."

"Sounds good." She was watering it down because she'd

been burned by getting her hopes up before. But the camera footage could give them a break in the case. It might have even captured Don Lambert's killer. That's if they stalked him from a distance and followed him down the alley.

"We can hope. Now as for the vic's car, I've been informed it's being taken to the crime lab in Manassas where it will be processed."

She nodded. It wasn't ideal as it would cause some delay, but she had no control over the matter.

"We were told that Don Lambert had possible affairs too," Trent said. "We could benefit from looking at his phone activity."

Malone, ever so subtly, glanced at her. He must have picked up on how Trent had prattled that off without any attachment. "I don't see any issue with getting that warrant approved. In fact, I'll personally make sure that's handled."

"Thanks," Trent said.

Malone dipped his head. "Anything else or was that it? I'm going to assume you served notice to your... uh, Lambert's wife. How did that go?"

Trent stiffened but he beat Amanda to responding. "We came to tell you that we have Gertrude Lambert in for questioning."

"Oh?" Malone again looked at Amanda, but then leaned forward and clasped his hands on his desk. "Is she a viable suspect?"

"I want to say no," Trent said. "But she's being rather evasive in her answers to our questions."

Amanda admired her partner's restraint and how he was fielding all Malone's inquiries with a cool detachment. She just feared he might be overcompensating for how he was truly feeling.

"Good call bringing her in then. Keep me posted on how it goes."

Amanda led the way from Malone's office, to the interview room where Trent's aunt was waiting for them.

Gertrude was seated at the table, hunched forward, her forehead resting in her left palm. She looked up when they entered the room and sat across from her.

"Was all this really necessary?" Gertrude's question was plainly leveled at Trent, her eyes drilling through him. Her spirit might have been wounded, but she had some fight left. She had probably been strong-willed and resilient to start with. No one was exempt from falling victim to abusive relationships.

"It was necessary," Amanda said firmly, stepping in for Trent. He dipped his head toward her as if thanking her. Amanda let silence stretch out for a few seconds before speaking again. "Mrs. Lambert, you told us Don sometimes goes out at night and doesn't come home. How often does this happen?" Trent had asked a similar question back at the house, but his aunt had sidestepped it.

"Not often, and with no regularity. Usually he just pops out for a bit and comes home."

"And during those times, how long is he usually gone? Do you know when he leaves and comes back?" Amanda asked.

"He'll pop out around eleven thirty and return shortly after midnight. I usually stir awake when he gets into bed."

Amanda nodded. "How often does this happen? Every week? More than once a week?"

"A couple of times a month."

"And do you know where he goes?" Amanda anticipated the answer she'd receive, but she had to ask anyhow.

"Not my place. He'd knock my teeth out," she added at a lower volume.

Trent flinched beside Amanda, but she didn't act like she'd noticed. It was heartbreaking to imagine how many women and children lived in constant fear. Sadly, that self-preservation also didn't help the case. Gertrude could have had enough. On another note, they would have to figure out some other way whether Don routinely frequented the alleyway and why. That could help lead them to a suspect, someone familiar with Don's schedule who took advantage of that knowledge. Whatever business Don had on those nights didn't take long though. A mere thirty to forty-five minutes, give or take. Certainly long enough to hook up with a prostitute or score drugs. But they weren't going to get further on this matter with Gertrude. "Did Don have any friends? Maybe he went out with them sometimes?"

"Fridays and Saturdays for beers." The way she shared this news was matter-of-fact, just rolling off her tongue.

Amanda straightened up. This could be a good starting point. "Where do they go?"

"I don't track Don." Gertrude was staring at the table, her eyes glazed over as if her mind were elsewhere.

"Then you're saying you don't know?" Amanda wanted to cut through the veneer of Gertrude's response.

"Uh-huh."

Don might have berated Gertrude to "know her place," but seeing sparks of her character coming through, Amanda found it highly unlikely the woman had no clue. But so far, moving the questioning to Central hadn't had the desired effect on Gertrude. She was just as closed off as she'd been at home. "What are their names?"

"I don't know that either."

Trent smacked the table, and his aunt flinched. The energy swirled in the room, a tangible entity that expressed his instant regret.

"Mrs. Lambert," Amanda said in a soothing voice, "I'm sure you can understand why it's hard to believe you wouldn't know their names. Don never mentioned them?"

She shook her head. "He never talked to me much."

Amanda still wasn't sure she was buying that Gertrude

didn't have names to give them. The question was why she was withholding them. It was time to take this interview in another direction. She pointed at Gertrude's injured hand. "It's time you tell us what happened there."

Gertrude looked down at the white bandage. Her face sagged, and tears filled her eyes.

"It's all right, Gertrude. You can talk to us." Amanda did her best to sound kind and reassuring. All the while, her heart was frozen in her chest. She hadn't yet released Gertrude from suspicion. In fact every time she refused to answer a question or deflected, her distrust only increased. "Mrs. Lambert," she prompted.

The woman sniffled and unwound the bandage. The room was silent except for Gertrude's quickened breathing as the bandage dropped onto the table. This was one of those times when saying nothing said it all. Was she about to confess to murder? That she'd burned herself when she doused Don with gasoline and lit him on fire?

Eventually, after what felt like several minutes, Gertrude said, "I deserved it. I made him angry," and held her palm across the table.

Amanda sat back. The flesh was seared, raw, and angry. "Did Don do that to you?" Amanda wanted the matter cleared, without any chance of misinterpretation. Gertrude could have burned herself in the execution of Don's murder and her words could be her twisted way of coming to grips with what she'd done.

"He..." Gertrude wiped away tears from her cheeks. "He held my hand against a hot stove burner."

Trent jumped up and paced the end of the small interview room. The soles of his boots slapped against the flooring.

Amanda didn't need to look at Trent to feel his rage. The situation had her back up too. It also had her feeling conflicted. It was easier to fight for justice when the victim was a good person, or at least possessed some redeeming qualities. They had yet to uncover one for Don Lambert, but she had an oath to uphold regardless. "When was this?" She could barely get the question to scrape from her throat as her empathy for Gertrude burned in her chest.

"This past weekend."

Amanda's inclination was to offer sympathy and express remorse for what Gertrude suffered, but she had to remain objective. That past weekend was recent enough to spark motivation in Gertrude for her to finally act. Don's abuse could have fueled her imagination. He burns her, and she retaliates and one-ups him. "I need to ask you again, where were you last night between midnight and six AM?" The timestamp on the parking ticket was three but they hadn't yet spoken to the parking enforcement officer to get his statement. He could have been and gone by the time of the murder.

"I told you. I was home asleep." She rewrapped her injured hand.

"And no one can corroborate that?" Amanda volleyed back.

"Of course not."

Amanda took a few seconds to process what was being said and what wasn't. It was apparent Don held power over Gertrude from the grave. She was defensive and posturing. But was it out of some sense of obligation toward Don, or was she protecting herself? After all, she'd have ample motive. With that thought, a potential hole in her defense grew into a chasm. She was surprised it hadn't clicked into focus before now. "You told us you went to sleep last night at nine o'clock, like you do every day?"

"That's right."

"Okay, so if you're always in bed at nine, how did you know that Don stepped out a couple of times a month, and for how long?"

"I... *I* hear the front door open and close." She stumbled over her words.

"And last night?" Amanda clasped her hands, quite confident in her conclusion, but she was just building to her point.

"I heard him leave."

"So you were awake then, not asleep. Did you, by chance, get out of bed or leave the house?" Amanda caught Trent glance at her in her peripheral vision but kept her focus on Gertrude.

The woman shrugged.

"You were home *all* last night?" Amanda asked, stressing a key point.

Gertrude threw up her arms and huffed. "That's what I've been telling you."

"And you're sure about that?" Amanda certainly wasn't. Trent was now boring his gaze through the side of Amanda's head, but she refused to acknowledge him.

"I swear."

"Then there's no way you were anywhere near the plaza?" How Gertrude answered these questions would establish a foundation for the investigation. If she said no, and they uncovered evidence to the contrary, Gertrude would have some explaining to do.

"No, I wasn't. Why would I be?" She laid a hand on her chest.

Trent cleared his throat. "Detective Steele, can we talk in the hall?"

Amanda got up. "We'll be right back," she told Gertrude and left with Trent.

He shut the door behind them. "You're going at her awfully hard, don't you think? I'm telling you she never killed Don. She's not capable of murder."

"Really? How can you not see the holes in what she's already told us? Then there's what she isn't saying."

"Whatever, Amanda."

"Don't *whatever* me. You might not like this, but we're all capable of murder. Including your aunt."

"See, that right there."

"What?"

"You're convinced she killed him."

"I'm not, but I am keeping an open mind to the possibility she did."

"Are you suggesting that I'm not?"

"I never said that." *In so many words...* "But your aunt is hiding something. That seems obvious, whether you wish to admit it or not."

"Judge and jury now, Steele?"

She narrowed her eyes. He never hauled out her surname. "No judgment passed. Just experience from being at this job for as long as I have. She only answers what she feels inclined to. For everything else, it's 'I don't know.'"

Trent paced, circled back. "Next thing you're going to tell me is she's lying about how her hand got burned."

A dark cloud settled between them with that statement, and Amanda shook her head. "I believe her about that." The truth had been in the woman's broken expression and her tears.

"There's a miracle. As for her managing her responses, she's probably battling with being secretly pleased the bastard's dead. I know I am."

Amanda bristled. It wasn't so much the admission but the cavalier way in which it was dispensed. "So because the man was physically abusive, it justifies murder?"

"I never said that."

"It seems to me that's exactly what you're implying." She could be reading more into his words and body language than was being said, but she followed her gut instinct.

"Don't pretend you have no insight into how I'm feeling. I'm sure you've been right here."

It didn't take much effort to read between the lines. He'd

been witness to her reaction at the murder of the man who had taken her family away. To say that she didn't feel some justice had been done would be a lie. She'd even found some adverse pleasure in the fact he had suffered like her family had in their last moments, like she had in the years since. But she still didn't like to acknowledge these feelings that pitted cop against grieving widow and mother. Regardless, she eventually said, "I have."

"Thank you for your honesty. I bet you also took some satisfaction in his death." He raised his brows, his questions now piercing her to help him justify the turmoil he was in.

"I did." Voicing this admission was unsettling and cleansing at the same time. "But you should know that it never brought me lasting peace. In the end, my husband and daughter... my unborn child... they were still dead. His death didn't bring them back." It had only been in more recent months that she started to process the loss of her unborn son and the fact the accident had left her unable to conceive. So far, she was *managing* that one.

"I'm sorry I brought this up for you." He pressed his lips, emphasizing his apology. "I just want to know I'm not alone. I'm not used to feeling this way... like the victim got what they deserved. It goes against who I am, but Don was scum, and that's putting it mildly. But I'll do my job regardless and find the person who did this. If only to prove my aunt's innocence."

She nodded. Again, this situation mirrored what her own had been. She'd been focused on clearing her name and her family's. There was just one fault in that. "I understand but, Trent, what if the evidence doesn't tell us what you want to hear?"

"I swear you have no need to question my integrity to the badge. But my aunt is innocent. I know her."

It was his defense on repeat, and to argue the point again would be futile. She hoped he'd come to realize the years of separation from his aunt could have made her into someone he no longer knew. But that was for him to acknowledge. "All we can do is follow the leads we get, go from there."

"I agree."

Her phone pinged, and she checked on it. "It's a text from Liam telling us that the autopsy on Don Lambert will start this afternoon at two thirty."

He checked his watch. "It's around noon now. Wow, it feels later than that."

"It's been a tough morning," she said and meant it in more ways than one. It had been emotionally, physically, and mentally draining starting with the sight of charred human remains.

"Do you want to head there for that or—"

Pounding on the interview room door interrupted Trent. They unlocked the door, swung it open, and Gertrude stumbled out. She was breathing heavily and gripping her chest. Her face was pale and beaded with sweat. "I... I..." She collapsed to the floor before either of them could break her fall.

NINE

To say the investigation was off to a rocky start was an understatement. Amanda and Trent had called for an ambulance to take care of his aunt. Thankfully, it turned out to be nothing more than a stress-induced panic attack, but her fall had hurt her other hand and made her tailbone tender. But all things considered, it could have turned out much worse. Amanda kept telling herself none of this was her fault, but she was having a hard time whitewashing her conscience even if everything she'd asked Gertrude was necessary. But maybe she could have been kinder in her approach. Though, Gertrude's adverse physical reaction only strengthened Amanda's suspicion she was hiding something. Whether that was murder, only further investigation could reveal.

They had stayed at the hospital while Gertrude was treated, and miraculously the turnaround had been quick. Her chest pain had moved her up the list of priority, as did arriving by ambulance.

It was one thirty by the time Trent pulled down the street for Gertrude's house. When they had been there earlier, Amanda had noted it was a storybook neighborhood where homeowners tended to the properties. Cars were in most drive-ways as the residents here were predominantly retired. And most of these were luxury vehicles. Considering Amanda's knowledge of what took place behind the closed doors of the Lamberts' home, she couldn't help but note the contrast to the surroundings. Things weren't always as they appeared.

A black Lexus LX was parked at the curb a few doors down from Gertrude's house, a man behind the wheel. He turned away when they drove past.

Probably means nothing, Amanda thought and let it go.

Trent turned into Gertrude's driveway. He'd taken off his seatbelt when Gertrude spoke from the backseat.

"You don't need to come in with me."

"I was just going to make sure you got inside all right," Trent said.

"I'll get in like I have every other time I've come home in the last several years."

Amanda could feel Trent's energy take a nosedive, and she wished there was some comfort she could give him. But their relationship was their business and didn't need her interference.

Gertrude stepped out of the car, and Amanda prepared for a hard slam of the door behind her. Instead, she poked her head through and mumbled, "I do appreciate you getting me to the hospital and sticking around to drive me home though." Then, she closed the door without giving Trent a chance to respond, but he appeared stunned by her words. It hadn't exactly been a thank-you, but the implication was there.

Trent's hands were both on the wheel as he watched his aunt make it to her front door. He was so still, it didn't look like he was breathing.

"Are you all right?" Amanda cursed herself for asking such a stupid question when the answer seemed obvious. How could he be with such tension existing between himself and his aunt? And that was just the personal side. In the larger picture, she hadn't been cleared as a suspect. That had to be weighing on his mind too.

"I just hate leaving her. She's all alone now. Don saw to it that she lost her family and friends."

"She's not alone, Trent. She has you."

Trent looked over at her and smiled. "And she always will."

She returned the smile, letting it sink in how Trent's loyalty to those he cared about was reliable. Not everyone was like that.

"I blame us though," Trent said, breaking the silence.

"Blame us for what?" She swallowed roughly. So far, he'd managed the scare with his aunt's health expertly, but as the adrenaline from fear was wearing off, she could feel his mood shifting.

"We shouldn't have pushed her so hard." He looked over at her.

What he really meant was *she* shouldn't have, just like his accusation moments before the aunt had collapsed. "I don't think we did. If anything, we went easy on her."

"Really? You essentially accused her of lying to us. You questioned her statement about going to bed how many times?"

"If she was anyone else, we wouldn't be dropping her off at home. She would be back in an interview room at Central." Amanda hated feeling boxed into a corner, but like a wild animal she was ready to defend herself. "You were in that room, right? One minute she's asleep in bed and heard nothing. The next she knows exactly when her husband goes out, including last night. You must admit that looks fishy. She's hiding something. If you don't see that, well..."

"Well what?"

"You're blind," she spat without apology. "If you're not able to let the personal tie go, then I'm going to suggest you recuse yourself from the case, Trent. I say this as a friend and your partner." She held up her hand as if petitioning peace.

"Huh. Yet, you're not sounding like you're keeping objective, Amanda. For one, we don't have a solid case against my aunt, and two, we need to consider that someone else may be behind Don's murder. The guy was a dick. I'm sure he made a lot of enemies, people who'd love nothing more than to see him dead. And meet a violent end, to boot."

She weighed his argument and nodded. "I agree it's possible. It would be great if we could track down Don's friends."

"It won't be through his phone records. We're still waiting on those."

"If we knew what bar he'd go to, that might help," she volleyed back.

"Just one more thing we don't have, but we do have Don's place of work. Someone there could give us some names."

"It's definitely worth a shot."

"All right then."

Trent reversed onto the road, and Amanda's eye was drawn to Gertrude's house when the curtains fluttered in the front window. Gertrude was looking out at them, and Amanda had this curdling in her gut. What if their leniency toward her became their downfall?

TEN

Amanda and Trent didn't say anything as he drove them to Don Lambert's workplace. Handyman Building Projects was in Woodbridge and was a hardware and lumber store. They serviced retail customers in their store but also offered online shopping.

They were greeted by Garth, a man in his forties, his name embroidered on his shirt.

"Is there anything that I can help you find?" he asked and offered a genuine smile that touched his eyes.

Amanda and Trent held up their badges in perfect unison, and it had Garth stepping back.

"What can I do for you... officers?" Garth's voice took on a higher octave.

"Detectives," Amanda corrected. "Is there someplace we could talk that offers more privacy than the sales floor?" She figured that Garth was as good a person to start with as anyone.

"Ah, sure." Garth took them to a remote corner of the store. "What's this about?"

"We have questions about your coworker Don Lambert," Trent said.

Garth's shoulders lowered, seemingly relieved they weren't there for him, but his mouth rested in a frown. "Did something happen to Don? He didn't show up to work today and the boss is really pissed off."

"Something did," Trent said coolly. "Don Lambert's body was found this morning behind Patriot Plaza."

"He's... ah... dead?" Garth rubbed his throat, and his complexion turned ghostly white.

"We offer our condolences," Amanda said, empathizing with how Garth was reeling at the news. "Hearing this comes as a shock to you?"

Garth swallowed so roughly that it had his Adam's apple bulging out. "Ah, yeah."

"So you two got along?" she asked.

"All right, I suppose."

"Do you know of anyone who might have had an issue with him?" Trent pulled out his tablet and powered it up.

Garth's eyes flicked to the device, then to Amanda. "Woah, hold up. Are you asking me if someone had reason to... Someone *killed* him?" His voice rose in volume, pitching his last question as a loud outburst.

Amanda cringed and held up a hand. Other customers milling about the store didn't need to overhear their conversation. Also, what part of Don being found behind a plaza spoke to natural causes? She shook that aside as shock shutting down his logic.

Garth lowered his voice and said, "I'll keep it down. It's just shocking is all. But in answer to your question, I didn't know much about Don and wouldn't want to point you at someone."

She raised her eyebrows and angled her head. His uncertainty sparked her curiosity. "Then someone is coming to mind?"

His eyes snapped to hers. "Sure, but I don't have a name to give you."

"You'll need to spell that one out for us," Trent said.

"It really might not be anything, but there was a guy who came to talk to Don sometimes."

"And what can you tell us about him?" Amanda wasn't sure whether it was worth getting swept up by the cloak and dagger.

"He drove a black SUV, but that's about all."

Goosebumps laced down Amanda's arms. *A black SUV...* Like the Lexus LX she saw parked near Gertrude's house? "Can you give us the make and model?"

"Nah, I'm not good with that, but I think it was a luxury vehicle."

She nodded. It could be the same vehicle then, and by extension, the same man. It was certainly a lead they needed to pursue. "Tell us more about this man and the SUV."

"That's all I know."

"You probably know more than you realize," she said and flashed him an encouraging smile. "Do you remember what the nose or the grill of the vehicle looked like?"

"It wasn't a Beemer or a Mercedes, I know that much. The body shape was rather boxy, and oh, the grill was silver. There were lots of horizontal lines."

A fit for the Lexus LX... "Okay, that's helpful. When was this man last here for Don?"

"I saw him, uh, last week. Friday, I think it was."

Last Friday was May 3, but was there any significance to that? "You said this man showed up for Don sometimes. Do you know who he was to Don? A friend?"

Garth shook his head. "I didn't get that feeling. Not that I have any clue what business they had together."

"And why that feeling they weren't friends?" Trent had his finger poised over his tablet, ready to document Garth's answer for the record.

"He was always miserable after talking with the guy. More moody than normal, and that's saying something. He'd snap at any little thing. Although, I guess you're not to speak ill of the dead."

"It's fine," Trent said. "We just want the truth."

Amanda glanced at her partner, then asked Garth, "And was that the case last week? Don was moody after this man's visit?"

"Oh yeah. Even more cantankerous than other times."

"Do you have any idea why?" She kept the questions firing quickly, baiting Garth to respond just as fast. The quicker they returned to her, the more authentic and genuine.

"He wasn't telling me, and I wasn't asking."

Just Garth's impression of the situation between the mystery man and Don didn't settle well. The stereotype about dark vehicles might not be helping her objectivity either. "Did this man ever come into the store?" If a surveillance camera captured his face, they could have it run through facial recognition databases.

"Not that I saw."

Amanda studied Garth and got the sense he was being straight with them. He didn't know the identity of the Lexus driver, if that's who this guy was. Time to move along... "We heard Don liked to go out drinking on Fridays and Saturdays. Do you know who he went with?"

"Nah, sorry." Garth rubbed his forehead. "We weren't exactly pals. He worked in the warehouse, and my job is on the retail floor. Speaking of, I should get back to work." Garth's eyes widened with a petition.

She nodded. "Thank you for your time."

"I wish I had more to tell you," he said before leaving them.

Me too, she thought, but she and Trent weren't walking away with nothing. Amanda turned to her partner. "Maybe it was just a coincidence, but when we dropped your aunt off there was a black SUV, a Lexus LX, parked a few houses down from your aunt's."

"I saw it too, didn't think anything of it. I could have been too quick to dismiss it."

"What I've been thinking about myself, though it's not like we had context that would flag its presence."

"Until now. Should we go back and see if it's still there? Have a talk with this guy?"

Amanda debated whether they should. "We will, but since we're here, let's speak with Don's boss first. He could give us something."

The clerk at the counter told them the manager was Jim Roman and informed him that PWCPD detectives were wanting to speak with him. Within a minute of her hanging up, a fifty-something man was walking briskly toward them. He took one look at them and their badges and waved them back to his office.

The space was bright with one wall mostly being floor-to-ceiling windows, but otherwise the room had a masculine and utilitarian feel. The desk was metal with black trays and a black monitor on its surface.

Jim smoothed down his tie and took a heaving breath. His stiff and rigid posture told Amanda he was bracing for bad news, while trying to remain grounded. "How can I help?"

"Your employee Don Lambert was found murdered this morning behind Patriot Plaza." She included *murdered* just to erase any possibility for a misunderstanding on manner of death. "We're hoping you might be able help us."

"Ah, me? I'm not sure how. Murdered, you say?" His voice cracked.

"We appreciate this must come as a shock to you," she said.

"Damn straight—" He snapped his mouth shut and blushed. "Excuse my language. But, yeah, it's a shock. The guy didn't show up to work today. I've been on the warpath since I haven't been able to reach him, cussing his name. Yet all this time he's been dead." He leaned back and swiveled in his chair. "Murdered," he added in an undertone.

"We found out he had a buddy turn up here sometimes. He drove a black SUV," Trent started, clearly taking liberties about the relationship Don had with the mystery man. "Guess him and Don could get into it sometimes...?"

Amanda appreciated that Trent was stretching Garth's testimony to see how Jim would react.

"News to me, if so. Do you think that...?"

"We're just covering all our bases here," she said firmly. "Anyone you can think of who had a problem with Mr. Lambert?"

"I don't get involved in the personal lives of my employees. I like to keep things professional." Jim's lips twitched as if he were regretting that decision.

"Unfortunately, as much as we try, we can't always leave our personal lives at home. Was Don acting any differently in recent days, say the end of last week even?" It was a long shot, but a person doesn't just wake up one day and decide to torch someone. In that vein, Don must have been aware someone had it out for him, and surely, his fear must have manifested in his behavior.

"I wouldn't say so. Though, he did one thing out of the ordinary. He asked for a two-week pay advance last Friday."

Her mind was whirling with theories, trying to piece together the mystery man in the black SUV, Don's moodiness, and this request. Was it connected? It seemed too coincidental not to be. Friday was the day that Garth last saw the mystery man with Don. "Did he say why he wanted the money?"

"I asked, but he refused to answer. Not that anything he said really would have made a difference. If I gave him an advance, other employees would find out and expect the same treatment. No business can afford that."

"And how did Don take it when you turned him away?" Trent asked.

"He stomped out, mumbling under his breath, something about what was he going to do now."

Her stomach churned from an infusion of adrenaline as a theory took shape in her mind.

They inquired about the names of Don's friends or where he might like to drink. Jim had nothing to offer in either regard. Amanda and Trent thanked the manager and left him with their sympathies.

Back in the car, she did up her seatbelt. "I think I've figured something out."

"You and me both, but go first."

"We have a black Lexus LX. Not a cheap set of wheels. We take that, combine it with a mysterious driver who shows up at Don's work and, presumably, at his home. Then Don asks for a pay advance the day of this guy's last visit. The timing could be a coincidence, but I don't think so. Don throws a tantrum when his boss turns him down and mumbles his frustration. Add all this up, and it sounds to me like Don owed money to the wrong person."

"Yep, exactly what I was thinking, and if that's the case, my aunt could be in danger."

ELEVEN

If Don's actions had placed his aunt in danger with thugs, it was a good thing the man was dead. For him and Trent. What they learned at Don's workplace painted a rather clear picture. Don borrowed from the wrong person and found himself in too deep to pay back the money. While it shifted the spotlight from his aunt, what if these people now came after her? They could view her as a built-in insurance policy. Kill Don and collect from the widow.

Trent felt a glimmer of relief when he pulled down his aunt's street and didn't see the SUV. He wished he could discount his worry as nothing, but even the absence of the man left him with a bad feeling.

He parked in the driveway and rushed to her front door. No response when he pressed the doorbell. He tried knocking. "Where is she?"

"I'm getting a bad feeling, Trent," Amanda told him.

"You and me both." He could have done without her expressing her concern. It only validated his own. He tried to peer through the sidelight but couldn't see anything. His heart was racing as he rang the bell again and knocked right after. If his aunt didn't come in the next thirty seconds, he would break in. He was prepared to do just that when footsteps came toward the door, and it was opened.

His aunt sighed dramatically at the sight of him, and her reaction might as well have been a spear to his heart. Why did he keep putting himself through this drama? Letting himself worry about her well-being when she clearly detested him?

"What are you doing here? I was trying to get some rest like the doctor advised me to."

Right... His cheeks heated, feeling embarrassed for his wild trip down Worst-Case Scenario Lane. "I'm sorry to wake you, but this can't wait. We have more questions and need to take a look around." On the way here he told Amanda he wanted to handle the questioning.

"And this really can't wait?"

"No, it can't," Amanda inserted.

"Good Lord." His aunt threw her arms in the air but backed up to let them inside.

They wiped the bottom of their boots in the entry but kept them on in case they had to leave fast. "Is there anything I can get you, Aunt Gertrude?" The question left his lips without thought. Showing respect and care for her as his aunt seemed his default setting despite her bitter tongue.

"Some peace and quiet. But since that seems too much to ask for..."

Does every word out of her mouth need to be dry, sarcastic, and loaded with malice?

"We won't be long," Amanda mediated.

They returned to the living room, to the spots they took up that morning.

"I had nothing to do with what happened to Don," she said. "Tell me you believe me." She met Trent's gaze. Her eyes were a brewing storm kicking up hurt, regrets, and fear. Those were just the few emotions he could identify.

"I do," he said, feeling Amanda stiffen from across the room. But what did she expect him to say to his aunt's face? Besides, he spoke his truth. Don wasn't a great guy and would have made enemies. While most remained faceless, this mystery man in the SUV seemed a solid place to start. After all, they needed a clearer picture of Don's life. "Did Don borrow money from a loan shark?"

Her mouth pursed into a tight line, then she opened her mouth to reply.

Trent butted in, "Before you tell us you don't know, we've found out about his *friend* in a black SUV that comes around for him at his workplace and here. We saw him on your street earlier today." Trent was running with the assumption that the SUV they saw was *the* one. But really, the chances they were different were slim.

His aunt licked her lips and defiantly stuck out her chin. "It seems to me you have the answers. Why ask me?"

There were times, like now, he barely recognized the aunt he had known. Physically, the bruising and other injuries aside, she resembled the woman. Recognition was lost on her attitude and demeanor. She'd turned into a bitter older woman. Though his empathy could excuse that considering the abuse at Don's hands, it didn't make it easier to endure. "Did Don get in over his head? Owe money to the wrong types?"

"You tell me, Trent." His aunt primly gathered her hands in her lap.

Her timid response and body language had him faltering some. "We think he did, but we thought you could tell us for certain."

"I'm not trying to be difficult." She drew her gaze from him to Amanda and back. "It's just that..." She closed her mouth, clearly changing her mind about saying more.

Don was still in his aunt's head, playing mind games, even from the grave. "You don't have to fear Don anymore. He's gone, and he can't hurt you." After the words left his mouth, he feared his aunt might retreat behind her wall, possibly even defend Don as she had earlier that morning. *That morning...* Time was a cruel joke today the way it seemed to expand and engulf so much in a handful of hours. It felt like so much longer ago when they had spoken with her last.

"I know that. It's just..." She took a deep, staggering breath, and her eyes glistened with unshed tears.

His heart was breaking for her. Despite how she'd treated him from the moment he'd showed up at her door today. It wasn't her fault though. It was preconditioning. Don was the only one to blame for the estrangement and the current tension. But he couldn't continue to dwell on this, or he'd quickly go mad. *Focus on the job*, he thought, recalling his mantra from earlier. "We think that whoever Don owed money to might have killed him." Maybe if his aunt was assured that they weren't suspecting her at this moment, she'd relax and speak more freely.

"Yes, all right. I'm sure he placed bets on sports events... not through legal channels."

Trent could read through that easily enough. It had recently become legal in the state of Virginia to bet on sports, but only if made online or through mobile apps. "He made wagers with a person, or a bookie, who then placed the bets?"

"Probably. If he bet online, he'd need money upfront, wouldn't he?"

"I think so." Trent didn't know a lot about the world of gambling, but usually a stake was needed. That being money put down that the gambler would either forfeit or grow depending on the outcome. He imagined if Don worked with an illegal bookie, that person might extend him some credit at a high penalty for failure to pay on a loss. That could explain the Lexus hanging around and Don's request for a pay advance. "Has he been miserable lately?"

"Hard to tell with him. His moods were all over the place. Super high some days. Others, he was absolutely insufferable." She gestured to her bruised cheekbones and indicated her burned hand.

White-hot fury pulsed through Trent, but he let it flow through him before speaking. "Reflecting his wins and losses."

"I think so. I mean, it makes sense."

Every time she justified Don's treatment of her, it seared Trent's soul. "No, Aunt Gertrude, it doesn't make sense. None at all. He should never have laid a hand on you. No man should ever lift a hand to a woman, or talk down to her." If only there was a way to suck all the years of abuse and hurt from her system...

"I know that."

Trent sat up straighter at that acknowledgment. She didn't look at him when she said it, but he'd still take this as a win. His aunt's light was starting to shine through. "Do you know who this bookie is? What he looks like? Where to find him?"

She shook her head. "Honestly, I have no idea."

Trent nodded, but her phrasing soured some in his gut. *Honestly...* As if before now she hadn't been completely forthcoming. He'd sensed it for himself, but Amanda's observation of this fact chose now to shuffle to the front of his mind. He hadn't wanted to acknowledge it, still didn't. "A look at Don's things might help us. Did he have an office or a place of his own in the house?"

"His den." His aunt popped up and led him and Amanda down a hallway and into the basement.

It was a masculine space but also dated with its wood-paneled walls, mounted dartboard, and retro bar. In front were two stools, their plush pleather tops cracked from age. Behind, a gold-flecked mirror and glass shelves housed several bottles of alcohol. None of them top-shelf brands.

Trent and Amanda stepped into the room, but he stopped

and turned around noticing his aunt had stayed in the hallway. She was hugging herself. "Aunt Gertrude?" he prompted.

She shook her head and started to tremble and cry. Trent shot one look at Amanda and rushed to his aunt's side.

"What is it?"

"I'm not allowed in there. Ever." Her chin was quivering, and tears beaded on her lashes.

"Remember he can no longer hurt you." Trent reached out to touch his aunt's arm, hesitant to do so, assuming physical contact wouldn't be welcome. But his aunt stepped toward him, and he took that as permission. He opened his arms to her, and she tucked against him, putting her arms around him. Tears burned his eyes, and he tried to blink them away, but it was of no use. A few fell. When their hug ended, he wiped his cheeks.

They stood there looking at each other for a few seconds, the silence between them speaking volumes. It was as if the moment swallowed all the years they'd been separated and mended all the hurts. There would be so much catching up to do for Trent and his entire family. His mother was going to be so happy to be reunited with her sister. Don's death was a blessing, as dark as that might sound.

"Trent," Amanda said, breaking the spell.

"Yeah?" He turned, and Amanda was behind the bar holding up a laptop in gloved hands.

"That's his computer. If it still has a password, I can't help you. I tried to get in it before with no luck," his aunt offered.

"We'll figure it out," Trent assured her.

"What had you trying?" Amanda asked.

"I... ah, I was just trying to find something out."

"Aunt Gertrude, be straight with us. Please," he petitioned her, feeling like he'd found some solid ground with her. "Tell us the whole truth, about everything we ask."

"When your uncle died, I came into a bit of money from his life insurance."

"How much is a bit?" Trent asked, a bitter acid swirling in his gut with a hunch of where this might be going.

"Two hundred and fifty thousand."

"And Don took this money from you?" Forget bitter acid. Rage reared its head.

Aunt Gertrude nodded. "I think so. He told me he'd keep it safe and help it grow for me by investing it wisely."

Trent was trembling and couldn't keep his hands still. He stuffed them into the pockets of his pants. "How long ago did he take control of this money?"

"I made him a co-signer on the account right after we got married."

That gave Don full access to the money from his uncle's death. That thought alone made him sick. "So you tried to get on his computer to see how much money you had left?"

She nodded. "I was curious. Whenever I'd ask him about it, Don would hit me. Eventually, I stopped asking."

Trent flinched, as if physically wounded himself. He also didn't care for what Don's strong response likely indicated. He'd guess Don had burned through his aunt's money. *I hope he continues to burn... in Hell!* The thought was charged and dark, but he didn't regret it crossing his mind. What reasonable person, in his position, would blame him?

"Did you try going to the bank directly?" Amanda asked.

"Uh-huh. But I got cold feet and left before I got to speak with the bank manager. If Don found out I was asking about the account, he would have beaten me badly."

Trent's hands formed into fists inside his pockets. "I can find out what's happened to the account, if you'd prefer I handle that."

"Thank you."

"Don't mention it. I'll just need the bank and account info," he told her.

"I'll get it for you." With that Gertrude left, and Trent joined Amanda behind the bar.

Neither of them said anything, and she pulled out an accordion file organizer.

"This was with the laptop." She started emptying the contents and set everything on the bar.

There were invoices for utilities, but there were a lot of unopened envelopes stamped *Past Due, Final Notice, Going to Collection*.

"Well, if we had any doubt that Don was experiencing financial problems, I think this confirms it for us." He gloved up. Most of the collection notices were for credit card debt, but one was far more serious. It was a bank statement showing that a second mortgage on the home had fallen into default. Now, after all his aunt had already suffered, she was at risk of losing the roof over her head. "The guy was despicable." He passed the statement over to Amanda.

She looked it over, shaking her head. "That he was, but let's keep focused. A bank isn't going to send someone to kill you if you don't pay up." She dipped back into the organizer and came out with a small piece of paper, gave it a once-over. "Now this is more like it."

He moved closer, cognizant of not coming into contact with her though. "What is it?"

"Looks like a bet slip to me. Obviously, nothing legal about that..." She met his gaze, and he nodded.

"I know the law. Online and mobile apps only."

"Uh-huh. So he likely didn't need money to put down, but *that* means he wouldn't have just *lost* money..."

"He'd have *owed* it," Trent finished. He peered at the slip. "Dated May first, that's last Wednesday."

"Yeah, and it isn't good. Don bet in favor of Miami Heat winning out over the Boston Celtics in the NBA conference semifinals in Thursday's game. Well, they lost."

"I didn't realize you were a fan of basketball."

"There's a lot you don't know about me, but I'm not. Logan likes the game, and so does my brother. Kyle even played in college. He came over to watch it, and the outcome was all they talked about for hours afterward."

Trent vaguely remembered that her brother played coming up before. But he hated how every time she said Logan's name it made him recoil. He had to let it go. Amanda wasn't his and never would be. It was ridiculous stressing himself to think differently. "It's unlikely a coincidence that this mystery man comes to talk with Don on the Friday, two days later, *and* Don asks for a pay advance. Especially now we have that." He gestured to the slip. "Can you tell how much Don would have owed?"

She took out her phone and punched numbers into the calculator app. "Ten K for this bet, not accounting for what interest might have accumulated since Friday morning. The rate isn't posted on the slip, no surprise. The fact there's even a paper trail is a bit of one though."

"They'd want it in writing, but the trail kept to a minimum. Regardless, it sounds like motive to me."

"It certainly doesn't appear that Don had any way to pay the bookie off either. Not looking at all these past due bills. Unless Don had hidden money socked away..."

"I get that gambling is an addiction, some even consider it a disease, but I don't understand why anyone would risk everything on the hope it will pay off."

"You essentially said it, though. It's the rush that comes with defying the odds. Any small win can trigger the gambler, who will crave that *high* again and again."

"Well, people have been killed for less. There's definitely no bookie's name on there? Any clue to their identity?"

She pressed her lips into a straight line and shook her head. "Not on this slip."

"That bad feeling from earlier is intensifying." There was nothing to stop this bookie from sending his goons to harass his aunt.

"I feel it too, but let's step back and ask how they'd benefit from killing someone who owes them money. Dead men can't pay off their debts."

"Neither could Don when he was alive. Heck, he was about to lose the house. But this doesn't rule out the bookie. Killing Don would send a message to others who haven't paid up yet. But it's another thought that scares me. They could have killed Don because they figured they'd still get their money. Through my aunt."

"If that's the case, she could be in real danger, Trent."

TWELVE

Amanda wished she could have offered Trent reassurances, but the truth was Don had placed Gertrude in danger when he made a bet he couldn't cover. The fact a luxury SUV was lurking around did nothing to calm her nerves. "I'll call Malone to arrange for an officer to watch over the house," she told Trent. "We should probably get a warrant for all of Don's financials too." She called Malone and ran through all the bullet points that got them to this juncture. Less than a minute later, she was hanging up with good news. "Malone will make sure a uniform sits on your aunt's house twenty-four hours a day."

"That helps me breathe somewhat easier."

"Me too. Your aunt's had a rough go in life." And that was putting it mildly. Knowing what she had suffered at Don's hands made Amanda appreciate her own blessed life even more. The men in her world treated her with respect and admired that she was strong-willed and independent.

"She is pretty great."

She considered saying something about what she'd witnessed a moment ago between him and his aunt. But it was none of her business and would be crossing a line.

Trent was working with the laptop trying to get in. He had it powered up, but couldn't get further than the password screen. "I just thought I'd try..."

"Don't give yourself a hard time. We have people who can get in." She was thinking of Digital Forensics, a unit of the Prince William County PD, that specialized in technology. Unlocking devices was child's play for them. Heck, they could resurrect deleted data.

"That we do, but it means having patience. And if something on here could help us find the bookie..." He sighed as he powered down the laptop and shut the lid.

"We'll find him another way. We just need to think like a bookie to catch a bookie." She smiled at him, an expression he returned.

"And how do you propose we do that?"

"Well," she dragged out, "your aunt said that Don goes out with friends on Fridays and Saturdays, but a couple of times a month he's only gone for thirty to forty-five minutes."

"Plenty of time to place a bet."

Amanda resisted playing devil's advocate by pointing out it was enough time for a sexual hookup too. But they were thinking along the lines of a bookie. "Because this bookie's business isn't legal, he's not going to splash it in a public place. I can't even see him conducting business in the alley behind Patriot Plaza."

"Though it's not like anyone would question him if he did. We're talking about sex workers, drug dealers, and their clientele."

"I suppose, but I'm thinking more about what else is in the area. We feel that Don was targeted, so it's entirely likely he was in the vicinity of the plaza on a predictable schedule."

"Well, there are a lot of residential homes in the neighborhood. It's possible the bookie lives in the area. Then again, Don's murder might have zippo to do with his gambling debt."

"Let's just follow this angle through before we discount it," she said despite feeling less confident than before. They were running on an assumption, but some farfetched theories paid off. And this one wasn't even that far out there. "There is a coffee shop near where we found Don's SUV. Java Stop, if I remember right. He might have met up with his bookie there. I mean, the coffee shop seems like as good a bet as any."

"Bet? Don't even joke around about that."

She held up her hands. "Sorry. I just meant..."

"Nothing by it? I know. I'm just so angry and conflicted about what to focus on first. Don screwed my aunt over in so many ways. He took my uncle's ring, and then stole the insurance money from her."

"We don't know that he took the money."

"Please, Amanda, I know you prefer to give people the benefit of the doubt, but Don doesn't deserve that kindness. My gut tells me that he emptied the account, and she's been left with nothing to start over."

"That's where you're wrong, even if that is the case. Your aunt will always have you and the rest of her family." She gave him a tight smile, and he nodded.

"She does, and we'll never let her do without." He shook his head and frowned.

Witnessing Trent going through this testified to the resilience of his character and the depth of his loyalty. It wasn't dispensed from a sense of obligation but was how he was wired. Her phone rang, and it was Rideout. She answered on speaker and said, "Trent's with me."

"Well, hello to both of you. I thought you'd appreciate an update on a few more immediate findings. Our vic, you identified as Don Lambert, had carbon monoxide in his blood and soot in his lungs. There was also trace of gasoline on his flesh. I can confidently tell you that he was alive when the fuel was ignited."

Amanda cringed at the grotesque horror Don must have experienced, the excruciating pain. No one deserved to go out that way, not even someone who had abused his wife physically and possibly robbed her. She couldn't bring herself to look at Trent, to see his reaction to this news. She feared he might look appeased as if it were an atonement for Don's sins. She cleared her throat and asked, "Would death have happened quickly?"

"Definitely, and I can also tell you time of death was between midnight and three AM."

Three AM was the time on the parking ticket left on Don's car. It was possible the enforcement officer had seen something or someone that might advance their case. "Do you think the killer could have burned themselves in the execution of the murder?"

She saw Trent through her peripheral vision turn to face her, but she didn't return his gaze. If he surmised that she asked because of his aunt's burned palm, he'd be correct. Technically, she hadn't been cleared as a suspect. But of all the things Gertrude had said, Amanda believed her when she said Don had burned her hand. She'd only asked Rideout for due diligence.

"It's possible but not necessary. The killer could have flicked a match at him and jumped back before the gas caught fire." Rideout paused for a few seconds, and added, "On another note, there was a wallet and the husk of cell phone, but I doubt the lab is going to get anything useful from either."

"Thank you for the updates," she told him, and Rideout ended the call.

"You just had to ask, didn't you," Trent said.

"It was worth asking," she defended. "Our job is to follow the evidence, not our desires or wishes."

Trent shook his head. "So even after talk of the bookie, you still think my aunt could have killed Don?"

"In light of the *evidence*," she stressed, "she hasn't been cleared, but she's not our prime suspect either."

"I guess that will have to do."

"What we can confidently conclude is Don was targeted. This murder method would have taken premeditation too, and I'd wager carry a deeper meaning. Don wasn't torched to hide his identity or conceal cause of death. Its sole purpose wasn't to eliminate forensic trace either. I believe the killer's priority was to inflict pain and torture. Possibly even serve as punishment."

"Or as a message," Trent said, "as I'd suggested before. That could fit with a pissed-off bookie."

"It could." While she could appreciate why Trent preferred to consider the bookie the prime suspect, there was a flipside to that. If the bookie killed Don, what was to stop them from killing Gertrude?

THIRTEEN

Before Amanda and Trent left Gertrude, she told them she had changed her mind and decided to go to the bank herself. Malone called soon after to confirm he'd requested the uniform sergeant send officers out to canvass Gertrude's neighborhood to see if anyone could provide more details about a man lurking around who drove a black Lexus LX. If someone had even a basic physical description to give them, it could go a long way to tracking this person down. Of course, a license plate would be preferred.

They dropped Don's laptop off at Digital Forensics, and then grabbed a quick bite from a drive-thru, planning to eat in the parking lot. They'd long passed lunch, and it was already after five thirty in the evening. Though it shouldn't come as a surprise. The day had been jam-packed. In the ideal world, she'd be headed home for the night, but it didn't work that way this early in an investigation. The strongest leads came within the first twenty-four hours.

"I just need a minute," she told Trent and stepped out of the car to make a call.

Logan answered on the third ring. "Let me guess. You need me to pick up Zoe?"

She'd tease back that he was a mind reader, but there wasn't much talent or gift involved with his prediction. It was one based on precedent. When she called any time after five, it was pretty much a given it was a heads-up that she'd be home late. "If you could." She winced, hating that she had to rely on him so often.

"I'll handle it."

Zoe stayed with Libby DeWinter after school. Libby was a teacher at Zoe's school, so it was convenient, but their relationship exceeded that. Libby and her life partner, Penny, were essentially Zoe's extended family. They had been close friends with the girl's parents, who were murdered when Zoe was six.

"How late will you be, or can you say?" Logan asked, some grit in his tone.

It felt like the unpredictably of her schedule might break their relationship someday. But he'd never asked to sit down for a talk. It was possible this stress point was built up more in her head than a real issue. "I wish I could say, but you know how—"

"How it works? I do by now, or I'd be an idiot. It makes me thankful for my eight thirty to five."

"Stop trying to make me jealous," she teased. Logan worked in the trades for a large development company. Great money, healthcare benefits, and best of all, reliable hours. But Amanda wasn't about to make a change in vocation any time soon.

"Just get home when you can. Zoe and I will be here when you do."

"Thanks, Logan."

"Don't mention it," he said and ended the call.

There had been a subtle strain in their relationship since last December, and they had been working to repair it. Even if that meant avoiding the root cause. She certainly wasn't going to raise the issue when she was the one who messed things up in the first place. In some ways, it might have been better to kiss Trent and *not* tell Logan, but her conscience wouldn't bear it. Logan had forgiven her, but she had to work at regaining his trust. That was a hard task when Amanda spent most days and some nights with the *other man*.

Amanda pocketed her phone and got back into the car. She dug into her burger. Between bites, she and Trent discussed the case. The plan after leaving his aunt's had been to talk to the parking enforcement officer and hit the coffee shop. Then, depending on how all that shook out, return to the plaza to see if anyone was around. They might find eyewitnesses and at least one willing to talk to them.

After they finished eating, they got on the road. It was only a short five-minute drive to the address for the parking enforcement officer. It was a medium-size apartment building in Wood-bridge, and there was a list of tenants next to the intercom buttons.

"Cole Dorsey, right?" she asked, certain she'd remembered correctly.

"Yep. That's him—"

Their fingers touched as they reached for Cole's button at the same time.

"Sorry." She withdrew her hand, cursing herself for reacting so quickly. *And for apologizing...*

"Me too. Go ahead." He gestured for her to hit the button, and she did without hesitation. It would be nice if these little awkward moments stopped happening.

"Hello?" A man's voice came over the speaker, groggy, sounding like he'd just woken up.

"Detective Stenson, Prince William County PD," Trent said. "I need to ask you a few questions. It should only take a minute or two."

No verbal response, just the buzzing of a lock being released. Trent held the door for Amanda, and they headed up to the fifth floor. The hallway was a mix of food smells, including onion, Cajun spice, garlic, chicken, and pork, but it was the dinner hour.

Apartment 512 was a few doors down from the elevator bank on the right-hand side, and a man in his late twenties, with short spiky hair, was waiting in the doorway.

"Mr. Dorsey, this is my partner, Detective Steele," Trent told the man.

Cole dipped his head in acknowledgment but said nothing.

Trent continued. "We understand that you work in the area surrounding Patriot Plaza."

"That's right."

"And you worked until seven this morning," Trent said.

"Ah, yeah."

At this point, Trent suggested they sit down, and Cole took them to the living room. A first-player shooter video game was paused on the TV screen, and a controller was abandoned on the coffee table in front of the couch.

Without a place to sit, Trent just got started. "When you were working Ingrid Street, did you happen to notice any suspicious people hanging around?"

"You at all familiar with that neighborhood? It's creepy as hell down there at night."

"We understand there are certain types that frequent the area," Trent said.

Cole smiled. "That's nice talk for hookers and druggies, but respect for not judging people. Rare to find these days."

"Let me rephrase Detective Stenson's question some," Amanda said. "Did anyone in particular stand out to you last night?"

"I don't think so."

"So no one toting around a small red jerry can?" Trent asked.

"Seems rather specific, but no. I never saw anyone on the sidewalk or street. What's this about?"

"What time were you in the area, and what time did you leave?" Trent didn't bother to respond to Cole's question.

"Well, I started on Ingrid Street about three, and it didn't take me long to walk the entire street to the next block. I only doled out one ticket right at the start. It was for a blue SUV. A Buick, if I remember right."

Don's Encore GX. "Did you smell anything unusual in the air?"

Cole shook his head, but stopped. "Barbecue? Though, come to think of it, three in the morning is a rather strange time of day to be firing up the grill, but to each their own. Am I right?" He looked at Trent, who nodded.

Amanda and Trent left Cole with their thanks, a business card, and a request he call if he thought of anything or anyone else after they left.

Back in the car, she turned to Trent. "He didn't have a lot to offer, but we can now say with some authority that Don was dead by three AM." Or as Rideout would say, *a crispy critter.*

Her phone rang, and she answered on speaker when she saw CSI Blair's name on the screen. It would save Amanda from repeating everything to Trent.

"I've got a quick update for you on the victim's SUV," Blair started.

"Great. Hit us," Amanda said.

"There was some minor blood trace," Blair offered. "Obviously, I don't have your aunt's DNA, but the blood isn't a type match to Don."

"And where was it found?" Trent asked.

"On the front mat, passenger side."

It seemed like a strange location to find blood. But it was possible Don had struck his passenger, more than likely Gertrude, and it was castoff from that. Amanda didn't want to suggest this, knowing it would torture Trent, but she needed more information. "Is there anything more you can tell us about this blood? Was there a lot? Do you think it was the result of someone being hit in the car?"

"I'd think in that case, there would be more, but it's really hard to say."

"There isn't much blood then?" Trent asked.

"Hardly any."

"Is there any way of knowing when the blood trace was left?" Amanda was aware technology was making strides every day.

"With this small of a sampling, near impossible."

"It is what it is," Amanda said, even if the answer was disheartening.

"Exactly, and a possible lead. That's why I thought I'd call you as soon as possible. Well, that and two other finds. One was an ATM slip. It looks like the vic withdrew fifteen hundred dollars as a cash advance from a credit card."

"What was the timestamp on that?" Trent asked with a side-glance at Amanda. If she was reading his mind correctly, he was wondering where Don had found available credit considering all the past due notices from credit card companies. She was.

"It was taken out last night at eleven fifteen."

"Presumably, moments before he parked on Ingrid Street." She'd pick up this thread with Trent after they were off the phone with Blair. "You said there were two things...?"

"Uh-huh. There was also a crumpled cash receipt under the seat from JJ's. It's a bar in Woodbridge, in case you haven't heard of it, and there was a to-go cup from Java Stop in the console. Suppose that would make three more things. But most of the coffee was gone. What was left was cold and skinned over."

There was proof Don had been to the coffee shop at one

point, but Amanda's mind was fixed on JJ's. It could be the bar where Don went with his friends.

"And that's it for now," Blair said. "We might have more, as we're still busy cataloging all we pulled from the alley. In the least, I intend to have a list of what we collected over to you in the morning."

"Sounds great," Amanda responded. "Thank you."

"Just doing my job." With that, Blair said goodbye and ended the call.

"He got his hands on fifteen hundred dollars within hours of his death," Trent said. "Don may have been planning to meet his bookie and hand over an installment. But did they ever meet up? If so, where? The alley or the coffee shop? Somewhere else?"

"And if he did offer a payment, was it enough to satisfy his bookie?"

"His murder would suggest it wasn't."

"Assuming the bookie is behind it," she corrected him. "But we follow the leads. Java Stop is the coffee shop where we were headed anyway. What do you say? Now as good a time as any?" She gestured out the windshield, and Trent put the car into gear.

"Works for me. When we're done there, let's go over to JJ's. It could be the bar Don liked to frequent."

"Great minds." She smiled at him and tapped her head. What he didn't realize was she was rooting for his aunt to be innocent just as much as he was. She hated the thought of Trent going through what she had when she put cuffs on her own flesh and blood.

FOURTEEN

Java Stop certainly didn't pose any business threat to Starbucks. Their menu choices were limited. Coffee or coffee. Well, likely tea and hot chocolate too. And no drive-thru either. From the looks of it, none of this curtailed business. There was a steady stream of customers going in and out, considering it was early evening. Most tables were occupied, and Amanda and Trent joined the line at the counter.

Trent was breathing deeply, as if he were utterly exhausted. All this stress with his aunt was clearly taking its toll. Amanda leaned in toward him. "Are you going to tell the rest of your family what happened to Don?" There was plenty of time to ask and listen to his answer. The woman at the front of the line sounded like she was placing an order for ten people.

"I will when the time is right. Probably once the case is closed, and after I've spoken with my aunt to see if she's up for a reunion." He didn't meet her eye as he spoke. He kept his gaze forward, his eyes carrying a faraway look. His mind was busy, possibly contemplating how that conversation would go.

"That's a smart idea." She didn't envy any of them that path. Reconciliation wouldn't come easy or fast.

"Next," the man behind the counter called out, waving for the man immediately in front of them to step to the side.

Amanda held up her badge, and so did Trent. The clerk appeared to be in his late thirties, with a crewcut and scruffy facial hair. He had a hook nose and ears that stuck out. He had the absent, glassy gaze of a drug addict.

He moaned, his entire body sagging. "Seriously? I don't have time for this."

"Really? That's how you talk to the police?" Amanda put her badge away. "Are you afraid of us, Tanner?" She took his name from the tag pinned to his shirt.

His lips curled in a sour expression. "I'm not afraid of anything, but I am working. So unless you're going to order something..." He was looking right through them, but given the unfocused and dilated pupils, he might have been watching pink elephants dancing behind them.

She looked over her shoulder, and there was just one man in line behind them.

"Do you recognize him?" Trent stuck his phone in Tanner's face, and it had the clerk pulling back.

Amanda surmised Trent was showing Tanner Don Lambert's license photo.

"Maybe."

"How about you show us some respect and start talking? Honest, *open* communication." Amanda smiled at him.

"With cops? Not likely."

Amanda snapped her fingers for his attention. Eventually, his gaze landed on her. Then, she spoke. "How about you cooperate with us, and we don't start digging into you? Just a hunch, but you're high as a freakin' kite right now. If we were to bring you in, say, for public intoxication, we'd have the right to search your person. I'm going to guess we'd find drugs or drug paraphernalia on you. Then you know what would happen, right?" She rolled her hand, encouraging audience participation.

"I'd go to jail."

"Very good. So my partner is going to show you that picture again, and you're not going to get smart or cute. You're going to answer honestly. Do we have an understanding?" She snapped her fingers again.

"Ah, yeah, sure."

"Excuse me," a man said as he tapped on Amanda's shoulder. She turned around. "Could you hurry up? I've got things to do."

"We'll be finished up here shortly," she told him.

He threw his arms in the air and left mumbling, "Unbelievable."

"Hey," Tanner dragged out, "you're scaring the customers away."

"Focus," she said and gestured for Trent to show Tanner the picture again.

With his screen in the man's face, Trent repeated his earlier question, "Do you recognize him?"

"Uh-huh. He's a reg... u... lar." His speech was becoming a touch slurred, but Amanda found it hard to conjure empathy. In some ways he'd done this to himself. But at the same time, it was sad he resorted to this choice.

"Now, that wasn't so hard, was it? Well, your regular customer is dead," Amanda said. "When did you last see him?"

Tanner paled and swallowed roughly. Amanda stepped back thinking he was going to vomit on the counter. Thankfully, he seemed to be keeping his stomach contents down.

"I saw him last night."

Amanda perked up. "And you're sure?"

"Uh-huh."

"Was he alone?" Trent asked.

Tanner's left eye started twitching. "I don't want to say, and you can't make me."

The clerk was sharing more than he realized. Whoever had been with Don terrified Tanner. "What is the person's name?"

"Couldn't tell ya. I don't collect 'em. Don't need 'em."

"Is this other man also a regular?" Trent asked.

Tanner shook his head, but the action was delayed.

Amanda read that as a druggie who had to think first, which meant it wasn't an honest response. "He doesn't need to find out you talked to us."

"He has ways of finding things out. He's totally screwed in the head."

That aptly described someone capable of pouring gasoline on a person and igniting them while they were alive. "How often is he in?"

"Remember, keep it to yourself." Tanner leaned across the counter. "He's here a couple of times a week, no set days that I could tell ya. Usually it's at night though. Say eleven until midnight."

"When was the last time you saw them here together?" she asked.

Tanner scratched his neck. "Last night."

Could they have actually found their bookie? After all, the times the man came in also lined up with when Don would slip out of the house. Was their meeting last night and Don's murder purely coincidental? She didn't believe so. "Do you have video?"

He nodded slowly and took them to an office next to the kitchen. There he brought up the video from last night. He no sooner had it on screen than a man shouted from the front.

"Hello? Anyone working here?"

Tanner left them to tend to the customer but gave them a verbal go-ahead to check the footage.

Trent sat down and forwarded to eleven o'clock. From there, he sped up the playback and reverted to live time when Don entered the coffee shop at eleven forty. He got a coffee, then joined a man at a table. His companion was wearing a baseball cap, the bill low and covering his eyes. Still, it could be made out that he had a square jaw. His torso was trim, and he was a bit shorter than Don. It was impossible to guess his age without seeing more of his face.

Nothing much was said, and Don slid an envelope across the table.

The man picked it up, looked inside. He tucked it into the interior pocket of his light jacket but, if his grimace was any indication, he wasn't pleased.

"That's likely the fifteen hundred dollars," she said.

"Uh-huh, and the guy doesn't look too thrilled by the meager instalment."

"Agreed. Obviously, we don't know what was said, but Don's body language is growing more guarded and the stranger's more aggressive." She had watched as Don leaned farther back in his chair, while the man inched forward. "There's definite tension there. But enough malice to facilitate murder?"

Trent hit pause. "Without being mind readers, it's impossible to know, but why not?"

"But do we think the bookie did the dirty work himself? Or did he call in an enforcer, who somehow lured—or followed—Don behind the plaza and proceeded to burn him alive?" She wasn't expecting that Trent would have any answers to these questions but just wanted to verbalize them.

Trent resumed the video. The bookie left at 11:50 PM, and Don left five minutes later with his coffee cup in hand.

Amanda pointed to the screen. "Possibly the coffee that Emma found in his SUV."

"If so, that raises more questions. That would suggest Don returned to his Buick. If he had plans to get with a prostitute, he would have left his coffee on the table."

"Right, so what had him getting out of his vehicle and going into the alley?"

FIFTEEN

Amanda and Trent watched the video from the coffee shop a second time. It wouldn't seem they'd missed anything. There wasn't a single shot of the bookie's face that was good enough to get them a hit in any facial recognition database. At least, Amanda didn't believe so, but she still had Tanner email her a copy of the video file. She then forwarded it to Emma Blair. Hopefully, the investigator would see something she and Trent hadn't. The fact this man had been with Don in his last hours had propelled him to the top of the suspect list.

But their day wasn't over yet, and without solid evidence against the man, she and Trent needed to keep tugging at threads. Trent took them to JJ's, the bar noted on the receipt in Don Lambert's car. If luck turned in their favor, Don's friends might be there and be able to give them the name of Don's bookie.

It was rather early in the evening, and, as indicated by the parking lot, JJ's hadn't found its stride yet. But it wasn't exactly a go-to for dinner, and most of the bar's clientele would have a meal on their mind this time of day. They mostly catered to the over-forty crowd, who would likely turn up around seven and leave for home at a decent hour to get to bed.

Inside, modern country music played through the speakers at a moderate volume, and it was more crowded than the lot had indicated. Peanut shells were crushed on the floor and made for slippery footing despite the spilled beer that made it tacky on the soles of her boots. One of Amanda's feet slid out from under her, but she managed to recover with her pride intact and without face-planting into a table or chair.

Amanda nudged her head toward the bar to let Trent know that's where she was headed. Of anyone here, the bartender should be able to offer them something about Don.

She squeezed between two patrons seated on stools and flagged the tender down.

"What can I get ya?"

She held up her badge, and while she couldn't hear the groan, she sensed it. "Detectives, Prince William County PD. We have some questions about a regular." It was a leap based on a single receipt, but she gave it a try.

The man, in his late forties, glanced at the customers within earshot. All of them were watching him in return, seemingly interested in how he was going to respond.

"Ah, sure, but I can't talk long." He gestured for them to follow him to the end of the bar. It was too high traffic, though, with the order system there. They were bumped around as servers cut in to print checks and close out tabs.

"Maybe somewhere a little quieter would work better for our conversation," Trent suggested.

"Ah, sure. Let's see what we can find." The bartender pointed toward a vacant table that needed to be cleared and wiped, and they sat down. The man gathered the empty beer pitcher, glasses, and a plucked-apart plate of nacho chips to one corner. "I don't have a lot of time," he began, "so if we could get to the point. Who is the regular?"

"Before we get to that," Amanda said, "who are we talking to?"

"My name's Micah Lutz."

She nodded and introduced herself and Trent. "The guy's name is Don Lambert. That ring any bells for you?"

The man shook his head. "I'm not so good with names. I'm much better with faces, though I ascribe people to memory based on their drink orders. You wouldn't happen to know his go-to, would you?"

"Can't help there but..." Trent had pulled up Don's license photo on his phone and showed the screen to the bartender.

"Oh yeah, I recognize him. Boilermaker. He mostly orders Budweiser, sometimes with a whiskey chaser. Sometimes just whiskey on the rocks."

Amanda didn't care what Don had drunk, but this proved he was a regular. Micah might be useful for the investigation. "How often does he come here?" Gertrude had told them he drank with his friends at a bar on Fridays and Saturdays. She was curious if Micah's answer would line up.

"Mostly once a week... Friday nights with a couple of his buddies, and sometimes on Saturdays."

"Sometimes?" Trent asked, catching the discrepancy.

"That's right."

"Is he alone when he comes in on Saturdays?" Amanda was just following a hunch.

"How he usually arrives, but he sometimes attracts company as the night goes on."

It didn't take looking at Trent to feel his anger. "By company, I assume you mean women?"

"Yep. Quite sure he leaves with some, but it's none of my business. Other nights, he's holed up at the bar all night chatting with Bernie."

Don's character was painted in a worse light with every revelation. He wasn't just a cheater, but he'd have sex with strangers. That made it more possible he'd employ prostitutes. But she was also interested in another tidbit Micah had given them for a couple of reasons. One was that this Bernie could be a friend of Don's, and two, the bartender just said he didn't remember customers' names. "You know Bernie's name. What is so special about him?"

Micah smiled. "The man's a legend. He's in every night and has been since the bar opened."

This place had been in business for decades. Bernie's liver was likely pickled by now, and if he was around from the beginning, then he'd probably be an older man. She looked at the bar, eyeing all the different faces, old and young, round and lean. "Is Bernie here?"

"No, ma'am. He doesn't show up any time before nine, then he stays until closing at two. He loves his gin and tonics and just sips 'em as if each drink will be his last."

We all have to go sometime... The cynical thought struck Amanda, and got her thinking more deeply. Was it better to live like you were dying or live like you'd go on forever? Arguments could be made for both, but she wasn't letting her mind distract her. "You wouldn't happen to know the names of Mr. Lambert's other buddies, would you?"

"I'm not sure I'd call Bernie Boilermaker's friend, but Fridays he comes in with Bud and Whiskey." He gave a lopsided grin.

"Anyone else on staff who might be able to give us their real names?" Amanda asked.

Micah looked over his shoulder toward the bar. A man, in his thirties, was behind the counter pouring out drafts of beer and setting the filled glasses on trays. "Jake, that's the barback, probably could. I can send him over."

"Sounds good. Thank you." Amanda smiled at Micah.

"Just don't hold him up for long, please." Micah stood, flagging the attention of a passing server and pointing out their dirty table, before he hit the bar.

The server barely acknowledged Amanda and Trent while she loaded everything from the table onto a tray. She quickly swiped a damp cloth over the surface of the table and was gone.

Amanda wasn't going to test her theory, but she suspected the table would be sticky to the touch. She leaned back farther in her chair, only straightening back up when Jake ambled over. Deep dimples carved into his cheeks as he grinned broadly at her.

"Micah said you wanted to talk to me?" He settled his gaze on Amanda.

"*We* both do," Trent interjected. "Prince William County PD."

"Yeah, Micah might have mentioned that." Jake winked at Amanda and sat where Micah had vacated.

"He told us you might know the names of Don Lambert's friends," Amanda began.

"Yeah. Noah Peterson and Elton Kent."

That was easy... "Good memory. You must serve dozens of people in a day."

"My father taught me that customers are the foundation of any successful business and drummed it into my head to be observant. It was important to him to call his patrons by name, so I do."

The bar's name was JJ's, and Amanda now suspected one of those Js might have stood for Jake. "*Was*? He passed away?"

Jake nodded somberly. "Last year in a snowmobile accident. He left me the bar though, and I decided to leave my corporate job and live his dream."

With the father gone, that better explained why Micah was training Jake. "I'm sorry for your loss."

Jake brushed off the sentiment. "Why are you interested in those guys anyway?"

Amanda debated whether informing him that Don Lambert was murdered was the way to go. Her concern was he'd tip off Noah and Elton before she and Trent got to them. He said he just had their names, so presumably he wouldn't have a way of reaching them. She wasn't willing to take a chance he did though. "We can't say, but we greatly appreciate your cooperation, Jake." She added a smile to sweeten her otherwise bitter words.

"Okay, well, I understand. Police business and all." His dimples were back. "Is there anything else I can help you with?"

"Actually, Micah said that Don Lambert sometimes picked up women here. Can you give us any names or point out any who might be here now?" She held her breath as she waited for a reply. Sometimes the long-shot questions paid off. She smiled when Jake nudged his head toward a woman in her late fifties or sixties sitting by herself.

"Her name's Iris. She's drinking a whiskey and pop, so it's a good night."

Amanda was tempted to ask what she drank on a bad one but resisted the urge. "Thank you."

"Any time." With that, Jake hefted himself up with yet another wink and another wicked grin.

He was certainly a heartbreaker, and Amanda suspected a lot of women would have fallen victim to those dimples. But her focus was more on Iris. Would she give them something that would break the case wide open?

SIXTEEN

Trent was already warm, but his temperature edged up another few degrees hearing about Don picking up strange women from a bar. Though why should he be surprised? It wasn't news that Don was a cheating bastard. His aunt had even told them as much. To hear it from other people just made it more real, he supposed. Don had found a way to humiliate his aunt beyond using his fists.

Iris shot back the rest of the drink as he and Amanda reached her table. With the glass still pressed to her lips, she signaled a passing server. The woman walked backward, and Iris held up her empty glass. "Another," Iris said.

"You got it." The server took the glass and left.

Amanda stepped up in place of the server. "Iris? We're Detectives Steele, and Stenson."

Iris looked from Amanda to Trent, and her expression softened. The woman was old enough to be his mother, but she had a rebellious, younger streak as testified to by her big hoop earrings and lip piercing. Her tanned, leathery, and wrinkled skin suggested she was a sun worshiper as well. "And which one are you, handsome? The Steele or the—"

"Stenson," he said coolly. Having women hit on him wasn't new, but he got the impression Iris would take a run at any man with a pulse. "We just need a few minutes of your time."

"Sure. Make yourself comfortable." Iris gestured to the spot next to her and smiled. The expression bunched up the skin around her mouth, drawing a series of fine lines. She might be a smoker too.

He sat across from her, and slid over to make room for Amanda.

"So what do you want with good ole Iris?" She started to lean across the table but sat back when the server returned with her new drink. Iris happily plucked it from her hand with a curt, "Thank ya."

"We understand that you and Don Lambert were acquaint-ed," Trent said through clenched teeth. That was as close as he dared go or he'd risk imagery snaking into his mind. If it did, white-hot rage would envelop him, and he'd lose his self-control and any shot at detached professionalism.

"Acquainted?" Iris laughed the deep-throated laughter of a lifetime smoker and then coughed. "Honey, is that what they're calling hookups these days?"

Just focus on the job... focus on the job...

"Tell us how well you knew Mr. Lambert," Amanda requested, and he was thankful for the time to work on his composure.

"Besides Biblically? Not much." She slurped some of her drink.

Trent formed fists under the table.

"We had sex just the once, and it wasn't that great." She leveled her gaze at Amanda. "You ever been with a drunk guy? It's a miracle if they get it up, and if they do it's not impressive."

Just when Trent didn't think he could be more uncom-fortable...

"The only thing that came close to rescuing the night was a

little blue pill." Iris smiled. "Even then, it was *not* worth the wait, let me tell ya." She cackled, which led to another brief coughing fit.

"Then there's nothing you could tell us about his personal life?" Trent began. "How to reach his friends or whether he had dealings with anyone shady?"

"Shady?" Iris pointed a paper straw, still in its wrapper, at him and narrowed her eyes. "Why are you two here asking about Don anyhow?"

Trent noted that Amanda hadn't mentioned Don's murder to the bartender or the barback. He'd follow his partner's lead. "It's pertaining to an open investigation. Could you give us names of anyone who might have an issue with him?"

"Ah, he's dead, isn't he?"

Trent glanced at Amanda, who nodded. "Yes," he said. "Don was found murdered this morning."

"Oh, dear." Iris sat back and took a few hefty swallows of her drink. Her eyes were glassy and not just from the booze.

"This news upsets you?" He was surprised it might because of how casual she made things sound between her and Don.

"Ah, yeah, I slept with the guy, and now he's dead."

The skin tightened on the back of his neck. Just a hunch, but he'd see it through. "Your response suggests you think there might be a link there."

She held up her hands. "Hey, just shocked is all. I don't know nothing about his death so don't look at me."

His brief hunch about Iris was likely wrong, but it marked the budding of a theory. If Don was sleeping with everyone and anyone, what's to say his actions didn't hurt other people? Maybe he was taken out by a jealous lover, or a lover's signifi-cant other. "Are you seeing another person who might not have been happy you slept with Don?"

"Hell no. I am happily and blessedly single. I like my life simple and uncomplicated, and I certainly don't want to be picking up after a man. Been there, done that, back in my twenties. The prick cheated on me to boot. I kicked him to the curb and never looked back. Never let myself get conscripted to any exclusive relationship since either. Why bother when most men cheat anyway? If you're ever interested in a good time..." Iris bobbed her eyebrows at him, and he winced inwardly.

"I'm flattered," he lied, "but I'm involved with someone."

Amanda went rigid beside him. He'd told her he was seeing someone but didn't talk about Kelsey much. And their relationship was certainly far less serious than he'd made it sound to Iris. He just needed to make the line abundantly clear so the cougar wouldn't cross it again.

"Figures. The cute ones always are." Iris shook her head at Amanda.

"Do you know who else Don may have hooked up with? Possibly even a married woman or someone who was already spoken for?"

"I don't ask those kind of questions. I'm more of a live-in-the-moment kinda girl. But Don sleeping with a married woman wouldn't surprise me. He struck me as a guy who went after what he wanted and normally got it. His confidence was the most attractive thing about him. It's why I gave him a chance and took him back to my place."

Hearing that Don had been confident didn't come as a surprise. The abusive ones often hid behind that and charisma at the onset, but Trent was finished talking about Don and his lady friends. He stood and gestured toward Amanda. "If you think of anyone or anything later on, call Detective Steele."

Amanda must have read his cue because she gave Iris her card. He certainly wasn't leaving his contact info with her.

Trent and Amanda left the bar armed with tangible leads. At least the moments of discomfort had yielded benefits.

The evening air was a touch cool with the sun starting its retreat. A quick look at his phone told him it was already seven.

He stepped to the side of the bar's doors, and Amanda joined him.

"You all right?"

He shook his head. "Not really. It never gets easier to hear how Don mistreated my aunt. An abusive asshole and a pig. Maybe my uncle Tom returned from the beyond and killed Don. I wouldn't blame him." At that realization, he was taken aback by anger that rose against his aunt. How could she disrespect Tom's memory by marrying Don? To think he had looked up to them as a couple. Just as he had his parents, considering them an example of what love and marriage should be like.

"I don't really know what to say to that, but it probably didn't start off that way. Don probably made your aunt feel incredible at the beginning."

"He did. It's just too bad it didn't last." Trent remembered how his aunt lit up when she talked about the new man in her life. Sadly it wasn't long before the shine was tarnished. "Don's wandering penis deepens the suspect pool even more. What's to say he didn't piss someone off by hooking up with their woman?"

"It's a possibility, one you weren't exactly subtle about in there." She smiled at him and continued. "If we're looking for a jealous lover, though, we'll need to figure out how to go about finding them."

"Uh-huh. Just how to do that?"

SEVENTEEN

The hands on the clock were spinning around, but Amanda and Trent still had a few hours ahead of them before they'd go home. Amanda had pulled a brief background on Noah Peterson and Elton Kent using the onboard computer in the department car. They got their addresses and intended to knock off interviews with both of Don's friends tonight. After that, they'd pop back around to the alley to see if they could speak to anyone there. She couldn't give the stretch ahead too much thought or she'd curl into a ball from exhaustion. But it was the first twenty-four, and true to form, it was proving to be a long haul.

Her tired mind was full of colliding thoughts. Some about the investigation, but also her personal life. Just the thought of Logan and Zoe at home made her jealous that she couldn't be with them. Then there was the revelation at JJ's. Trent had a girlfriend. He'd mentioned seeing someone "nice" before, but this time he made the relationship sound far more serious. He used the word *involved*. But good for him really.

Her phone rang, pulling her out of her head. It was Malone, and she answered on speaker. "You've got the two of us."

"Good, less repetition that way. Have any updates for me before I head home?"

It was a late hour for Malone to be tapping out, but her heart ached at *home*. Such a glorious fantasy, if not an option for her. She filled him in on her and Trent's last couple hours and the next steps they planned to take.

"Sounds like you have it all under control, not that I'm surprised. I wanted to let you know what has come back from the canvassing uniforms in the Lamberts' neighborhood. Some people did mention, and I quote, 'questionable characters,' around the house at times."

"Whatever that means," she pushed out. The feedback wasn't exactly earth-shattering.

"Anyone mention a black Lexus SUV lurking around?" Trent asked.

"Not specifically. However, the neighbor across from the Lamberts' noticed a man at their front door on Monday night."

She couldn't get excited about that news. It could have been anyone for any purpose. "That's rather vague. Nothing beyond that?"

"Just that he was on the short side for a man. But apparently, it was after nightfall, around ten, too dark to see much. The front light never came on either."

The timing of the visit seemed noteworthy. Not suggestive of a friendly call. "Did anyone come to the door to talk to the guy?"

"Sounds like Don did, but whatever their discussion, it was brief. The man was on his way a minute later, if that long."

The fact Don never turned the light on indicated his visitor hadn't been welcome. The brevity of the interaction also supported that. It could have been the bookie or his enforcer. "Did this neighbor see where the man went from there?"

"They saw him leave in a dark-colored sedan that was parked on the street."

"Huh." Had two men been at odds with Don, or were they looking at one man who had two sets of wheels?

"There's still a car sitting on my aunt's house, right?" Trent parked in front of a modest detached home that must belong to Noah Peterson.

"There is, Trent," Malone told him. "She'll be safe."

Amanda glanced over at Trent, but he was looking out the windshield. His facial profile had the tightened expression of a person deep in thought. "Anything else?" she said to Malone. "Any update on Don's phone records or that doorbell camera footage?"

"No ETA for the phone records, but the video file should be in our hands by the morning."

That was potentially great news, but she'd hold off celebrating until it was in their hands to see if the lead panned out. Amanda thanked Malone for the updates and ended the call. Trent cut the ignition and reached for his door handle.

"She'll be okay, Trent." She offered this because she had a hunch that despite Malone's assurance he was still worried about Gertrude. Amanda would have been in his place. There was always room for things to go wrong. A cynical viewpoint but true.

"I hope so."

They banged on Noah's door in the absence of a doorbell.

"Hold your horses," a man said, swinging the door open. The momentum stopped when his gaze landed on their badges. "Can I help you?"

"Detectives Steele, and Stenson," Amanda said. "We're looking to talk with Noah Peterson. Would that be you?" Not that she needed to ask as his image closely resembled his driver's license photo.

"Ah, yeah." He bunched up his face and angled his head. "Something I can do for ya?"

Amanda found his response reassuring. It indicated a cooperative spirit, and suggested Noah was a straight shooter with nothing to hide. If he did, he'd have countered with something defensive. "It might be best if we sat down for this conversation. If we could come inside..."

"Yeah, that's... well, I was just watching TV with my wife. Let me tell her..." Noah retreated into the house, leaving the door open for them to follow and waved them along with an arm.

Amanda and Trent remained in the entry while Noah spoke with his wife in a nearby room.

"What do the police want with you?" she asked him.

"I guess I'm going to find out. Just watch whatever you want, and I'll be back."

"Okay," the woman dragged out, clearly not impressed by the interruption.

Voices and music were coming from the room by the time Noah rejoined them. "We can go to my den," he told them.

He took them to a room in the basement, clearly designated as his man cave. It had an alcohol cart and a mini fridge in one corner of the room. Noah switched on a floor lamp, but it didn't do much good. It mostly cast the room with shadows, offering just enough light to make out the furniture in the room. A puffy navy-blue fabric couch with pillows at the back instead of cushions, an adult-size beanbag chair, a dinged-up oak coffee table, and there was a large flatscreen mounted to the wall. The cords dangled from it to an amp and game console on the media stand beneath it. College students would be quite comfortable here.

"Please, take a seat," Amanda encouraged with a gesture toward the couch.

Noah dropped down on it. "What is it? Should I be worried?"

Amanda remained standing and so did Trent. "Don Lambert's body was found this morning." She served the base notification without embellishment.

His eyes widened and glassed over. "His what now? How did he...?" The last question was left to dangle, as if forming the entire thing would make it more real.

Amanda normally didn't shy away from mentioning cause of death, but Don's had been brutal. She'd stick with the basics. "He was murdered behind Patriot Plaza sometime between midnight and early this morning." They had him on video leaving the coffee shop at eleven fifty-five. It would take under five minutes to walk from there to the alley, but the time was close enough.

"Huh." Noah rubbed his jaw, scratched his nose, sniffled. "I'm speechless."

"We're sorry for your loss," Amanda offered. "We understand you and Don were friends."

"We are... ah, *were*. I can't believe that's he's... gone. Wow. Does Elton know? He's another guy we hang out with."

It was interesting that he was more concerned about Elton than Don's own wife. Though he could have assumed Gertrude had already been informed about Don's death. Still, he hadn't bothered to inquire after her well-being. "We'll be speaking with him next, but if you could let us be the ones to tell him, that would be appreciated."

"Sure. No problem."

Noah was clearly in shock from the news, and that kept him off the suspect list. She was just about to ask if he had any insights to offer about Don's romantic entanglements or the bookie when he spoke.

"You never did say how he was... killed."

It was human nature to want this knowledge, likely a crucial part of acceptance and the healing process. "There's no easy way to say this, but he was burned alive."

Noah cried out, "What the—? Are you being serious right now?"

"This must be hard to hear," Trent said, talking for the first time since they entered Noah's house.

"*Hard?* It sounds like I'm in some movie or a bad nightmare."

"I assure you this is real life, Mr. Peterson," Trent said firmly. "As a friend of Don's, you may offer a unique perspective that helps us find who did this to him."

"Ah, sure, whatever I can do. Not that I have any idea how I can help. I have no clue who would want to do that to him."

It was understandable why Noah had gone there. Anyone who watched crime dramas on TV would know it was one of the first questions cops asked. *Do you know who had it out for the victim?* But it was a solid inquiry for good reason. "And you're sure of that? We've found out that Don was sleeping with other women. Did you know about that?"

"I was aware of them, yes, but it's not my place to tell a man how to run his life."

"Did any of these affairs turn sour? Maybe Don hooked up with married women or those involved in relationships," Trent said, painting the scenario.

He swallowed roughly. "I think he even preferred them, like it was more of a challenge."

This admission had Amanda's attention, and it added merit to Trent's theory the killer may be a jealous lover out for revenge. "You know for a fact some of these women were in relationships?"

"Uh-huh." Noah wasn't looking at her or Trent now, and she had a strong suspicion he was holding back.

"Talk to us," she said, earning his gaze. "Is someone specific coming to mind?"

"As I said, I don't have names. But there was some guy that was right pissed with Don last Friday."

"Tell us about him," Trent pushed out.

"He came up to Don at JJ's and started yelling at him."

"What time was this?" Amanda interjected.

"Probably about nine or ten. But this guy's face was all red, and his nostrils were flaring. He was right pissed off and told Don he should have stayed away from *her*. No name, but I got the feeling it was a boyfriend or husband of some woman Don had slept with. The confrontation wasn't exactly a discreet affair."

Yet the bartender and the barback didn't mention a thing... "Then what happened?"

"The guy left."

"Just like that?" It was hard to believe.

"Yep. Don said something to him, that I couldn't hear, then pointed at the bartender. The man went on his way."

It would seem just the threat of intervention sent the man away. But how did that make sense if he was so hopped-up on anger? "Did Don say anything afterward?"

"Just that the guy was nothing but hot air and to forget about him."

"But that's not the impression you had?" Amanda asked, going on a hunch.

"Nope. The guy seemed homicidal."

Tingles spread over Amanda's arms. Had he returned for Don, this time at Patriot Plaza, to burn him alive? If so, it would indicate two things. One, Don did frequent the alley. Two, this man was privy to his routine. But, again, the question rose, why had he just retreated at the bar? "Do you know what might have had Don in the alley behind Patriot Plaza between midnight and three AM?"

Noah shook his head. "I don't."

"What about in general?" she countered. "Did he make a habit of going there?"

"No."

"You sure about that?" Trent kicked out. "Prostitutes work back there. He hook up with any of them?"

Amanda cringed at Trent's cool tone but wanted to hear Noah's answer.

"I don't think hookers were his thing, but..."

"Then you don't know," Trent concluded. "From what we've gathered, Don slept with anyone he could. Paying for sex wouldn't be a stretch."

"Yeah, I can't say."

"Yet you confessed to knowing about his sleeping around. You would have known he was married...?" Trent's jaw clenched.

"Of course."

Amanda sensed Trent unraveling. "Detective Stenson, maybe—"

Trent interrupted her. "But you didn't try to stop the affairs?"

"As I said, not my place."

"Did you know that Don beat his wife?"

"Ah." Noah looked at Amanda to be rescued.

"Detective Stenson, it might be best if we could stick to questions pertaining more directly to Don's murder." Amanda was pissed that Trent had put her in this position. Sure, she understood Trent's anger toward Noah. He could well be aware of the domestic abuse but had remained silent about it if he was, just like he had Don's affairs.

Trent snapped his mouth shut, his lips pressed in a firm thin line.

Amanda proceeded. "You mentioned JJ's. You often go there with Don?"

"Every Friday night. Our other friend Elton joins us."

"Was this past Friday the last time you saw Don?" she asked.

"Yes."

Trent's lack of control seemed to have Noah retreating somewhat. He was responding to questions, but now his tone was curt and his answers short and crisp. "How was he overall? Moody, his normal self? How did he recover from that altercation?" She was tiptoeing into bookie territory, wanting to know if Don confided in his friends about his financial burdens.

"I guess you could say he was *off*. But Don was often moody. He had highs and lows, but Friday, he was rather dark and quiet, which wasn't his normal."

"Did you ask him why?" Amanda glanced at Trent. He hadn't said a word since she'd stepped in. He wasn't looking at her either, but his gaze was drilling through Noah.

"I let it go. Figured he'd talk about whatever it was if he wanted to."

"Well, we've come to find out that Don had some money problems," Amanda began.

"Oh. That might explain why he wrangled Elton into covering his tab on Friday."

"Were you aware that Don placed bets with a bookie?" Trent asked, finally reinserting himself into the interview.

"I have no clue." Noah responded to Trent's question but wasn't looking at him.

"Did you ever see a black Lexus SUV lurking around, or a dark-colored sedan?" The latter was vague but necessary to include in her inquiry. Its driver had visited Don at ten o'clock at night.

"I can't say any that stood out to me."

Amanda nodded, thanked Noah for his cooperation, and handed over her business card. "If you find out the name of the man who confronted Don on Friday, call me immediately. Same too for anything else that you feel might help us find Don's killer."

"Will do."

She and Trent saw themselves out. Once they were in the car, she faced Trent. "What was that in there?"

"What was *what*?"

"You lost focus."

"I'm just angry," he seethed, his hands on the steering wheel balling into fists.

She felt more than just anger. The pain emanating from him was intense and impossible to miss. But they had a job to do. "That's not an excuse to lose your cool. The investigation requires keeping a level head."

"Yeah, I admit that I screwed up in there. It won't happen again."

"Oh, it will." She met his gaze. "You're only human, Trent. This case, well, it's a bitch especially for you. But just try to keep a better handle on your emotions, okay?"

He nodded.

"Now, we need to talk to Elton Kent. Maybe he'll know who that guy was from the bar last Friday."

"And whether he was angry enough to torch Don days later."

"That's the thing. And if he was so mad, why would he just leave? Also, why didn't Micah or Jake from JJ's mention this? We're just talking about last Friday."

"Let's see if we can find out. We'll stop at the bar on the way to Kent's." Trent got them moving, and Amanda settled into the passenger seat, leaning her head against the rest.

She closed her eyes for a second, sorry that she had. Her conscience started nattering at her. Trent was losing control, and if that kept up, she couldn't continue to keep quiet about it. His temper had already caused an uncomfortable situation with Noah Peterson. What if it ended up truly jeopardizing the case? Unfortunately, if Trent couldn't get himself together, she'd have no choice but to report him. Even if she viewed it as the last resort, she didn't want to give much thought to what that could do to their relationship.

EIGHTEEN

A quick stop at JJ's told Amanda and Trent that Micah and Jake had witnessed the man yelling at Don, but the situation deescalated quickly on its own. For that reason, neither of them saw it worth mentioning. Security video also wasn't an option because last week was already purged from their server.

Next, they talked with Don's friend Elton Kent, but he didn't give them anything they hadn't already learned from Noah Peterson. Until they had more to go on, the theory of a jealous partner was a dead end.

It was nearing ten o'clock by the time they got to Patriot Plaza. Police presence was gone from the alley, but that didn't mean the earlier activity hadn't scared the sex workers and drug dealers away. Though from the looks of it, some did return. Shadows lingered along the side of the grocery store, distinguishable due to dampened moonlight and dim spotlights mounted to the eave.

Whether any of these people would be willing to talk to them remained to be seen.

She pointed out the people to Trent. He parked closer to the plaza, and they walked over. Amanda felt their eyes on them as they approached. Their faces were obscured by shadows but based on shape and body size, she pegged them as three women and one man.

The man was standing off to the side of the women, smoking a cigarette. Its tip was glowing and waving through the air, as he lifted it to his mouth and then lowered his arm, like an air traffic controller on a tarmac. He could be the girls' pimp, but she didn't get that feeling.

"I'll handle him." Trent gestured toward the man, who had since stomped out his cigarette and was starting to walk away. "Sir, I need to ask that you stop right there," Trent called out, trailing after him.

"Ain't gotta do nothin'." The man waved an arm over his head and kept moving.

Trent pursued, and the man eventually stopped walking and turned around. Amanda watched until it was clear her partner seemed to have the situation under control. Though she never let her guard down. Things could go sideways in a flash, and she was braced to act if needed.

She put her attention on the trio of women. One woman stood braced against the wall, one leg up and bent. The two others stood in front of her, both casting slender figures. She flashed her badge. "Detective Steele."

"Congratulations," one of them said, and the other two chuckled.

"Nice to see you have a sense of humor. That's a good start," Amanda responded. "At least that means you're talking to me. So tell me, were any of you around between midnight and three AM this morning?"

The seeming spokeswoman for the group shrugged, causing her shirt to fall over her shoulder. "What's it to you?"

"You may have heard a man was killed behind Patriot Plaza during those hours I just mentioned. Any of you see anything?" She let her gaze travel over the three of them. The one who had already spoken made defiant, yet blank eye contact. She was unquestionably high on something. The woman beside her was chewing her bottom lip aggressively enough to strip the lipstick, her gaze in space, and the one against the wall shook her head and kicked off.

She deadpanned, "Never saw a thing. Girls, I'm gonna bounce."

As much as Amanda would have liked to stop her, she couldn't force her to stay and talk. Nothing pointed toward an angry prostitute going to the alley armed with a jerry can of gasoline and torching Don.

Amanda stepped in front of the woman who had yet to speak. She tucked close to the spokeswoman. "What about you?"

She hitched her shoulders and wouldn't look at Amanda.

"No worries if you didn't see anything. Just let me know." She didn't want to come across as threatening and intimidate her into silence. It felt like the other woman was doing enough of that.

"Yeah, well, she doesn't talk much. None of us do. Especially not to cops." Again, it was the spokeswoman.

"I'm sure she does have a voice though?" Amanda gestured toward the woman still going at her lip.

"I told you"—the spokeswoman stepped in front of the jittery one and squared her shoulders—"she's *not* talkative."

The aggressive positioning, and the fact this woman spoke on her behalf communicated she was in charge of her. Amanda's intuition was screaming that she needed to get the timid woman alone. If her gut was right, she had seen something. But since Amanda lacked grounds to bring her in, she'd have to bide her time. "Okay, then, have a good night." She pivoted to leave, but as she was midturn, the lip biter made brief eye contact with Amanda.

Amanda walked away, but kept her senses at high alert,

braced to respond to any sounds or intuitive feeling that she was in danger. As she moved, she glanced over at Trent. Things appeared to be calm on his end.

She reached the parking lot before stopping and looking back. The two women had moved farther along the building, putting themselves out of sight. The third was standing against the store at the opposite end. Apparently, one bent leg was her default pose.

Trent finished up with the man and was heading toward her. They didn't talk until they got back into the car.

"How did you make out with the ladies of the night?" He faced her from the driver's seat, the engine still not on.

"*Ladies of the night?*" She smiled. "Do we still call them that? But I swear one of them knows something. I just can't get her to talk as long as the other one is hanging around."

"Do you think she saw the murder happen?"

"The way she practically bit her lip off and avoided eye contact, it wouldn't surprise me."

"Then we need to figure out a way to get her alone."

"It's the only way we're going to get her to talk, but we can't bring them back to Central for standing next to a building. Even if it's obvious what their business is, any lawyer would argue we can't presume intent. Our only choice is to get comfortable, stick around, and hope to catch her in the act."

"I'm game if you are."

She pulled her phone and woke up the screen to check the time. *10:30 PM*. It was impossible to gauge how long they'd need to hang around, but that woman could hold a key to solving Don's murder. "It could take a while," she griped.

"But it might pay off, so we don't have much choice."

"Suppose you're right." She was flushed with guilt. She already would have missed Zoe's bedtime and reading to her. It was something they had done from the beginning, a tradition that Amanda had continued after the murder of Zoe's biological mother. Logan would still be wide awake though. A true night owl, he stayed up every night until midnight. He was probably wondering when Amanda would get home, maybe even anxious about the fact she was with Trent. She took a deep breath. Dwelling on her personal life wasn't helping right now. "So, what transpired with the guy?"

"Nothing to say. Guy was a druggie, already high as a kite, and looking to score. Again, can't bring him in for making bad life choices. Besides if he saw anything, he might have already killed the brain cells housing the memory." Trent leaned against his head rest, and she looked out her window.

Nothing happened for the first half hour, but then an older sedan pulled into the lot. The driver cut its headlights as it drove slowly toward the grocery store. With the department car off and parked in front of the plaza, the new arrival might not have noticed them.

"I'm going to check on this. You stay here. If he picks up a girl, I'll text you. Just be ready to pull him over." She left the vehicle and quietly closed her door behind her. She peeked around the corner and watched the sedan stop near the store. Faint lights from the dash outlined a sizeable shadow for the driver. It was definitely a man.

Amanda ducked against the side of Patriot Plaza, seeking out a section left in complete darkness.

The spokeswoman and the lip biter approached the car, putting obvious effort into the sway of their hips. The girls chatted him up at the driver-side window for a few beats, but it wasn't long before the lip biter got into the passenger seat, and the car was circling back toward the exit.

She pulled her phone, quickly dimmed her screen, and texted Trent, *He's heading out.*

She slinked along the plaza, no longer concerned about being spotted. The man's focus would be on the street, and it was too late for the spokeswoman to step in.

Amanda saw the nose of the department vehicle, then its strobing lights. The older sedan came to a stop a mere ten to twenty feet from the road. Gratefully, the man hadn't been an idiot and led them on a chase. She'd guess he'd been through the process before though because he put his window down and stuck both his arms out.

Trent was chatting with the john when Amanda came up on the vehicle. The passenger door sprung open, and the woman bolted out.

Amanda took off after her. "Stop! Prince William County PD!"

The woman was struggling to keep momentum, and the three-inch heels on her feet probably weren't helping. Every time she glanced over her shoulder, her steps faltered, but she'd recover. Amanda was counting on the woman's luck to run out and didn't have to wait long.

The woman flew forward, her arms pinwheeling, but to no avail. She fell to the concrete with a wail.

Amanda caught up and stood over her. "You're under arrest for prostitution." She laid out the Miranda rights as she hauled the woman to her feet. She didn't feel sorry for her either. She'd given her the chance to talk before. If she had, Amanda and Trent might have long been on their way.

"Lawyer," the woman said as Amanda slapped on cuffs.

The night just got longer...

NINETEEN

It was twelve fifteen by the time the woman's court-appointed lawyer arrived at Central. While they waited Amanda and Trent had gathered what information they could on her. Jill Swanson was her legal name, and she had no record. All of twenty-two, Amanda found her heart going out to her. Had a bad childhood turned her to prostitution? Had she been groomed? Or was she so desperate to eke out a living that she saw this as the only way? She couldn't have been in the game for long because she didn't have the vacant gaze of most sex workers. Jill's still held a glimmer of light. A quick look at her background revealed she lived in a poor area of Woodbridge.

Amanda stood at the one-way mirror and watched Jill consulting with her attorney. "She looks too innocent to be caught up in this life."

"Agreed," Trent said. "She just doesn't have that hardened look."

"What I was just thinking."

The lawyer nodded toward the glass, expecting they were on the other side, and signaling for them to come over.

Amanda entered first, a folder in her hands with Jill's basic background and a list of personal effects taken from her person at the time of her arrest. Not exactly extensive. Just a purse containing condoms, a cell phone, and lipstick. At this point they had no legal rights to access her phone. That could change depending on this interview. "Jill Swanson, I'm Detective Steele, and this is my partner, Detective Stenson."

Jill's long eyelashes fluttered, but she didn't raise her gaze to meet Amanda's. She was madly chewing her bottom lip like she had earlier. Her nervous energy only strengthened Amanda's feeling she had seen something in relation to Don's murder.

"And I'm Mac Sawyer," the lawyer said. "Now that we're all acquainted, can we get to the point here?"

Amanda could appreciate Mac wasn't being paid much money for being here, but the budding attorney was acquiring experience. "Your client was arrested for prostitution. When we apprehended Ms. Swanson, she was in the company of Levi Bell. How are you and Mr. Bell acquainted?"

Jill made brief eye contact with Amanda. "He's my uncle."

Amanda admired her spunk and her stab at fabrication. Levi Bell was forty-one and could have been her relative, if not for the circumstances surrounding her arrest. His rap sheet showed he'd paid for sex acts in the past, and he was clear about his intention tonight. When she and Trent had talked to him, he'd cracked under a modicum of pressure without even requesting a lawyer. "This conversation is only going to work if we're honest with each other."

"You have proof he's not her uncle?" Mac challenged.

Amanda angled her head and regarded Jill, deciding to play along. "And why was your uncle picking you up near Patriot Plaza at eleven o'clock tonight?"

"I..." Jill looked at her lawyer and resumed chewing her lip.

"Detective, let my client go." Mac's grating voice resembled the caw of a parrot.

"I don't think so. Her *uncle* told us all about tonight. But

Levi Bell isn't your uncle, is he?" Amanda leveled her gaze at Jill.

"No."

"Thank you for your honesty. Can you tell us why you were in his car tonight?"

Jill's cheeks flushed red, and the reaction had Amanda feeling bad for the woman, but she wanted to make it clear the trouble that Jill was in. Maybe if she appreciated that she'd be more willing to disclose what she'd seen in the alley. Then a deal could be struck. Of course, that was assuming she'd seen something, but Amanda trusted her intuition. "Ms. Swanson," she prompted.

"You don't have to say a word," her lawyer cautioned.

"It's nothing to be embarrassed about," Amanda said, no judgment in her tone or body language whatsoever.

"He was going to pay me for sex." Jill's voice was small, broken, ashamed.

She certainly wasn't the typical representation of a sex worker. "How long have you been doing this?"

Jill's eyes met Amanda's. There was so much sadness housed in them, Amanda glanced away. She'd wager Jill hadn't been working the streets for long.

"Please, Detective, what is the relevance?" Mac said. "And if you have proof Jill was going to turn a trick, let's see it, and call an end to the dramatics."

Amanda sat back, slowly sinking more into her chair. Technically, their case against Levi Bell and Jill Swanson was fallible. They didn't have proof of the intended transaction. They hadn't witnessed an exchange of money take place or any sex acts. "We are willing to work out a deal for your client. That's if she's willing to help us with something."

Jill's eyes lit at this prospect. "Anything, whatever it is. I need to go home." The desperate plea spilled from her lips.

"I might be able to make that happen," Amanda said, her

tone even. "But first you need to answer some questions. Do you often hang around Patriot Plaza at night?"

"Uh-huh." She started chewing her bottom lip again.

"Were you there Wednesday between midnight and three AM?"

Mac flailed his arm in the air. "Relevance?"

She patiently turned to the lawyer. "We're not in court, Mr. Sawyer."

A pink hue splashed his cheeks, and he pursed his lips.

Amanda prompted, "Please answer the question, Ms. Swanson."

"Yes, I was there."

Mac huffed. "Please tell me what the hell is going on here, Detective."

While she wasn't impressed by the lawyer's adolescent approach, she would answer regardless. "A murder took place behind Patriot Plaza during the hours I just mentioned." She turned her focus back to Jill. "Did you see the murder happen or anyone suspicious?"

Jill nodded.

"Are you willing to share any of this with us?" Amanda asked. "As I said, there is potential for a deal."

Mac shot his client a quick look, then held up a hand to Amanda. "If my client talks, you let her walk."

Amanda smiled. "Let's see what she has to say first."

Mac narrowed his eyes, recognizing the noncommittal response.

"You'd really let me go?" Jill's voice pierced the room.

"It all depends on what you can offer us."

Tears hit Jill's cheeks as she nodded. "It was horrible. I haven't gotten a wink of sleep since. I just keep..." She sobbed, gasping for breath. She swallowed roughly. "I keep thinking that I imagined it, but I... I didn't. It was the most horrific thing I've ever seen and, oh my god, it stunk so bad."

Mac was seated against his chair, shoulders square, back straight. He flipped out his tie, as if he were moving simply to defuse his discomfort. They hadn't told him how Don had died.

Amanda inched forward on her chair. It sounded like Jill had witnessed the entire thing. "You saw it happen? Including who lit the man on fire?"

"Yeah. The whole thing." She blanched like she was going to vomit.

A rush of adrenaline made Amanda lightheaded. "Can you tell us what the person looked like?"

Jill shook her head. "It was pretty dark."

"Tell us what you can remember," Amanda said.

"He was dressed in black."

"Are you sure it was a man?" Trent interjected, finally getting involved in the interview.

Jill looked at him. "Actually, I don't for sure."

"Were they of a bigger build?" Trent asked.

Jill shook her head. "No, smaller. That's why I'm not sure. It could have been a woman."

Yet Jill's instinct told her the killer was a man. There had to be a reason for that. If only Amanda could jog that loose somehow. "Tell us what else you can remember. Was anything said? If so, with any accent?"

"I'm sorry, but I can't remember anything else. I was in shock then and couldn't believe what I was seeing. Mostly everyone else left. Please, you said you would give me a deal. I don't want any more to do with this. I just want to get home now." Her shoulders were trembling.

Amanda didn't get the feeling Jill's desire to go was entirely selfish. "You have someone waiting on you, don't you?"

"My baby. She's two, and she's my whole world. I only do *this* for her and her future. It's practically impossible to support a kid as a single parent these days, and I want her to have what I didn't."

Amanda's heart ached for Jill, for how she obviously felt like she was forced to make the decision she had. "There are other ways, if you wish to see them," she said gently and pulled her card. "You can call me if you need help. Anytime. All right?"

Jill took her card and tears welled in her eyes. It felt like something shifted in her, then she said, "There is something else. I not only saw that man's murder, I have it on video."

TWENTY

The next morning, Amanda's mind was still replaying the video from Jill Swanson's phone. It pinned the attack and subsequent murder at precisely 12:15 AM and captured the whole, ugly mess. There were no Hollywood effects, but it appeared dramatized for a viewing audience. Just the grotesque nature of the crime accomplished that. Regardless of Don's life choices, no one deserved to go out like that. His screams were surreal, high-pitched, otherworldly. It was surprising no one else had come forward but, then again, it wasn't a neighborhood friendly with cops. They were lucky that one resident had offered up their doorbell camera footage, even if they requested a warrant before they'd hand it over. Jill had confessed that she hadn't wanted to get involved and wouldn't have if there wasn't a deal on the table for her release.

"You got in late last night," Logan said as he sat next to her at the kitchen peninsula with his second coffee of the day, and it was only seven thirty.

"What can I say? I picked up a new case yesterday." She didn't feel the need to reiterate ground they'd already covered. Just how vital the first twenty-four hours of an investigation were. She attempted to smile at him, but the expression wouldn't form, and she pressed her lips to her own cup to hide the awkwardness. She'd like to chalk her mood up to exhaustion, but she was on the defensive. Her job had created problems between them before, and she wasn't confident that issue was resolved for good, just like the Trent thing. Logan said he'd forgiven her for kissing Trent, which had been months ago, but the road back to where they had been prior was full of potholes. Though she suspected the forgetting part of forgiveness was the tough part.

"Well, I better hop in the shower and get moving," Logan said. "You good to drive Zoe to school today?"

"You bet." Amanda looked forward to doing so. It would give her some time with Zoe she hadn't had last night.

Logan popped up, kissed her forehead, and took off down the hall toward the bathroom.

Amanda checked in on Zoe to make sure she was getting ready for school. She'd already eaten breakfast, and Logan said she'd had a bath last night.

Amanda found her bedroom door closed and knocked as she slowly opened it.

Zoe was dressed but seated on a small chair near her bookshelf, hugging her stuffed dog, and holding on to a Curious George book. Something was obviously troubling the girl. The dead giveaway was the stuffed dog. Sir Lucky was its official name, and Zoe had decided about two years ago that she was too grown up for him. Her holding on to him meant she was seeking comfort.

"I see you have your old friend out," Amanda said gently as she approached the girl with cautious steps.

"Not that he's helping me." Zoe stuck out her bottom lip, and her eyes filled with tears.

Amanda sat on the floor beside Zoe, suspecting the source

of the girl's sadness but asked anyhow, "What's wrong, sweetie?"

"I just..." She hiccupped a sob. "Miss them and when you" —she leveled a chilling look at Amanda—"aren't home, it makes me miss them more." She sobbed, and the sight and sound broke Amanda's heart.

Amanda wasn't sure where to start, how to respond. Words fell short at a time like this. Zoe regularly saw a therapist to talk out her feelings about her parents' murders, but that still didn't erase the pain altogether. This was the first time the girl blamed Amanda's absence for triggering her grief. But she had a job to do. It wasn't like she was purposely choosing to stay away. "Your parents are always with you, even if you can't see them." She wasn't about to mount a defense and caressed a hand over Zoe's head and her long blond locks.

"Do you really believe that?" Zoe looked at her, the eyes of a child, calling for the truth.

The direct question, and her gaze pierced Amanda like a stake. *Do I...?* "I would like to."

"But you don't?"

Nothing gets past this girl... "It doesn't matter what I believe, sweetie. Everyone needs to believe what is right for them. But I can confidently say your mother and father will always exist right here." Amanda laid a hand over Zoe's heart. "I feel Kevin and Lindsey in mine."

"All the time?" Zoe blinked, her soaked eyelashes splashing tears onto her cheeks. "Because I don't. I'm afraid I'll forget them."

If only there was a way to suck all this hurt from her, but Amanda knew only time helped lessen the sting. "You'll never forget them. There will be things that happen, and it will trigger a memory." Like how coming into this room could unexpectedly flood her with memories of her daughter Lindsey.

"Then you don't think about them all the time?" Zoe set the dog and book on the carpet at her feet and palmed her cheeks.

Amanda shook her head. "It's only natural, sweetie, as time goes on, for us not to think about them as often. That doesn't mean they never mattered or that we're bad people for moving on."

Zoe didn't say a word, just pierced Amanda's eyes. Both relief and sadness danced in the girl's gaze.

"Come here, sweetie." Amanda opened her arms, and Zoe nested against her chest. She held the little girl tight. "I'm always here for you," she whispered against Zoe's head and pecked a kiss there.

Zoe pulled back and jumped to her feet. "But you're not! You're always at work. All the time."

The accusation burned as acid, more truth than fiction. She didn't have an excuse to offer, just an explanation. "I'm catching bad guys, trying to make the world a safer place." She grappled for something that would smooth this over. She'd even used words Zoe had said before.

"We need you too, Mandy." Zoe snatched her backpack from a small table in the room and headed out.

It took a few minutes before Amanda could scrape herself off the floor. She could barely breathe. She'd hurt the person most important to her, and there would be no taking that back. She felt like such a failure. To make it worse Zoe had obviously seen the effect Amanda's long hours had on Logan too. She had included him in her grievance.

She found Logan getting dressed in their bedroom and told him what had just taken place with Zoe.

"She is right, you know. We both miss you when you get new cases, but I know, it's your job. We understand."

For some reason every time Logan said that it made her question its authenticity. Was it an auto-response? What he felt *she* needed to hear? "I'll try to be home earlier tonight, but I can't make any promises."

"Do what you can. We'll be here." He pulled her into a hug and kissed her temple, then her lips. "Just if it's possible, carve out time this weekend for us...?"

"I will do my absolute best." She refused to promise, only to possibly break it, but she would hold the intention.

They parted with well wishes for the day. Amanda dropped Zoe off at school, and she left the car without so much as a good-bye. *Ouch!*

Amanda got into Central at about eight twenty, beating Trent. With all that had transpired with Zoe this morning, Amanda already felt emotionally spent. It had effectively kicked the graphic video of the murder from her mind, but being at her desk brought it back. There was an email in her inbox advising her the footage from the doorbell cam was on the department server to watch. But she'd wait for Trent.

She decided to view Jill's video again. She popped in Bluetooth earbuds, not looking forward to the all-immersive experience, but she might pick up on something she hadn't before.

Don entered the alley from Ingrid Street ten minutes after midnight. A dark-clad figure was following carrying a jerry can. Its bright-red color was tamed by the darkness of night, and the person's clothing made it impossible to ascertain whether their shape belonged to a man or woman. They appeared to be a few inches shy of Don's height, which was six foot even, so that aspect wasn't conclusive either.

Don was heading toward the dumpster when the killer must have said or done something causing him to turn around. Unfortunately, the video hadn't picked up what that was. The next thing she saw was a ball of flame lighting the screen seconds later. The killer must have doused him with the fuel out of the video sightline. Other figures in the alley dispersed in silence.

Don ran some, flailing arms accompanied with screams.

Only a moment later, all fell silent. But smoke and flames continued to shoot above the dumpster where Don had gone down.

Amanda paused the video, noting the key takeaways. Don's killer had unquestionably targeted him. They also didn't show any signs of hesitation. Did that mean they were an experienced killer or simply on a mission?

But none of this released any of their current suspects from the frame. The bookie, a possible enforcer, a jealous lover, and Trent's aunt were still viable.

"Hey there." Trent set a coffee from Hannah's Diner on her desk.

"Thank you! You're a lifesaver." With everything that had transpired with Zoe, stopping for coffee had been the last thing on her mind. She eagerly pulled back the tab on the lid and took a tentative sip. Too hot to gulp, unfortunately, but she'd have longer to savor it.

"I see you're a glutton for punishment." Trent flicked a finger toward her monitor where the end of the video was frozen. "I never need to see it again. It's here." He tapped a fingertip to his head.

"Same here, but I just watched it once more to see if I missed anything."

"And...?"

"Shouldn't have bothered." She winced as the graphic imagery layered in her mind. Then there was her earlier thinking about the mystery person, how it could have been Gertrude. Surely, he would have seen that possibility too. "Ah, how did you sleep last night?"

"Sleep? Doesn't that sound like a luxury reserved for those outside of law enforcement?"

She bobbed her head and smiled. "I hear you." She didn't need to add that her rest had been unsettled too. "So the doorbell cam footage came in. Want to start with that?"

"Works for me." Trent wheeled his chair in from his cubicle. She moved over to make room for him next to her.

As she opened the directory on the server, an email notification popped up in the bottom corner of her screen. It was from CSI Blair with the subject "You'll want to know this." That was too tempting to ignore. "Just one brief detour..." She clicked on the message.

Trent leaned over. "It looks like the evidence list of what was collected from the alley, but it looks like she flagged—"

"If you don't mind." She smiled at him, but he was encroaching on her personal space. He was pointing at her screen, his arm in front of her face.

"Oh. Sorry." He lowered his arm, adding a smile.

"But, yes, she did flag something..." Amanda paraphrased the find. "A fingerprint, on the bottom side of the jerry can, survived the fire."

"Was there a hit in the system?"

"Not that she says, and I'm sure she would have. But once we get a suspect, it could help button up the case."

"It's better than nothing, I suppose." Trent sank against the back of his chair and drank his coffee.

"Don't you sound impressed." Complete sarcasm.

"Well, it's not exactly an earth-shattering find. It has potential, sure. But there's no way of knowing when that print was left. It could belong to the attendant who filled the jerry can at a gas station for that matter."

"True enough." In seconds, he'd managed to suck her dry of any faith in the finding. She closed the email window and brought up the doorbell video. As they were told, it was from the house where Don had parked on Ingrid Street. She forwarded to eleven thirty when Don's Buick Encore turned up. He parked and walked up the hill toward the coffee shop.

Amanda forwarded the video in slow motion. No foot or street traffic until eleven forty-two when a red Kia drove past.

Just like the car that Gertrude has... She glanced at Trent, but he didn't look at her, and she would let it go for the time being.

The Kia seemed to slow as it passed Don's Buick, but it picked up speed again and disappeared.

She paused the video and gave him seconds to say something. When he didn't, her impatience bubbled up. "Are we just going to ignore this?"

"The red Kia? No, I saw it." He took a sip of his coffee.

"We can't just pretend we don't know what it might mean. Your aunt has a red Kia." She resisted her impulse to add more to that statement. After all, this combined with Gertrude's white lies and obvious withholding of information didn't help her case. Tag on to that the fact Gertrude fit the size of the killer.

"A lot of people have Kias, Amanda."

"But I doubt all of them would have motive to want Don dead."

"Now you're getting carried away. We don't know the driver of the Kia is the killer."

"Fine." She held up a hand, realizing he made a good point, but the coincidence that one of their prime suspects had a red Kia continued to niggle. "But you know how dodgy she's been when we've questioned her. What if she wasn't in bed like she told us? Can we believe a word she says?" Part of her wished to retract the last question when Trent's eyes darkened.

"You're always telling me we follow the evidence. Where's the evidence this is my aunt's car? The angle doesn't let us see the license plate. Let's just watch the video, *please*." He gestured toward her monitor, and she hit Play.

Several minutes later, at 11:57 PM, they were rewarded with the sighting of the dark-clad figure from the murder video. Unfortunately, their face was covered, but there was a jerry can in their hand. They came to a standstill at the Buick's rear bumper and just stood there.

"He's waiting for him," Trent said.

He... It was too soon to leap to the gender of their killer. He might not have meant anything by it, but she felt it was intentional to push focus from his aunt. But surely he had to acknowledge Gertrude could have parked down the street and walked back. "Let's just watch."

A few minutes past midnight, Don ducked into his Buick, dropped off his coffee cup, and then shut the door. He started walking toward the alley, seemingly oblivious to the mystery person lingering behind his vehicle.

"That son of a bitch," Trent pushed out. "He was going to hire a prostitute."

"If it's any consolation, it didn't end up happening."

"Last night anyway," he mumbled.

On the screen, the mystery figure left their post and set off after Don. Soon after, both figures were out of the camera's line of sight. But they had what happened from there.

She stopped the video and swiveled to Trent. "Whether you like it or not, we need to bring your aunt in for further questioning. We have no other option."

He blew out a staggered breath. "Just let me take the lead with her, please."

She nodded and shut down her computer, prepared to stand by his side whatever was to come.

TWENTY-ONE

The little boy inside Trent wanted to shut his eyes, plug his ears, and dismiss what he had seen. He wasn't going to let on to Amanda, but he was certain the red Kia on the video was his aunt's car. Hers had a scuff mark on the front passenger-side quarter panel, just like the one on the footage. Aunt Gertrude had lied right to their faces. *His* face, her own nephew's. She hadn't been at home in bed. He wasn't sure whether he was more angry or disappointed. But he wasn't going to lose sight of the bigger picture either. Just because his aunt had lied, it didn't mean she was the mystery figure and Don's killer. "Even if it was her, I'm sure she has an innocent explanation." He heard how weak and pathetic he sounded the second the words left his lips. After all, the lies indicated his aunt had something to hide. What if his aunt had killed Don?

"We'll find out what she has to say, Trent. That's all we can do for now."

He was sure Amanda was looking at him, but he couldn't bring himself to face her and witness pity in her eyes.

Trent drove slowly down his aunt's street, keeping an eye out for a black Lexus LX. None were in sight. Neither was a police cruiser. "I thought my aunt was under twenty-four-hour watch."

"She was supposed to be. Let me check in with Malone." Amanda got on her phone.

Trent would have expected to be informed if the surveillance detail had been pulled. Yet moments ago, they'd been in Malone's office, and he'd said nothing about that. Though, he also hadn't suggested they have the officer bring Gertrude into Central.

Trent pulled into his aunt's driveway behind her Kia.

"Thanks." Amanda hung up.

"So?"

"Malone thought there was a uniform assigned to watch over her. He's going to follow up on that right now."

Trent wanted to take Malone's word on the matter, but it didn't explain his other thought. "If he believed a uniform was on site, why didn't he suggest they bring my aunt in?"

"He did."

"I don't remember that."

"You hit the restroom on the way to his office, remember? I went on ahead to keep things moving along..."

The pitstop had been a delay tactic to allow himself a few precious seconds to gather his thoughts and his emotions, regain perspective. "Right."

"And I told Malone it was important to you that you be the one to bring her in."

"Oh, thanks."

"Don't mention it."

He nodded, appreciating that she was on his side, and they got out of the car.

As he walked up the driveway and passed his aunt's Kia, his gaze landed on the scuff mark, and it had a sudden dread washing through him. He rang her doorbell, and footsteps padded toward the door shortly after. His aunt's shadow darkened the sidelight.

"Oh bloody hell," she muttered loudly.

From the sound of it, she'd returned to her cantankerous self. *One step forward, two back...* "Open up, Aunt Gertrude. *Now.*" He refused to let her influence his emotions this time. He and Amanda were here on serious business, equipped with serious accusations. She needed to respond to them.

The deadbolt thunked, and the door was opened.

"What now?"

He was about to answer when the sight of her left him speechless. There were bright purple bruises on her forehead and a few cuts. "What happened to you?" He stepped inside the house without waiting for permission to enter. To hell with that. In this pocket of time, he was a nephew seeing to his aunt.

"I... It doesn't matter, does it? Does any of it?" She'd started off talking strong and defiant, but her confidence crumbled. Tears beaded in her eyes, and some fell.

"Tell us what happened," he told her. "We should get you checked out."

"No." She shook her head adamantly. "I'm not going anywhere."

He would have helped her to the front room, but she shuffled there by herself. Was her gait off or was he imagining it? He glanced over his shoulder at Amanda and raised his eyebrows. She offered a small shrug to denote she had no idea what might have happened.

They all took what were becoming their regular seats.

Trent sat on the edge of the chair cushion. "What happened, Aunt Gertrude?" His nerves were frayed, and adrenaline at the uncertainty of everything had his entire body pulsating.

"I was..." Her gaze traveled from him to Amanda and back again. "I don't want to trouble you with my issues."

Trent tensed at that remark. When would she realize she wasn't alone? That she had people who cared about her? "No trouble. Just talk." He gathered his composure and added, "Whatever you can tell us could help you."

Her eyes snapped to his. "What does that mean?"

"Let's just say it's in your best interest to be open with us from this point forward," he told her.

"I had a visitor last night." She sniffled, and a few more tears fell. "He roughed me up pretty good."

Trent tensed, all his bad feelings from yesterday brewing up with a vengeance. "Who? Don's bookie?" He wagered a guess and glanced at Amanda.

"Him or one of his men." His aunt hiccupped a sob. "He told me what happened to Don was just the beginning, and if I didn't pay his debt, he'd make sure I hurt too. Then he knocked me around some to get his point across." She sniffled and pinched the tip of her nose.

Trent got up, fetched her a tissue, and returned to his seat. "They told you they killed Don?"

His aunt blew her nose and held the bunched tissue in her palm. "What I gathered."

Trent considered the phrasing *what happened to Don was just the beginning*. He held eye contact with Amanda for a few seconds. He knew his aunt hadn't killed Don. She wasn't that type of person. Despite all the years of abuse, a kind heart still beat in her chest. "What else did he say?"

"He'll be back at one o'clock today, and I better have twenty K waiting for him. If I don't, he promised things would get a lot worse for me."

"Did he elaborate on what he meant by that?" Amanda inserted.

Trent shot her a look. Why was she forcing his aunt to relive this moment in time? "I think we get the gist, Detective Steele. He was essentially threatening her life. You were afraid for your well-being?" He directed the last bit at his aunt, and she nodded.

"I don't have that kind of money. I..." Fresh tears welled up. "I decided to go to the bank after you left yesterday. My account was closed two years ago. All of Tom's money, what I got from his life insurance, gone. Don stole all of it."

"I'm so sorry to hear that," Amanda told her when Trent didn't reply.

He was a million miles away, immersed in rage.

"Trent?" Amanda said, rather loudly. He couldn't be sure how many times she tried to get his attention before her voice finally cut through his thoughts.

"Yeah?" He slowly looked at her, and the pieces clicked together. She was doing her best to honor her promise of letting him handle the questioning, but he'd let the situation distract him from their original purpose. But could his aunt really be considered a suspect after what they'd just heard? After all, it sounded like his aunt's unwelcome visitor had confessed to the murder. "Aunt Gert, we originally came here to ask you something," he began.

His aunt's tears dried up, and she was staring at him unblinking and pale.

He continued. "We got our hands on some video footage from a doorbell camera on Ingrid Street for Tuesday night into Wednesday morning..." He wished his aunt would save him some grief and step in, but she didn't. "Can you tell where I might be headed with this?"

"I have a feeling."

"You were there, around the time of his murder," he said.

She nodded.

"Why did you lie to us? To *me*, when we asked if you were home all night?"

"I never figured you'd find out I was in the area. And I really wanted to avoid this conversation."

Her defense was pathetic and insulting. "I am your nephew, but even more importantly an officer of the law. I swore to uphold my oath, and if you had let me help you any of the hundred times I had tried in the last several years, you'd know I take it very seriously. You'd also know I'm damn good at my job and take the time to get to the truth. Now tell me some. Please."

His aunt's face pinched from his onslaught of words, but he didn't feel regret. He said what had needed saying.

"Why were you there?" he pushed out when she still hadn't spoken.

His aunt stuck out her chin. "I followed him. That's all."

"Please. Stop insulting me." He was flushed with rage and shot to his feet. "You want us to believe you followed your abusive husband, a man you were terrified of? And that's *all* there was to it?"

"Trent." His name came from her lips as a strangled cry and wrested him back from the ledge.

"What did you do?" He steadied himself for the truth, not sure if he could handle it. He'd been so insistent on defending her, but despite flesh and blood, she was more a stranger after all these years. That fact was just starting to sink in for him.

"I swear that I only followed him. I was careful to keep my distance, so he didn't see me."

"Why were you following him?" Maybe he didn't want the answer. But if she had killed Don, how did that reconcile with the man who threatened her last night? He'd as good as admitted to killing Don. Then again, it was his aunt's word that had taken place. He was learning he couldn't always rely on what she told them.

"I wanted to find out where he went when he left the house late at night. For the record, I'm still in the dark."

"I can't say this was the case every time, but we believe he placed bets with his bookie when he'd step out briefly at night." He was going to leave out all mention of sex workers.

Seconds ticked off, then his aunt eventually sat back and said, "Ah."

"Did you think he was meeting up with another woman?" he asked. She'd already voiced her suspicions regarding adultery, and he hated to refresh the wound. But her answer could give them some insight into her state of mind.

"I did."

"And what was your plan if he had? Was it still just to follow him?" He didn't relish being in the place of an accuser, but his guard was up.

"Yes. That's all. I swear."

"That would have been enough for you? Just to confirm what you felt you already knew? Or did you wait next to his Buick to confront him?" Trent had to slip into cop mode. It was the only way he could drill down to the truth, but he was pissed that his aunt was forcing him to go there. She wasn't responding to softer attempts, so he had to try a tougher approach.

"I drove by his car and returned home. That's all."

It wasn't necessary for her to have driven past again. She could have taken a side street near the coffee shop and gone down another one, avoiding Ingrid Street a second time. She might be speaking the truth. There was also the matter of the man who had roughed her up. The physical evidence backed up that story. It was feasible she was being honest about what he told her too. "Detective Steele, a minute in the kitchen?" It was at the back of the house, and would offer some separation so his aunt wouldn't overhear their every word.

"Sure." Amanda gave his aunt a look before leaving the room, as if she hesitated to leave Gertrude unattended. But it wasn't like she was going to run. She wasn't even walking right.

Once Amanda joined him in the kitchen, he said, "We need to have my aunt taken to Central, I understand that. I acknowledge that she's being cagey, she even lied to us, but we can't ignore what else she told us. The guy who threatened my aunt made it sound like he killed Don, and he's due back at one. When he gets here, he needs to find us instead."

Amanda held up a hand. "I'm not about to argue, but let me play devil's advocate for a second."

"Okay," he dragged out.

"You seem convinced this man who paid your aunt a visit killed Don, but he didn't say that."

"He did." He racked his brain for the language his aunt had used, but his mind was so cluttered with everything it wasn't coming to him.

"No, he didn't. Not in so many words. It was an implication, not a confession. He could have just found out what happened to Don."

"How is that?"

"Word travels on the street, for one thing. We won't know for sure until we have a chat with him."

"Yeah, just before we put him behind bars for attacking my aunt."

"No argument there."

"Good." He was heaving for breath, prepared to defend his aunt again, and hating himself for how wishy-washy he found himself at times. One second, he was prepared to defend her, and the next, ready to bring her in. But he'd be lying if he denied a tangle of emotions was affecting his vision. Maybe he should remove himself from the case. But then who would protect his aunt? Besides, he'd stepped back from her life for long enough already, failing to shelter her from Don. No, he owed it to his aunt to stay put. "I also think one other thing is clear. Dead or not, the bookie plans to collect Don's debt. And we must make sure it's not my aunt who pays the price." Trent choked up on that. The man had already roughed her up. There was no saying what he was capable of if she didn't hand over the money. It was a good thing they'd never have to find out.

TWENTY-TWO

Amanda watched Trent's face as they briefed Malone back at Central on the situation with Gertrude and their plan to get their hands on the bookie or his enforcer. Malone was guarded. His forehead was tight, and his gaze focused.

"If you think this mystery man killed Don, then why bring in Gertrude?" Malone leaned forward, looking at them across his desk.

Before coming to the sergeant's office, they'd set Gertrude up in a holding cell, surprisingly at Trent's request. He argued that it might help her appreciate what was at stake for her.

"Due diligence," Trent said stiffly.

"Hmm. Well, I suppose she may have more to say. It seems it's like pulling teeth to get her to talk, forgive me for saying this, Trent."

"No, you're right." Trent remained poised, sitting on the edge of his chair, shoulders square, chest out.

"All right, well carry on." Malone plucked a folder from his desk and set it in front of himself, another signal the meeting was over.

"One more thing." Trent hadn't moved from his chair. Amanda was already at the doorway.

"What is it, Detective?" Malone kept his hold on the paperwork and looked up.

"Why wasn't a uniform posted on my aunt's house last night?"

Amanda flinched at Trent's sharp tone, not that she blamed him for wanting that answer.

Malone stiffened. "The sergeant from the uniformed division told me all units were diverted to a manhunt last night."

Trent's breathing deepened, and his nostrils flared. "With all due respect," he seethed, "we're talking about one car here. If that officer had stayed put, my aunt might not have been attacked and threatened."

"While I appreciate your viewpoint, there is no guarantee she would have been safe either. Now, please, shut my door on your way out."

Amanda hoped that Trent would take the direction, because Malone's energy was hardened, ready to fight. She'd known the sergeant for long enough to recognize when it was time to back down.

Trent stood, letting out a huff, and breezed right past Amanda into the hallway. She gave Malone a tight smile and closed his door.

"Just an excuse, Amanda." Trent pivoted, raking a hand through his hair.

"Your aunt is okay." Things could have been worse, but she didn't want to come right out and say that. It wasn't like that made what she had suffered justifiable either.

"Sure, relatively speaking. Though I didn't realize we were in the business of taking chances with people's lives."

Amanda wasn't touching that. "Let's just do what we can to get this guy. You and me, all right?"

Trent nodded.

They proceeded to arrange for backup to accompany them to Gertrude's house, but the stipulation was made clear that no cop cars were to be within a two-block radius. They didn't need the bookie or enforcer to get spooked. By twelve thirty, everything and *everyone* was in place.

Amanda and Trent waited it out at the kitchen table, but time was dragging out. It wasn't like she wanted to initiate conversation, as she could feel Trent's temper simmering beneath the surface.

At exactly one, the doorbell rang.

She cleared her throat. "You ready?"

"You bet." Trent led the way from the room, but hung back for her to answer the door. She was to give the impression of a housecleaner.

The doorbell rang a second time and was followed by a brisk, loud knock. Amanda reached the entry and took a steadying breath, checked her gun in the holster at her hip. Its bulk was hidden under an oversized shirt she was wearing. She wanted it handy and accessible, but the mystery man didn't need to spot it the second she came into view.

"Woah, hold up. I'm coming," Amanda called out, stomping toward the door. She flung it open and was met with a man large enough to block the doorway. Her five-foot-nine was dwarfed by his looming size. Her face was level with his chest. She had to pull back to look up. Bald head, muscled biceps, and forearms the circumference of her calves. He was far too large to be Don's killer. So how did he fit in? Or did he? "Can I do something for you? If it's religion, take it next door." She jacked a thumb.

The man grimaced and squinted. "Do I look like the religious type?"

"I wouldn't know what type you are, but you best state your business or leave the property." So maybe she wasn't so good at playing helpless and vulnerable. She was better fit to the role of protector of the castle.

"Where is the nice, quiet older woman? My business is with her." He was looking over her head into the house. The only way she could block his view would be to jump and wave her arms. And that wasn't happening.

Think small and mighty! Amanda peacocked her posture and pushed out her chin. "She's having a tea in the kitchen."

"Well, I need to speak with her. Who are you anyway?"

"Not really your business, but I'm the housekeeper."

"Hmph." He made a noise that was a cross between a groan and a grunt, sounding like a Neanderthal from the Stone Age, and stepped toward her.

She only moved out of the way to avoid being stomped on. "Excuse me. I never said you could come in here."

"This is none of your business."

"Oh, I think it's the lady's business. And mine." Trent came out from behind the door, his gun trained on the giant's torso.

Easy, Trent... Amanda thought. Trent hadn't been given cause to even draw his weapon yet.

"Prince William County PD, and you're under arrest for assault and uttering a death threat," Trent said.

The man responded in an instant, striking out with a round-house kick. His foot knocked the gun from Trent's hand.

Both men dived to the tiled floor and in a moment were fighting to seize the Glock. Her partner's regular-sized frame was swallowed up by his opponent. Physically, Trent was no match but that didn't appear to be stopping him. He continued to throw punches, even though the blows seemed to glance off the larger man. They both had a hand on the weapon, and then it went off.

Amanda ducked into the side room, where she pulled her own weapon. Then she popped back out. Thankfully the bullet had burrowed into a wall, and no one's flesh. But the sound of gunfire should alert their backup to move in. "Stop right there." Amanda stepped into the entry, leveling her gun at the man as he reached again for the fallen Glock.

The giant grunted and left Trent sprawled on the floor, heaving for breath, but there was a fire in her partner's eyes as he reached to retrieve his gun.

TWENTY-THREE

Amanda's heart was pounding, as the giant faced down his mortality, challenging her to pull the trigger. She hesitated just a millisecond too long. The giant twisted her wrist, forcing her fingers to release her hold on her gun. He claimed possession of it. She bravely, and stupidly, clawed at him. To no avail. He gripped her throat with one hand, holding her tightly against his torso.

"You're going to let me go," he said to Trent, "or I'll squeeze the life out of her." He tightened his grip, which was already cutting off her airflow. She slapped his arm, but she was about as effective as a fruit fly. Nothing more than annoying.

Her consciousness started to float, as her life flashed before her eyes. *Little Zoe...* She'd die with her girl mad at her. Not fair to Zoe or her. There had to be a chance to make things right. That was only fair. A single tear fell from Amanda's eye. Hadn't she learned a long time ago that life wasn't fair?

"Let her go, or I swear I will put a bullet between your eyes," Trent seethed. His voice sounded like it was traveling through a tunnel or a tin can. So very far away...

Her eyes rolled back in her head, her lashes fluttering. *This is it...* But his grip weakened as he started to walk backward out the door with her. She could finally get a solid breath, and she greedily gulped it into her deprived lungs. She craned her neck and made eye contact with Trent. His gaze was intent, cold, deadly.

Take the shot! She was screaming in her head, but if they killed him, the truth of Don's murder could go to the grave. Could Trent even pull off the shot? They were trained to shoot center mass. A chest shot would come too close to her head. If Trent missed... She didn't want to think about it.

Thankfully, it seemed Trent had done the calculations too and concluded, like her, they were out of immediate options.

The giant stepped over the threshold, onto the front stoop, and lost his balance. His hold on her loosened further, and she assumed the same would apply to his grip on her gun. "Get out of the way!" she yelled at Trent at the same time as she bit the giant's hand. Her Glock fell from his hand, and for a second, he remained standing there staring at her, stunned.

Trent stepped out of the neighboring room where he'd sought shelter in case her gun fired. He appeared ready to take his shot when the giant spasmed and fell to the concrete.

Officer Leo Brandt stood behind them holding a Taser, the prongs still in the giant's body. "The bigger they are, the harder they fall."

Amanda looked down at the sprawled mass, let out a long, deep breath and rubbed her throat. That had been a close call. She turned to Trent. "You all right?"

"Yep. You?"

"Still above ground."

He bobbed his head, as more officers rushed in to help Brandt collect the giant and load him into the back of a squad car. He grunted and groaned the entire time.

Amanda and Trent hadn't even caught their breath when Malone entered the house.

"What the hell happened in here? It was just supposed to be a simple apprehension."

It's never simple...

"Hello?" Malone waved a hand in the air. "Either of you want to brief me on what happened? Whose gun went off? The perp's?"

"It was mine, Sarge," Trent said. "I'll hand my service weapon in, write up a report."

"Damn straight you will. It's protocol."

Amanda would have to submit paperwork too because she'd pulled hers, but she was more surprised by Malone's strong reaction. The incident must have scared him more than he was actually angry. He wasn't often present when her and Trent's lives were in danger. In fact, she was surprised he was on scene, but it wasn't her place to question him.

"But don't make me wait on your report," Malone said. "Give me the overview now."

"It was an accident," Trent said. "The perp kicked the gun from my hand onto the floor, we both got a grip on it, and it fired."

"An accident? That's what you're trying to tell me? Was it day one of the academy? Get talking. Tell me how that hap — Oh."

Amanda and Trent remained silent as Malone's face turned to stone.

"Your gun was aimed at him, and you were too close," Malone stated in an even tone, but Amanda wasn't fooled for one second. He was pissed off and close to erupting. "What the hell, Stenson? Did he give you reason to fire?"

"Not at that point but—"

"*But* is the point. Jeez, Stenson, someone could have been killed. Unless he took threatening action that warranted it you never should have..." Malone shook his head and let out an exasperated sigh.

"His mere presence was threatening," Trent rushed out. "You saw the size of the guy, and he pushed past Amanda to get inside the house. He was bad news."

Amanda cleared her throat, not really wanting to get involved but a sense of loyalty to Trent was compelling her to speak. "Trent did what he felt he had to, Sarge. Simply flashing a badge at him would have done nothing to get his attention."

Malone leveled a glare at them both but settled it on Trent. "I have to wonder if the personal nature of this case isn't getting to you."

"It's not," Trent pushed out. "And it was just a fluke he knocked the gun out my hand."

Malone clenched his jaw. "You really expect me to swallow that? It was a *fluke*? Can I trust you, Stenson?"

"You can, I swear."

"Then do the job. By the damn book." Malone's cheeks fired bright red.

"You have my word that I'll do better."

"I'm still going to have to write you up for this."

"Do what you must, boss."

Malone left without another word.

"Well, he's pissed," Trent said once Malone was out of earshot.

"You think?" she kicked back. "And he has every right. What were you thinking?"

"Wonderful. You're against me too."

She held eye contact with him, holding her own suspicions about his behavior. He hadn't acted as a trained cop. He'd responded as a nephew stepping up in defense of his aunt. Trent had crossed a line, and she'd be keeping a closer eye on him from now on.

TWENTY-FOUR

The giant wasn't turning out to be much of a talkative person. Amanda and Trent had to obtain his identity through the registration in the glovebox of the black Lexus, parked on the street in front of Gertrude's house. Reid Sherman had served some prison time back in his twenties for assault and battery.

"This guy did it. He hurt and threatened my aunt." Trent was pacing in the observation room while Reid conferred with his attorney. Amanda was just hoping Trent would take a seat. All his moving around was making her head spin.

"Except you're forgetting something rather important." She raised her eyebrows wondering if his rage would lift enough for him to see clearly. He didn't respond so she made her point. "Reid Sherman must be six foot four. The killer from the video was nowhere near that tall. And with his record, his prints would have flagged when CSI Blair ran the one from the jerry can."

"So this Sherman guy isn't the only one working for the bookie. Remember a smaller man was at my aunt's house on Monday night, the day before Don's murder."

"I'll give you that. He could be another enforcer or one of Sherman's buddies. It also could have been the bookie himself."

"Damn right. I just feel it though. This guy is the ticket to getting my aunt off the hook." He stopped in front of the window, resting his hands on the frame.

"You mean to finding justice for Don?"

"Yeah. Sure."

She stepped up next to him, studying his profile. The firm set of his brow, the downward angle of his mouth, and his fixed gaze told her he was ready to have a go at the man. But if he stepped out of bounds the slightest bit, Malone would bench him from the case. Amanda butted her head toward the glass. "I'll handle the interview with Reid Sherman."

Trent turned to her. "Because you don't think I can keep my temper in check?"

"Honestly? No, I don't."

He didn't rush to deny the accusation, simply said, "I'm just protective of my aunt."

"And I get that, Trent, especially with all she's been through. But if there's a case to build against Sherman, we need it to follow procedure, so the charges stick. That means no room for emotion. Just cool, professional detachment and objectivity."

"I get it." He led the way from the room.

She followed him into the interview room next door and hoped that he'd honor her request to do the speaking.

Reid and his attorney looked up, stopping their conversation midsentence. The lawyer turned his chair to face them and straightened his tie. He was in his late forties, if not early fifties, with silver threads in his hair. "I hadn't finished speaking with my client," he said.

"That's too bad because we're done waiting." Trent took a seat, and Amanda sat next to him.

Apparently, he's not going to keep his mouth shut! She hated that his attitude put her on the offensive. "I'm Detective Steele, and this is Detective Stenson." Hopefully, Trent would take the hint she wasn't going to back off and he'd shut up.

"Gavin Roach, criminal defense attorney, with Roach & Pratchett." He produced a flashy silver business card from his suit jacket pocket and handed it to her.

Interesting name for a defense lawyer... She barely glanced at the card and slipped it into the folder she'd brought in with her. "Your client, Reid Sherman, was arrested this afternoon for assault against me and Detective Stenson. Charges are also pending for assault and uttering death threats against Gertrude Lambert."

"Who?" Reid blurted out.

Gavin smiled. "My client isn't aware of who this woman even is so why, in God's name, would he assault her or threaten to kill her?"

"Let's leave God out of our conversation, if you would," she fired back. Her relationship with a Greater Being never recovered after the deaths of her husband, daughter, and unborn child. "But your client surely wouldn't enter the home of a woman he doesn't know. Please give us more credit than that."

The lawyer stiffened but said, "My client must have gotten the wrong house. He doesn't know the name Gertrude Lambert."

Amanda gave Reid some credit. He'd laid down some deniability from the onset, asking for the 'nice, quiet older woman.' His main issue might have been with Don, but Amanda wasn't fooled for a minute that he didn't have Gertrude's name. "Right. Even so, he entered the home uninvited. Is your client in the habit of going inside strangers' homes?"

"He says that you invited him in before he could get to the point of his visit."

Her turn to smile. "I did no such thing. Your client practically walked over me to get inside. You see, we know that your client is quite familiar with the Lamberts. Neighbors have spotted your client's black Lexus LX in the neighborhood on several occasions, as well as outside the place where Don Lambert worked." That was a slight reach as Don's coworker just mentioned the vehicle, nothing past that.

"You must realize how many black Lexus SUVs there are," Gavin defended.

"Oh, please," Trent blurted out and rolled his eyes.

Gavin didn't acknowledge him. Amanda's insides were boiling. She wished her partner would just keep his lips zipped for the duration of this interview.

"With your client's criminal record, I'm sure he knows the benefits of being honest," she started. "It lays the basis for clear communication and cooperation. Without it, well, I'm not too inclined to extend any favors. Does your client admit to knowing Don Lambert?" she asked.

Gavin gestured for Reid to answer.

"Yes, I know Don."

She was surprised a bit that her mini speech had worked. "And how is that?"

"My client chooses to exercise his fifth amendment right," Gavin stepped in on Reid's behalf.

The fifth amendment of the US Constitution protected those on trial from saying something that would be self-incriminating. In this setting, it boiled down to the same thing. Essentially, Reid was asserting his right to remain silent, also a provision under the Miranda rights. "Huh. Okay, well, that's not exactly the cooperative spirit I was hoping for."

Gavin licked his lips. "Did you really think we were going to fall for your little speech? That it will get my client to bare his soul? You spoke of favors, but I didn't miss that there was no indication of what they might be."

The lawyer's eyes challenged her to do so now, but she wasn't in the mood to play. "What is your business with Don

Lambert?" She leveled her gaze at Reid, who met her with steady eye contact.

"Plead the fifth." He smiled, sly, like a reptile.

"Though I suppose I should have said, what *was* your business with Mr. Lambert? After all, he was recently violently murdered. Would you have anything to tell us about that?" She chose to hold back more specifics for now.

Gavin shook his head. "I don't like what you're suggesting, Detective. Unless you're charging my client with this Mr. Lambert's murder, I don't see what relevance any of this has."

"Oh, did I fail to mention that he is under suspicion of conspiring to murder as well? No, well..." She shrugged. "There you have it."

"You haven't exactly been honest and straightforward yourself, Detective," Gavin said.

Trent stood and pointed a finger at Reid. "He told Gertrude Lambert that she'd wind up worse than her husband. He knows something about Don Lambert's murder."

"Yeah, that he's dead!" Reid shouted. "That's all."

Gavin laid a hand on his client's forearm to calm his temper, but Reid shrugged him off.

"It would be a good idea if everyone calmed down," Amanda said matter-of-factly. She was so angry with Trent, she couldn't look at him. She only started to breathe easier when he returned to his chair and sat down. Still, she gave everyone a few beats, including herself, to regain composure. "How did you become aware of Don Lambert's murder?"

"Word got around."

She smirked. "More specifically, who told you?"

"I don't remember."

"That's convenient." She sat back and crossed her arms. "I'll ask again, nicely. What was your business with Don Lambert?"

"Plead the fifth," Reid muttered.

"All right. Have it your way." She fished out a copy of the

bet slip from the folder and pushed it across the table. "Look familiar?"

Reid flicked a brief glance at it, and a slight twitch tugged on his bottom lip.

"Yes? No?" she prompted, but his reaction gave him away.

"Plead the fifth."

"Where were you Tuesday night, let's say between eleven forty-five PM and Wednesday twelve thirty AM?" She padded the times between the mystery figure showing up on the doorbell cam and the murder. While he was too big for the figure on either video, if he had detailed knowledge of the murder, her question should gather some telling reaction.

He was blank as he reiterated, "The fifth."

"I see. Well, apparently, you're not inclined to talk to us, and that's fine. We'll get the information we need another way." She stuffed the bet slip back into the folder and got up.

"So my client is free to leave?"

Amanda ignored the lawyer's asinine question and left the room.

"What are you doing? We can't just walk away from that guy." Trent hustled behind her, as she returned to the observation room.

She spun on him. "Trust me, I'm not just walking away, but Reid Sherman isn't Don's killer. He did recognize that bet slip though, and I'm confident he's the bookie's muscle. We'll get a warrant to access his phone, and hopefully that will lead us right to the bookie."

"Good thinking."

"We'll also need to have your aunt ID him from a lineup for the charges relating to her to stick. And we'll need to take her prints, Trent, and run them against the one on the jerry can." She hated being the one to bring that up.

"I will."

A commotion in the neighboring room cut their conversation short. Reid was yelling at the lawyer and flailing his arms. He had pushed the chair into the table, and it had toppled backward to the floor. A uniformed officer who had been posted outside the door rushed in to get the situation under control.

What the...? Amanda rushed into the hall.

TWENTY-FIVE

A lot had transpired in the last ninety minutes, starting with Reid Sherman's conniption fit when his lawyer quit for reasons unknown. Amanda had secured the necessary authorization that allowed them to access Reid Sherman's cell phone. It didn't take any time to flag their next person of interest. The number tied back to Seth Dodger of Woodbridge, and he was the only contact Reid had in his phone. Seth didn't have a criminal record, but he did have a four-door charcoal sedan registered to his name. Was it the same one spotted near the Lamberts' house driven by Don's late-night visitor? Time would tell. Same too for whether Dodger was the bookie or another enforcer. Officers were dispatched to bring him in.

Trent had wrangled together a lineup, and Gertrude was quick to identify Reid Sherman as the man who had threatened and attacked her. Whatever his level of involvement with Don's murder, he'd be facing trial and prison time for that and the assault against Amanda and Trent. Satisfaction came with that. Reid was a threat to society and best kept off the streets.

She and Trent had also questioned Gertrude further about her presence near the plaza last night, and her story remained unchanged. Amanda was leaning toward believing her, but they had her fingerprints and they'd be compared to the one left on the jerry can.

Don's financials and phone records had also come through. Amanda was working through those while Trent submitted his report about the shooting incident and turned in his weapon. Since Amanda hadn't discharged hers, she didn't need to surrender it, but she had to complete a report. She had taken care of that before digging in.

Don's financials confirmed the picture that had started to form at the house. He was tapped out. There was one cash withdrawal for a thousand dollars on the third of the month, the Friday Don begged for an advance. Combining it with the fifteen hundred they knew about already would have only made for a very small dent against the money Don had owed the bookie.

Next, she looked at Don's communications. She started with Don's text messages and found quite a few abusive missives aimed at Gertrude. Most of them were controlling and demanding.

There were a few texts exchanged with his friends Noah and Elton, but nothing of striking importance.

His call history confirmed his boss had called a few times on Wednesday morning, but there were incoming numbers that weren't saved in his contacts. She looked these up in the system to see who they were registered to.

There was a knock on the frame of her cubicle. She looked up, and it was Officer Wyatt. "Dodger's in Interview Room Two."

"Okay, thanks. He demand a lawyer?" If he had that would buy her more time to carry on with what she was doing.

"Yep, and he's already here too. Gavin Roach."

That was the same attorney who had been with Reid Sherman. It couldn't be a coincidence that he was dropped as a client. It had probably been Sherman's reaction to the bet slip that doomed that relationship. "Good to know. Thanks." She smiled at Wyatt, and he left with a dip of his head.

Trent was walking toward her, and he pointed at his temporary gun assignment resting in his hip holster. Just another Glock. His regular one would stay with admin staff until his report was reviewed and he was cleared of any wrongdoing.

"Look at you. A regular ole cowboy." Her words were meant to be playful but twisted once they were out. The implication was there that Trent was quick to draw and fire. Not what she meant, but it was too late to backpedal.

Trent grimaced. "That's me. Just a gun-toting American with an itchy trigger finger."

"I was just fooling around, but it's time to move. Dodger's in Interview Room Two waiting for us. Oh, and the lovely Gavin Roach is in tow."

"The same lawyer Reid Sherman had? And I don't think I said as much, but Roach for a defense attorney is rather fitting."

Amanda just smiled before setting out for the interview room. She was armed with a folder that included Seth's background, as thin as that was.

"We meet again," Gavin said when she and Trent entered the interrogation room.

The term *again* could hardly apply since his cologne was still lodged up her nose from their last interaction. She and Trent didn't say a word as they sat across from him.

She set the folder on the table and leaned forward, clasping her hands on it. She introduced herself and Trent and said, "Do you know why you're here, Mr. Dodger?"

"Not really, no. I'm a good law-abiding American citizen."

As he spoke, she took in more of the man's appearance. Seth was under six foot and of a smaller build. He could be the man from all the videos they'd watched from the coffee shop to the doorbell cam to Jill Swanson's that captured the murder. He was also most probably Don's late-night visitor. It was hard to say why he'd have handled business when he had at least one enforcer, but stranger things had happened. "We have some questions for you." She intentionally held back mention of murder to avoid Seth shutting down right from the start. She pulled an enlarged copy of Reid Sherman's photo from her folder and set it across the table in front of Seth. "Do you recognize this man?"

Seth glanced at Gavin, who nodded for his client to go ahead. "I do," Seth admitted.

She smiled. "Good, good. It's great to see that we're off to an honest start."

"I don't like the implication, Detective," Gavin snapped. "Or the patronizing tone toward my client."

"Can you write down his name for the record, Mr. Dodger?" She paid the lawyer's comment no heed and gave Seth a notepad and a pen.

Seth scribbled his response and pushed the book back across the table.

In compressed handwriting was the name Reid Sherman. "Thank you." She nodded and exchanged Reid's photo for one of Don Lambert. "What about this man?"

Seth turned away, and the lawyer stepped in. "How about before my client talks, you tell us why we're here?"

"All right. We believe your client may be involved in the murder of this man." She pointed at Don's picture.

Seth appeared unmoved by the accusation.

"Do you have any response to what I just said?" she pressed.

"Besides the fact I didn't do it? No." Seth huffed.

"But you knew him, didn't you?" She leaned forward and jabbed a finger at the picture again.

"Uh-huh. But Don was a buddy of mine."

Was... Seth seemed to have transitioned to past tense

quickly. "For a *buddy* you don't seem too broken up by his passing."

"I'm pissed more like it."

"And why is that?" Amanda passed a side-glance at Trent. Had they found Don's bookie?

"Let's just say his death has left me hangin'."

She pulled a copy of the bet slip from her folder and put it on the table. "Did he owe you money?"

"I never said that," Seth defended.

She put the handwritten *Reid Sherman* beside the slip. "The writing looks quite similar. Both tight and cramped."

"Please, Detective," Gavin groaned. "Are you a handwriting expert now?"

"I don't need to be. Look." She pressed a finger to the bet slip, and then the notepad.

"Fine. So what? I issued the bet slip," Seth admitted. "What about it? That didn't kill him."

Amanda glanced at the lawyer, at first uncertain why Seth had confessed so easily. It made her suspect there was something else at play. Not that she had an idea what that might be yet. "You realize that taking and placing bets for other people is illegal in the state of Virginia? People need to take care of their own online or through mobile apps."

Seth shrugged. "Listen, I was just helping a fella out and trying to make a living."

"An illegal one," she shot back.

"Ah, a small transgression in the grand scheme. Live and let live. It's a free country, and I'm just an enterprising business-man. What America was built on." Seth flashed a smile.

Considering he'd just admitted to illegal activities, he was rather cocky. But her concern was more focused on Lambert's murder and the bookie's direct business with him. "Why were you at Don Lambert's house on Monday night?"

Seth blinked slowly and met her gaze, surprise registering in his eyes. A flitting smile also suggested he was impressed she knew. "I just went for a visit."

"And saw him again on Tuesday night?" she countered.

"We're buddies, so why not?"

She gave him credit. This time around he didn't even falter. "You went to his house then too?"

"Nah. Java Stop. It's a coffee shop."

"Right. I know the one. It's off Ingrid Street, about a block from Patriot Plaza?" She played dumb as if she hadn't teed everything up to get to this point.

"That's right."

Amanda glanced briefly at the lawyer, curious why he was letting his client talk so freely. There was definitely something else at work here. "What time was this?"

"Somewhere near eleven forty-five."

He'd just placed himself in the area at the time of the murder. "Rather late to drink coffee."

"It doesn't affect me like it does some people."

"Where did you go after the coffee shop?"

"Home to read a book."

"Anyone else who can testify to that?"

"I live alone. Big house. Neighbors keep to themselves."

No alibi with a motive. But did Seth take care of business for himself or delegate it? The existence of Reid Sherman would suggest the latter. And sadly, the lack of an alibi wouldn't carry the burden of a conviction. She'd move on for now. "What I gather from this bet slip is that your business with Don must have soured some recently. This bet alone lost him ten K plus interest." She touched the slip to draw his eye there.

"Sure. But he would have paid me back. He always has. Or he did. Listen, I can't be walked on, but I'm a reasonable man. Don knew this, and he showed up like clockwork to place a bet with me the first and fifteenth of every month. That wouldn't happen unless he cleaned up any previous losses."

"Is that why you were at his house on Monday? To collect what he owed you?"

"Nope, just there to visit a friend." His eye contact was overbearing suggesting that he was lying.

Amanda didn't believe a word. She figured Seth went when Reid Sherman's intimidation tactic at Don's workplace hadn't worked. Don likely arranged the meet at the coffee shop on Tuesday night. "Does that apply to coffee on Tuesday night? It was just friends catching up?"

"Just friends." A tight smile. "We often meet up for coffee."

"Then he didn't hand you an envelope with money?" They had the video from Java Stop, but it just showed a man in a baseball cap accepting an envelope.

"Where are you going with this, Detective?" Gavin stepped in.

"Here's the thing, my partner and I believe your client wasn't too happy with Don. We think he might have killed—"

"Nah. That's ridiculous," Seth burst out. "The bastard can't pay me back from the grave."

"The bastard?" she fired at him. "A moment ago he was your buddy, your friend, but that's a stretch. And after you killed him, you sent Reid Sherman to rough up his widow, didn't you? You thought you'd get the money Don owed from her."

"I—"

Gavin silenced his client with a gesture. "Let's stop with the accusations, Detective. My client is willing to discuss his relationship with Reid Sherman and testify to the fact he is a dangerous, volatile, and impulsive man."

And there it is... The gameplan she sensed was building beneath the surface between client and lawyer. They planned to flip all culpability over to Reid. She was listening but guarded. Anything Seth would say was to advance his own self-interest.

"Reid's a loose cannon," Seth put in.

"We'll need more than that."

"Well, so will you, Detective, to continue this harassment of a Prince William County citizen," Gavin said. "I'm inclined to file charges against you personally and the PWCPD for the treatment toward my client."

"Your client is hardly an innocent man, Mr. Roach," she said. "Reid told us he went to the Lambert house last night to shake down the wife on your client's orders." That was a complete lie, but if the bad guys could do it, the good guys should be allowed as well.

Seth's reaction came hot and fast. "That guy will say anything!"

"Tell us your version then," she said with practiced grace.

Seth took a few heaving breaths before he spoke. "Reid told me that Don Lambert was murdered. He didn't offer more than that, and I didn't ask for more. I didn't want to know. If he killed the man, that order wasn't from me. I will go on record saying that."

It wasn't missed that Seth completely avoided the topic of shaking down Gertrude, but it had Amanda thinking about the size of Don's killer. "We have the murder on video and—"

"Then you know it wasn't me," Seth cut in.

"What we know is someone your size killed Don Lambert. I'm sure I don't need to point out the physical differences between you and Reid Sherman."

"So... So Reid hired someone else to kill Don. I only ask him to put the fear of God in people... the ones who owe me money."

She resisted the urge to smile. In a panic to escape a murder charge, he'd just confessed to ordering Reid to knock Gertrude around. But there was another part to Seth's defense that had her taking pause. Viewed in a certain light it struck her as weak and convenient, but what if Reid had delegated this job? For that matter, what was to say that Seth hadn't hired someone besides Reid to kill Don? But she'd play along for now. "Does Reid Sherman have associates who would murder for him?"

"I wouldn't put it past him."

She wasn't sure what to make of his response. Seth could just be desperate and saying whatever it took to cast the light off himself. Still, for due diligence, they needed their hands on Reid Sherman's entire phone history, including communications he may have deleted. Seth's too while they were at it. "If only there was a way to prove you, or Reid, never killed Don Lambert..."

"Detective, it's your job to prove wrongdoing, but my client came here willing to cooperate."

Her call for them to show their hand just may have worked. She calmly clasped her hands on the table. "I'm listening."

Gavin gestured toward Seth.

"I can point you to where some bodies are buried."

She stiffened. "I'm hoping that you mean metaphorically..."

"Nope, I'm talking actual stiffs," he deadpanned.

"And who are these people?" She caught on to them scheming something but never expected this. It was also unsettling how detached Seth was about the topic.

"People Reid Sherman murdered."

"I figured that was the implication, but how can you possibly know this? Prove it?" She raised an eyebrow, skeptical. People came up with all sorts of things to push the light off themselves, but this was a new one.

"Ah, my client isn't going to answer that, but otherwise he is willing to cooperate. That is, in exchange for a deal, Detective," Gavin said. "You drop all interest in Mr. Dodger's business dealings, and he'll give you names and locations where you can find the bodies."

She wasn't about to make such a promise. "You are forgetting we haven't absolved your client of murdering Don Lambert. Exactly how many victims are we talking about?"

"He knows of three."

Amanda sank back in her chair. Three people whose families never received closure. The information, if it panned out, made the proposed deal a no-brainer. She gestured to the notepad and pen still on the table and got up. "We'll be back in five minutes."

She left with Trent, and they watched Seth scribbling wildly on the notepad through the one-way mirror in the observation room.

"Holy shit, I can't believe this." She put a hand to her forehead. "We bring him in for questioning regarding one murder, and now we might have three more bodies."

"No one can say our jobs are boring," Trent said with a smile.

"Say that again. But here's the thing, if Seth is telling the truth about the bodies, he's likely being honest about Don Lambert."

"Unless he's feeding us this shit so we think that. We can't just release him from suspicion."

"Oh, I never said we should. He essentially confessed to sending Reid Sherman to rough up Gertrude, and there's his illegal gambling business. Here's the thing that's working on me though. Why admit to those crimes and not killing Don?"

"Surely you heard the answer in your question. We're talking about *murder*," Trent said, stressing the last word. "It carries a life sentence. If he killed Don, it would make sense he's not in a hurry to make a confession. And all this about three bodies? Ask me, and he's trying to distract us."

She understood Trent wanted all suspicion off his aunt, but she could admit he had a point. "If that's his aim, it's working. He's also been cooperative and forthcoming. On the Java Stop video, Seth was the first to leave, but we're talking about a few minutes. How did he get changed, down the hill, and position himself behind Don's Buick before Don arrived? Not to mention where did he pick up the jerry can?"

"I don't have all the answers, but anything's possible, Amanda."

"Suppose it is. And it's also possible Seth or Reid hired the person who killed Don. That it wasn't Seth."

"It's possible." Begrudgingly.

This conversation only confirmed they had more work to do. They needed to contact the service providers for both Seth's and Reid's phones for their full histories and request their financials. Either avenue might provide a trail to a hired gun who could have taken out Don.

A tap on the one-way mirror from Gavin signaled they were ready.

"Here goes nothing," she said and returned to the interview room. "What have you got for us?"

"The list, as my client promised, in exchange for which you let my client go." Gavin handed over the notebook and pen.

"We'll need to verify this." There were three names on the page, but a location was only noted for the first. It was in a rural area within Prince William County. The following names had quotation marks. "And this?"

"You know... *ditto*," Seth said.

"So all three bodies are in the same place?" Trent cut in.

"Yep. Go dig 'em up, and let me get out of here."

"Umm. Not so fast." Amanda sat down. "You suggested that Reid may have hired someone else to kill Don."

Seth inched forward to the edge of his chair and folded his hands together on the table. "He probably did."

"Do you have any names for us in that regard?"

Seth shook his head.

"Do you hire other people besides Reid Sherman to do your... well, let's call it dirty work?"

Seth turned to his lawyer, who answered, "My client has just given you the names and locations of three murder victims."

"Allegedly," she said, pulling out a word defense lawyers loved. "But his knowledge also makes him accountable. The fact he's kept quiet suggests his involvement in some way. How do you know about these murders?" She leveled her gaze at Seth, but the attorney responded.

"My client asserts his fifth amendment rights on that matter."

Amanda wasn't surprised. It was this lawyer's standby for shutting down questioning. "And maybe I choose my right to ignore this." She waved the list. "Up to you. But if you want to be seen as cooperating with police tell us this, do you have others like Reid Sherman who you pay to do your dirty work?"

Seth turned to his lawyer, his mouth in a pained grimace. "Fine, yes, there is one other man. He's not in town right now though."

"Name and phone number?" Amanda fired back.

"Lyle McBride. I can write down his number."

"Now, that wasn't so hard. We'll take a look at this little list." Amanda downplayed its importance because she wanted Seth to sweat. She and Trent slipped out of the room. "We need to look into McBride and see what he has to say. We also need to move on warrants for Seth's and Reid's phone records and financials, as I said before." She was suddenly feeling overwhelmed. After all, if the list in her hands was legit, it was going to be another long night. Amanda hated to think of the further damage this would do to her relationship with Zoe. Would the girl ever talk to her again? Amanda's heart ached. She'd love nothing more than to go home and scoop the girl into her arms this instant, but her duty to the badge also beckoned.

TWENTY-SIX

Amanda and Trent found Malone in his office and brought him up to speed. His facial expression was priceless. Widened eyes, slack jaw.

"You're being serious?" Malone said. "Three bodies?"

"Yep, that's what they're saying anyway. Apparently, they are buried just outside the town limits. We have to go there to find out if he's telling the truth," Amanda said.

Malone ran a hand over the thinning hair on his head, then plucked at his groomed beard. "All right. We'll get a K-9 team out to scout the area, see what they can find. We can't ignore the possibility this is legitimate."

"As absurd as it all sounds, I think it is, Sarge," Trent chimed in. "Reid Sherman is prone to violence, which we saw with what he did to my aunt."

"Yes, I'm not disputing that, Stenson."

"But Sherman's not our killer. He's too large," Amanda chimed in.

"What is your take on Seth Dodger?" Malone leaned forward, taking them both in. They were seated in chairs in front of his desk.

"Like his lawyer, he lives up to his name," Trent quipped. "But he doesn't deny sending Reid Sherman to my aunt."

"An illegal bookie, who thinks it okay to rough up people who owe him money. Nah, this guy isn't getting out of jailtime by throwing his enforcer under the bus. There's no way I'm cutting him loose even if the list pans out."

"Technically, I never promised a thing," Amanda said.

"Good girl... Ah, good work, Detective." Malone corrected himself. It didn't happen often, but sometimes the long-standing friendship he had with her father influenced how he spoke to her.

"I didn't see I had a choice but to play along. If what he's told us is correct, we're talking about three homicides. That's three families who have never received closure. There can finally be some justice." As much as she didn't want there to be bodies to find, she knocked off two upsides if there were.

"When did these murders take place?"

"That he didn't tell us," Trent said.

"Regardless, we have enough to move. I'm going to get the dogs and their handlers dispatched to the scene immediately. I'll let you know if they find the bodies, but I want your focus to stay on resolving Lambert's murder."

Amanda was trying to process what that meant for her and Trent. "Does that mean we're not needed on site? Someone else will notify the victims' families?"

"That's exactly what I mean. You've done your part getting it this far and have your hands full already. If bodies are found, I'll assign the investigation aspect to Hudson and Ryan. They'll take care of notifications too once the remains are identified. But we could be hours or days out from that. All assuming, of course, there are victims to find."

Fred Hudson and Natalie Ryan were two other detectives in the Homicide Unit. She nodded, appreciating that Malone was right. They couldn't afford to let Don's murder case sit in limbo while they took the detour. But there was another aspect to that. "Ah, I would like to state one thing for the record, though, Sarge. Trent and I haven't fully released either the bookie or enforcer from suspicion in the Lambert case."

"I don't think you should." The phone on his desk rang, Malone answered, and waved them out.

"Since we're keeping our options open, I'd like to revisit what I was working on before Seth's arrival," she told Trent as they walked back to the warren assigned to Homicide. "I was looking at Don's phone records and trying to connect numbers with people. There are a few I haven't gotten around to."

"And you're thinking...?"

"As I said, just keeping our options open. We can't rule out Seth or Reid yet, but the same applies to that jealous husband or boyfriend that came up to Don at JJ's. It's possible one of those numbers may lead us to him. It's worth a shot anyhow."

"The guy could have gotten a hold of his number to threaten him. Sure, let's see what we can find."

"Actually, I was hoping you would get the documentation together to support warrants for phone records and financials on the bookie and enforcer."

"No problem."

"On the topic of financials..." She filled him in on the cash withdrawal Don had made for the thousand dollars.

"Assuming that was for Dodger too, in addition to the fifteen hundred, the bookie still wouldn't have been happy. That's not even half of Don's base bet."

"I had the same thought." But there was something else on her mind as well. She stopped walking and faced him once he stood beside her. "We also need to have a serious conversation about your aunt."

"Not this again. Please." He resumed walking.

She hustled to keep up with his strides. "You can't just

ignore that your aunt's Kia was in the immediate area of where Don was murdered, around the time he was murdered."

"She didn't deny that."

"No, initially she lied to us, telling us she was in bed."

"I'm well aware of what she had said."

"And she only admitted to being there after we told her we had her car on video. She said she was following him to see if he was meeting up with another woman, that she had no plans to *do* anything. I find that hard to believe."

"I don't. Because if she confronted Don, you know what would have happened. He'd have beat her unconscious."

Amanda didn't serve a rebuttal to that. Didn't Trent see that his defense worked against his aunt? The killer hadn't confronted Don, so much as faced him down, poured gasoline on him, and lit him on fire. They were the actions of someone who wanted the last word, of a killer who wanted to ensure that Don couldn't react. "What we know for sure is Don's killer knew he frequented the area."

"Like Seth. He said himself he'd often meet up with Don for coffee at Java Stop. He could have told Reid, his other enforcer, or Reid could have passed it along to someone on his payroll. And really, any other regular in that alley would have known Don's habit of going there."

She was getting a headache at the sheer number of potential suspects, but there was one way to whittle them down. "This person also needed a reason to target Don."

"To know him, is to want to... I'm just kidding around, Amanda. What I am serious about is there are other options besides my aunt." His voice was strangled, riddled with desperation. "She didn't do this, and we have nothing solid against her. So what she was in the area? We didn't even see her get out of her car."

She could argue that had happened off camera. She could also point out if they were discussing anyone other than his aunt, they would have already searched her property for a black outfit that could match what was on the video. "I *could* ask that you consider along with me that she *might* have killed him."

His phone pinged with a message, and he checked it. "Here you go." He held the screen toward her. "Blair just confirmed that my aunt's prints are not a match for the one on the jerry can. Now do you believe she's innocent?"

All Amanda believed was that the print wasn't a match. It didn't exclude the aunt from being Don's killer.

"I'm guessing not," Trent said.

"Even you said it before. It could have been picked up along the way at any point, even placed there by the person who filled it at the station. It wasn't necessarily left by the killer. Let's just bench talking for now and knock some things off our list."

And for the next hour and a half, that's what they did, starting with pulling a background on Lyle McBride, Seth's other enforcer. There wasn't even a need to confirm he was out of town because his license had him down as six foot two. There was no way he had set Don on fire.

Trent had submitted the paperwork to support warrants for the phone records and financials while she looked at the numbers on Don's phone. Nada there. Every one of the unknown numbers were spam calls. She shared this with Trent.

"We're obviously not finding the jealous husband or boyfriend from his phone, and maybe it's a waste of time pursuing that angle," Trent said.

"In a murder investigation, we don't have the luxury of picking and choosing potential leads. We follow them all. Besides, we'd be waiting forever if we expected the case to magically stitch itself together."

Trent angled his head and smiled. "Thanks for the brushup on being a detective. But I was trying to think of other ways we might be able to find the guy who confronted Don."

"We hit a dead end with Don's friends and JJ's, but we did only just speak to the staff..."

"Unless we're forgetting another pal of Don's, someone we've overlooked."

"Bernie," they said at the same time.

The barfly... "Yep, and people do a lot of talking when they drink," she said. "Who knows all that Don shared with the man? We might find out this guy's identity yet."

"I say we do it. He could help. But just one thing. We were told he doesn't come in until later at night. Nine, if I remember right."

She looked at the clock, and it was a quarter after five. There was time to go home and have dinner with Logan and Zoe and hang out some. She'd have a chance to set things right with Zoe. "How I remember it. Okay, so let's take a break for dinner. Then we'll meet up here about eight forty and head over."

"Sounds like a date. Like a *plan*," he rushed out.

She smiled, to relieve her own tension at his slip. Most of the time she could resist her romantic feelings for Trent. She could dispense them by thinking logically, but moments like now they surfaced and were hard to ignore. Her cheeks heated, and she quickly turned away. "See you in a few hours."

TWENTY-SEVEN

Amanda used the drive home as an opportunity to chastise herself. She had no right to cling to some fantasy of her and Trent being a couple. It was childish and foolish. She had a good thing going with Logan, and she deeply cared about him. No, she *loved* Logan.

She pulled into the driveway and parked next to Logan's truck. The prospect of surprising him gave way to anxiety. She was faithful in the true sense, but her thoughts strayed. Would he be able to see through her, somehow read her disloyal daydreaming? How did she even get to this place, where she cared for two men? She'd had a wonderful ten-year marriage to Kevin and never once entertained imaginings of another man. Her parents' marriage was what she'd looked to as an ideal to aim for. Maybe finding out her father had an affair blew up that image. Had that somehow altered her view on monogamy? Or was she using her father's slip to excuse her behavior?

The front door opened, and Logan stepped outside to greet her. "For a second, I thought I was seeing things." He smiled at her just before scooping her into his arms.

Tucked against him, the feeling of his warmth, made all

other thoughts fade. They disappeared completely when he pushed aside the collar of her jacket and shirt and kissed her collarbone.

The sensation of his warm breath sent a thousand tingles coursing through her body. "Would you cut that out?" She was laughing.

"We should probably take this inside." He winked at her.

Smiling, she said, "What has gotten into you? What about Zoe?"

"She's not here, and now you're home and so am I, so—" He smacked her butt playfully. She hustled inside, and he kicked the door shut, and pinned her against the wall. He trailed kisses around her neck, then met her mouth with the hunger of a starving man.

She desperately wanted to give herself over to the moment, but her mind was working against her. "Just one second. Where is—" Zoe? His teeth gently grazed on her collarbone again, and his hands traveled under her shirt and bra. He rubbed his thumbs over her nipples, and they sold her out. She'd sort out the Zoe thing after...

Amanda was dressed again and sitting on the couch, still catching her breath. "What the hell just happened?"

"If you'd like, we can have a refresher." He sat beside her and sucked on her earlobe.

"Cut it out." She batted him away and laughed.

"Here." He handed her a glass of water.

She gulped it down greedily. All that panting and moaning had made her thirsty. "Wow, that was quite the welcome home."

"It was a nice surprise. What can I say." He smiled and brushed a strand of her red hair from her face.

"It was." Her response was more in reference to the exuberant welcome home. She kissed him on the lips and drew back, studying the contours of his lovely face. "So, where is Zoe?"

"At Libby and Penny's for dinner."

Amanda didn't remember that arrangement, though she had been preoccupied with the investigation. "Oh."

"You wouldn't have known," he said as if reading her mind. "It was a last-minute thing."

She wished she could unsee how his eyes had darkened when he said that latter bit. It was just a subtle nuance she took as a dig at her unpredictability. As if *last-minute* was something she should be familiar with. Her gut clenched, and she went to the kitchen to top up her water glass at the sink. It wasn't that low, but she needed a few seconds of separation.

Logan came up behind her at the sink and wrapped his arms around her waist. "Please don't be mad at me about this."

She wasn't sure if he understood exactly what had her upset. He might even think it was making the decision for Zoe to stay at Libby's without consulting with her. She didn't say anything as she turned off the faucet and took a drink. If he had taken a jab at her for her unpredictable hours, then she had every right to be mad. He knew what the job was by this point. She turned in his arms to face him. "I'll let it go if you will."

"Works for me. Let me barbecue us up some dinner. I had a big steak out, plenty to split. Work for you?"

"Sounds delicious."

"All righty then." Logan tapped a quick kiss on her lips and started buzzing around the kitchen.

Once he cleared out, Amanda tossed a salad of fresh greens, cucumber, pepper, cherry tomatoes, crumbles of feta cheese, and balsamic dressing.

They ate on the patio, him with a glass of wine and her sticking with water. She still hadn't found the right moment to break it to him that she needed to go back to work even as they wrapped things up and headed inside. Part of her wondered if he suspected they were on borrowed time when she'd turned down wine. If so, he hadn't pursued it.

Her phone rang as she loaded the last of the dishes into the dishwasher. Malone's name was on the screen, and it probably meant he was calling with news about the burial site. "Detective Steele." She answered officially to send a not-so-subtle message to Logan that sometimes duty called, even when it wasn't convenient. "Did they find...?" She left *bodies* unsaid.

"Three, just as Seth Dodger said we would."

"Were they identified?"

"Surprisingly, yes. Turns out they were buried with their IDs, and these matched the names on the list. As I told you before, I assigned the investigation and notification responsibility to Hudson and Ryan. There's nothing you need to do on your end. I just wanted to bring you up to speed."

"Thank you."

"But I wouldn't mind hearing where things stand on the Lambert investigation. Any updates?"

She dared to look at Logan, who was watching her closely. Her supervisor had asked a direct question and she had to answer. Even if Logan wouldn't like what she was about to say. "There's potential for a solid lead that Trent and I will be pursuing later tonight."

Logan shook his head and left the kitchen. His footsteps were heavy as he disappeared out of sight. She pinched her eyes shut.

"Rather vague, but let me know if it pays off tomorrow. Unless it closes the case obviously. Then don't hesitate to call regardless of the hour."

"You got it."

Malone ended the call, but Amanda remained in place. She should go after Logan, but her legs wouldn't move. Her entire body tensed, as if by moving or breathing too deeply it would set off a colossal fight.

Logan returned, his face flushed, his eyes piercing. "You're going back out? Why didn't you say anything about that?"

She faced him. "I planned to. The timing just hadn't seemed right to bring it up yet."

"So you were going to wait until you were headed out the door? And you'll be with Trent?"

Amanda didn't like the implied accusation one bit. Yes, she'd betrayed Logan's trust by kissing Trent but he said he'd forgiven her for that. They were to be moving forward. How could they if he kept bringing up her past transgression? "He is my partner. Surely you can understand that—"

"I was understanding last night when you called to say you'd be working late with him."

"On a new case," she seethed. Did he really expect that she would voice appreciation for his understanding? "This is my job, and it doesn't have set hours."

"Isn't that the truth."

"What's that supposed to mean?" she pushed back.

"I'm quite sure you know, Amanda. You're rarely home for dinner. Weekends are hit and miss. There's always a case. Sometimes I feel like a glorified babysitter around here."

The impact of his statement stole her breath. She braced herself on the counter. He made it sound as if Zoe were an obligation. "If that's how you feel about..." She gripped her stomach, not believing what she'd just heard.

"I didn't mean it like that. I love Zoe." He reached for her, but she slapped his hand away.

"I thought you did." Her accusation had no merit. His love for Zoe wasn't really in question. She regretted what she'd said the moment the words left her lips. She was lashing out at him over his poor word choice when it was really herself she was mad at. She couldn't go on living like this, tiptoeing across a minefield.

"*Thought?* Unbelievable." He started to leave the room but

stopped and pivoted around. "If it's not too much trouble, Amanda, stop and think for one second about what's important to you. Is it me and Zoe or your job and Trent?" Pain bolted across his face and seared his eyes.

"You and Zoe," she rushed out. "And I shouldn't have said what I did... what I implied, about your feelings for Zoe. You just made it sound like taking care of her was a burden."

"Sometimes I feel like a single parent."

"I'll try to do better." The words felt hollow standing on their own. Only time and her actions would support this vow. Would he give her that chance?

"Zoe is an absolute blessing," he said, not even acting like he'd heard her. "She's funny and smart, has a really bright future..." His voice trailed off, and he swallowed roughly.

If she was reading his thoughts right, he questioned whether he'd be around to see what Zoe became. And Amanda couldn't answer that, even if the thought of letting him go hurt. She stepped toward him. "I realize things haven't been the same since..." She stopped there, realizing she didn't need to verbalize her screwup. "But we said we were going to put it behind us and make things work."

"That's the thing right there. *Make*... Love shouldn't be so hard, Amanda."

With her late husband, everything had come easy. They rarely disagreed, argued even less. "You're right." Warm tears filled her eyes, and while she did her best to blink them back, a few stubborn ones fell. She swiped them away. "I can't keep apologizing for what I did."

"And I don't expect you to." He closed the remaining distance between them and cupped her elbows with his hands. "Maybe we're putting too much pressure on ourselves to get back to where we were. Instead, it's probably best we just take things one day at a time without built-in expectations of where we should be, when."

She nodded, but how long did he intend to keep working on their relationship? Was there an expiry date? They'd already been on this road for over four months.

He spoke when she didn't. "And I think a good place to start is open communication. Can you tell me why you need to go back out tonight?"

"You know I can't disclose details about an active investigation, but I will tell you this much. There's someone we need to speak to that could greatly help the case."

"Can you pick it up tomorrow?"

She shook her head. "If I could, I wouldn't leave you. But we only have a way of reaching this person tonight."

"Could Trent question them by himself?"

She remained silent.

"I see." He let go of her.

"I don't think you do. We're partners, and we think differently. One of us could pick up on something the other one doesn't."

"There's always a reason."

"Don't be like that. Do you think I like being out all hours of the day? Not being home for dinner or on the weekends?"

His eyes shadowed. "You must, right? Or you wouldn't do it."

He'd crossed a line with that comment. It could be that it had such a ring of truth that it insulted her, or struck her as the words of a petulant child who wasn't getting his way. "Logan, I can't predict where a case might take me. And the first seventy-two hours are crucial. It's not a time to step away unless it's absolutely necessary. Yet here I am."

"Then I should be thanking you, but last night you told me how important the first twenty-four were."

"They are."

"But now it's the first seventy-two?"

"What do you want me to say? I saw a way to break away

for a few hours, and I took them. I chose to spend that time with you and Zoe."

"How thoughtful of you." Bitter and sarcastic, but she let it roll off her. He was hurting too.

Another tear fell and betrayed her, but her emotions were all in flux and conflicting. Normally she knew her own mind, but when it came to Logan, she wasn't sure where she stood. Sometimes what they had worked for her, but other times it didn't. But was any relationship perfect?

"I might never understand your job," he eventually said, crushing the expanding silence that had wedged between them.

"I'm not sure you will." The admission was bittersweet, but if he hadn't yet, he never would. Would he ever give her an ultimatum? If so, it would make her decision about their future an easy one. Being a cop was in her blood. She glanced at the clock on the stove. "I still have an hour before I need to head out." The words tumbled out born of awkwardness, of trying to reset the last five minutes. Not that they could be erased. Something had fractured between them, but was it beyond repair?

"One hour you say? All right then, let's make the most of it." He smiled, but it was small and didn't touch his eyes.

They spent the time bundled up on the patio and looking at the night sky. The words spoken were few. She had this very bad feeling that what remained unspoken had the power to destroy them.

TWENTY-EIGHT

Amanda was pulling into the parking lot at Central when her phone rang. It was Detective Hudson, and she answered after getting out of her car. Trent pulled in, and she waited for him and watched as he parked his Jeep Wrangler next to her Honda Civic. When he caught up to her, she pointed at her phone held to her ear.

Detective Hudson was saying to her, "Ryan and I are having a little chat with Reid Sherman about the three bodies he put in the ground."

"I'm not sure why you're telling me this." It was expected that they'd have him pulled for questioning. And honestly, she didn't have any bandwidth to spare. It was taking all her mental power to stay focused on the Lambert investigation as thoughts of her home situation kept creeping in.

"I need you to come in. He's refusing to say another word until he gets something off his chest to you. Lord, give me patience."

Amanda ignored his complaint. "Good news for you, I just arrived at Central. What room?"

"Interview two."

"See you in a minute." She hung up before Hudson could say another word and updated Trent on the bodies and Reid Sherman's protest.

Trent flicked a finger toward the station. "I'm to assume Sherman's inside?"

"You assume correctly." They started walking to the doors, and she glanced over at him. "Did you get your aunt home all right?" Before they had parted ways earlier in the evening, they made the executive decision to release his aunt again, and Trent volunteered to take her home. If solid evidence turned up against her, they knew where to find her.

"I did, and would you believe it? There's an officer posted outside her house now. For all the good that does her. The threat against her is over with the bookie and Sherman behind bars."

She held the door for them, and they headed to the interview room. She knocked, and Detective Ryan answered and stepped into the hall in a cloud of lilac perfume. How her partner or Reid Sherman weren't choking on the cloying smell within the small confines of the interview room was a miracle.

"Happy to see you, Amanda. Trent." Natalie Ryan dipped her head at him, as if he were an afterthought. "He specifically asked for you," she said to Amanda. "You may be aware of this already, but three bodies were exhumed from shallow graves and identified as the men on the list."

"Sergeant Malone informed me. Is there solid evidence against Sherman?" she asked.

Natalie nodded. "The victims were all shot with a nine mil, execution style. Same gun."

"Sounds like Sherman is a regular old assassin," Trent piped in.

Amanda turned to him with a slight smile. "Is there anything regular and old about an assassin?"

He shrugged.

To Natalie, Amanda said, "You admitted to having *solid* evidence against Sherman. Did you find the murder weapon in his house?"

"Uh-huh. An unregistered nine mil Beretta. The lab still needs to run a comparison on the lands and grooves to the rounds in the victims, but given that Sherman's sweatin' bullets in there... Yeah, he did this. A search of his home also revealed he keeps himself a little arsenal."

The markings she referenced were as unique as fingerprints, but until the lab's findings came back, what Natalie just told them was hopeful, not solid evidence. "All right, let's get this done. Does he have a lawyer with him?" She expected he would have hired a replacement for Gavin Roach.

"Nope, he waived his Miranda rights." Natalie rapped her knuckles on the door, and Detective Fred Hudson popped into the hall.

"Looks like the whole party's here," he said, eyeballing Trent.

"I'm ready to talk with Sherman," Amanda told him, not in the mood for dealing with Hudson tonight. On a good day, the man irritated her without trying.

Hudson gestured toward the closed door. "By all means, have at it. Cougar and I will be next door."

Natalie shook her head, and this highlighted just one reason why Amanda didn't care for Fred. He had little respect for anyone, including his own partner. Amanda never referred to the female detective by the juvenile nickname behind her back, let alone to her face.

Amanda entered the interview room with Trent. Reid Sherman straightened his huge frame at the sight of them.

"You remember my partner, Detective Stenson? He stays. Though I was told you specifically wanted to talk to me." She sat down across from him, and Trent dropped onto the chair next to her.

"What the hell is going on here? They've dragged me in here for three murders."

"Then you talk with Detectives Ryan and Hudson about that. Why did you request to speak with me?"

"Did that shit turn on me?"

She leaned back casually, crossing her arms. "You'll need to be clearer than *that shit*."

"Seth Dodger," Reid hissed.

"I don't see how that's relevant at this point. The PWCPD has the bodies and the murder weapon."

"You need to listen to me." Reid leaned across the table. "Whatever happened to those men isn't on me. Same for that woman."

"I will need you to be more clear."

"Don's wife."

"What about her?"

"Seth told me to rough her up a bit, scare her, get his money."

"And threaten her life?" she rushed out, hoping to cut off Trent from speaking. He was bouncing his left leg, the vibration from it spreading across the floor.

"I never did that."

Amanda angled her head. "Not what we heard."

Trent's leg stopped bouncing, and he leaned forward. "*You* assaulted her, not Seth. Don't sit there and tell me that Seth made you do it. You could bench press the guy." Her partner was scowling so fiercely a vertical line formed between his eyebrows. *If looks could kill...*

"I swear. He made me."

Reid's earlier edge was gone, replaced by tangible fear. It contradicted physics and logic. Reid Sherman, a giant of a man, was afraid of the slight-built Seth Dodger. "Detective Stenson is right. You made the choice."

"Fine, fine, but..."

"But, what?"

"Can you protect me from him?"

The inquiry suggested he had something to hand over. Was it proof that Seth Dodger killed Don Lambert? She managed her enthusiasm. "We'll see what we can do," she said nonchalantly. "It all depends on what you have to tell us."

"Okay, there's a storage locker at the bus station. Number eight seventy. The key is in the personal effects that were taken from me. Inside, you'll find a hard drive. It has audio recordings on it, conversations between me and Seth where he ordered, uh, hits."

His pale face told her he was serious, but it all seemed so convenient. Seth points his finger at Reid, then Reid points his at Seth. But she couldn't afford to ignore what he was telling her either. Especially when Seth Dodger hadn't been released from suspicion in Don Lambert's murder. What niggled was she wasn't sure how Reid expected to benefit from handing this over. "You realize if we get these recordings and they are what you just told us, it also implicates you."

"Sure, but it also gives me a defense. A jury will hear that I was told to kill those people who were dug up. It will show that Seth Dodger is homicidal, suggest I obeyed his directions out of fear for my own life."

"You're still not looking like a saint here."

"Yeah, yeah, I get that. But I felt like I had no choice. It was them or me. The jury would understand that."

Amanda wasn't so sure but wasn't about to say as much.

Reid continued. "Even if that fails, I'll be taking him down with me. He turns on me, well, he'll find out how that feels."

And there is the real reason... Vindictive revenge. The mental state was one Amanda could use to her advantage though. "Do you know if Seth Dodger killed Don Lambert?"

"Trust me, if I did, I'd tell you."

Her shoulders sagged, even though it was the response she'd

expected. She flipped things another way though. While Reid Sherman wasn't the mystery figure who killed Don, there was one suggestion that the bookie had raised that had yet to be explored. "Do you ever hire people to do your bidding? Knocking people around? Murder?"

Reid clenched his jaw. "Is that what Seth told you?"

"Wouldn't matter if he did." She shrugged. "I'll need you to answer my question."

"No. Check my phone if you want. My finances too if it helps."

"Oh, we will be. But this is your way of telling us you never contracted someone to kill Don Lambert?"

"I don't have those types of contacts. But if anyone is hiring anyone, I'd take a hard look at Seth."

They had and would dig deeper, but that was none of Reid's business. "When we spoke before you told us you heard about Don's murder because 'word got around.' You weren't too talkative at the time. You willing to tell us exactly how you found out now?"

"Why not? I went to Don's workplace and spoke with one of his coworkers. When I asked for Don, the man told me he'd been murdered. I figured that Seth got someone else to knock him off, then sent me to the widow to collect."

Presumably that coworker was someone other than Garth Wagner. Although he told them the mystery man hadn't come inside the store *prior* to Don's murder. "Then why not just tell us that from the start?"

"I hadn't planned to turn on Seth, but if he can stab me in the back..."

"Well, he did tell us that *you* told him Don was dead."

"Only because I thought he ought to know, not because I had knocked him off."

Amanda ignored his tantrum. "Seth admits sending you to Don's widow."

"Mark it down. He actually assumed an iota of responsibility for once."

"But it doesn't change the fact that you're a grown-ass man who struck a woman," Trent hissed.

Amanda held up a hand, hoping that Trent's outburst hadn't cost them Reid's further cooperation. But how much more could he have to share? The backup drive itself sounded like a goldmine. "Okay. We'll have this locker and the drive checked out."

"Thank you." Reid slumped in his chair, and Amanda and Trent got up and left the room.

They found Hudson and Ryan in the neighboring observation room.

"I assume you heard the entire thing?" Amanda asked them.

"You bet, and we'll take it from here," Natalie told them. "After all, it doesn't sound like Sherman's the guy you're after, and this backup drive is his main defense strategy."

"It would be great if you could handle that. Malone wants our focus on the Lambert case." Amanda dipped her head in thanks to her fellow detectives before leaving. She turned to Trent as they headed to the lot to sign out a department car. "This animosity between Sherman and Dodger might end up working out for us. At least for justice."

"If that drive has Seth ordering hits, that goes to his character. He could have killed Don."

"Not going to disagree. No alibi, and he was in the area."

TWENTY-NINE

Amanda and Trent arrived at JJ's only thirty minutes behind their original goal. It was a hopping place for nine thirty on a Thursday. One would think most people would be at home getting ready to tuck in to be ready for work the next morning. Then again, unemployment records were at a high.

Inside, country music was pumping out of the speakers louder than it had yesterday. Micah and Jake were hustling behind the bar.

She made eye contact with Micah, and he must have read her mind. He nudged his head toward an older man seated at the end of the counter cradling what could be a gin and tonic. She mouthed "thank you" and pointed the man out to Trent.

She'd estimate him to be in his mid-sixties. The hair he had left was dark gray and threaded with silver, resembling strips of tinsel. Deep lines on his face testified to a person who had been through a lot. He sat slumped forward, both elbows on the bar, one hand on his drink. His chocolate eyes took everything in and quickly landed on her and Trent.

He took a sip of his drink but didn't take his gaze off them.

"Bernie?" She stepped up to him. What she'd mistaken for him being slumped forward was a pronounced hunchback.

"That's me. But I haven't had a beautiful woman looking for me in a long time. Sit, sit." He pulled the vacant stool next to him closer and patted the seat.

She smiled at him and discreetly flashed her badge.

"Ah, figures." He took another sip of his drink. "Sit all the same if you must. I'm sensing a serious conversation on the horizon though."

Amanda returned the stool to where it had been, allowing herself more space, and sat down. Trent stood beside her.

"Bernie, we're Detectives Steele, and Stenson." She gestured toward Trent when she said his name.

"I'd introduce myself, but that seems unnecessary. Should it worry me that you know my name?" He smiled slyly and winked at her before taking another sip.

"Don't see why it should. We just have a few questions about a drinking buddy of yours," she said.

"Drinking buddy?" Bernie made a show of looking around, arms splayed out. "I'll need something more specific."

Trent took out his tablet, and Amanda caught a photo of Don Lambert on the screen before he showed it to Bernie. "You recognize this guy?"

"Sure do. Guy has a mouth on him too. He must love the sound of his own voice. He rarely shuts up long enough for me to have a lone thought."

Amanda resisted the urge to chuckle. Bernie was certainly what she'd call a colorful character.

"Well, you won't have to worry about that anymore," Trent said, pulling his tablet back. "He was murdered."

"You don't say..."

Amanda wasn't sure how to read the man's response or his body language. "You don't seem upset by that news."

"People die, that's life. It's shocking that he was murdered, but we weren't close. We'd shoot the breeze sometimes. Me with my gin and tonic, him with his whiskey or beer. Sometimes both. But our conversations were never anything deeply meaningful."

"That may be, but I'm sure you talked about your personal lives." Amanda would be surprised if they hadn't. One side effect of alcohol was loosened lips and oversharing.

"I'm a private person, but like I said, he was a talker." Bernie shook his head. "Just wowie, though. Murdered."

Amanda could appreciate it would take time to absorb knowing someone who was killed. "Did he ever talk about women he was seeing?" She'd keep her fingers crossed that Don had and that he'd mentioned names. If Bernie remembered them, it might get her and Trent to the man who had confronted Don on Friday night.

"Women were mostly what he talked about. Sometimes his job. But no names, or if there were any, they went in one ear and out the other. He had quite an attitude problem though. He often referred to women as the fairer sex. That bugged the crap out of me."

If that alone accomplished that, Amanda could imagine Bernie's strong response to finding out Don beat his wife.

Bernie carried on. "To make it all even worse, Don was married."

"Oh, you knew that?" Trent briefly balled his hands into fists, but Bernie didn't seem to notice.

"Sadly. And the guy was such a womanizer. Sexist, I guess it's labeled these days. You never treated a woman that way back in my time." Bernie took a drink, and Amanda noticed the simple gold band on his ring finger.

As this investigation kept reaffirming, Don had been a douche. But it was still their job to care about what happened to him, or at least slap cuffs on *who* had done it. "Are you married?" She flicked a finger toward his left hand.

"Widower. For twenty-three years now." He lifted his hand. "I still can't make myself remove the thing. Not even sure if I could. I think it's part of me by this point."

"Sorry to hear about your loss," she offered, appreciating while decades had passed, the grief was probably engrained.

He waved off her sentiment. "It was a long time ago, but she's still with me. You can never lose the love of your life. They live on. In you or—" He fluttered his fingers as if to indicate a spirit realm.

It had Amanda flashing back to her recent conversation with Zoe. Was there an afterlife? How could anyone alive truly know? But listening to this man talking about his dead wife had her examining her relationship with Logan. Would they stand the test of time? What they had worked, but was that enough? It wasn't fair to compare what she had with her late husband to what she had with Logan. Besides, no two relationships were the same, and it wasn't logical to expect them to be. But one thing was clear, she didn't want to remain stuck in the past like Bernie. She cleared her throat. "It sounds like you had something special with your wife. You really loved her."

"We did, and I still do."

This admission shone a light on her love life again, and she wasn't sure she liked what she saw. But it wasn't the time to dwell on it. "These women Don was involved with, did he ever say much about them? Whether they were single or married?"

Bernie gave a raspy laugh. "*Involved* would be stretching things mighty fine. But he slept with more than his fair share and, for a reason only God might understand, he had the desire to share sordid details with me. Now, I'm guessing why you're interested in women who were technically off the market has something to do with this one fella, from last Friday. Am I right?"

"We heard that a man yelled at Don to stay away from some woman," Trent said.

"Yep. Well, that happened. Saw it for myself, but I can't help you beyond that. You think this person killed Don?"

"It's an open investigation," Amanda said, "but you wouldn't happen to know the man's name?"

"Nope." Bernie sipped his drink. "But there is something you might be interested in hearing. Now whether it matters, I'll leave it to you to decide. Don used to get talking about this one woman he was with years ago. It took him at least seven whiskeys before he'd start going on about her."

"And what was so noteworthy?" Amanda asked, her interest piqued by the fact Don had to liquor up to talk about the woman and that Bernie saw her worthy of mentioning.

Trent stepped closer to Amanda. His hip brushed against her arm, and there might as well have been an electric charge buzzing between them. His eyes darted toward her briefly, telling her that he felt it too. She moved out of reach as quickly and discreetly as possible.

"Well, it may be nothing and have no bearing on his murder, mind you. I got the feeling the relationship dated back several years ago, but I found the story rather troubling."

"Please, if you would share it with us," Amanda gently prodded.

"Guess she was planning to leave him, but he wasn't going to stand for that to happen so he..." Bernie's complexion paled, and he took a large swallow of his drink.

Goosebumps rose on her neck and traveled down her arms. Her instinct was telling her what he had to say would turn out to be a crucial turning point for the case. "Bernie, what did he do?"

Bernie emptied his glass and signaled Micah for a refill. "He said that he drugged her and set her house on fire with her in it."

One sentence, words trailing each other in a steady rhythm, but the meaning was monumental. It implied Don had murdered someone.

"Just to be clear, he killed her?" Trent's voice barely rose above the din.

Micah came over with Bernie's fresh drink and said, "Hey" to Amanda and Trent. And whisked off just as quickly, taking Bernie's empty glass with him.

Bernie stared into the new drink but didn't sip it. "I think that was the plan, but..."

"She survived," Amanda said slowly, and Bernie nodded. Her body trembled with a flush of adrenaline. It wasn't someone getting payback for a loved one. Don's killer might be this woman herself. After all, it couldn't be a coincidence Don was burned alive when he'd tried to kill the same way. "Was this in town or somewhere else?"

"He never said that I recall." Bernie knocked back a solid mouthful of the new drink, his Adam's apple bulging as he swallowed. "If that's not all bad enough, he profited from what he'd done. He bragged about getting an insurance payout for the house. Can you believe that?"

Amanda was at the point where she'd believe pretty much anything unsavory about Don Lambert. "Can you remember if he told you this woman's name?'

"That one, yeah. It was Martha, Mary, something like that. Quite sure it started with an M."

"Did you ever get the rest of the story? What ended up happening to her? Where she might have gone?" Trent asked.

"No, sorry. And I don't think Don knew either. Just that she discharged herself from the hospital without his knowledge and vanished into thin air." Bernie angled his glass and stared into his drink again.

"A penny for your thoughts," Amanda said, hoping to tease whatever else Bernie had to say out of him.

He met her gaze. "Don made it clear if he ever ran into her again, he'd finish the job."

Amanda had heard enough. She lifted off the stool and handed Bernie her business card.

"Oh, she's giving me her number. I knew she liked me." Bernie smiled at Trent and winked at her.

Amanda's mind was too preoccupied to throw a smile his way. "Call me if you think of something after we leave. Her name or anyone else who might have wanted Don dead."

"Now that list would probably be a long one." Bernie tucked her card into his shirt pocket and dipped his head in goodbye.

They got out to the car, and Trent turned it on but let it idle in the bar's parking lot.

"The sick prick bragged about drugging a woman and trying to kill her. By fire," Trent stressed.

She understood her partner's need to reiterate what they'd learned. It was unfathomable. There really was pure evil out there, and it had lived in Don Lambert. "I don't think it's a coincidence that Don ended up a human torch. I think she may have returned for payback, and she carried it off."

"Bernie made it sound like this happened years ago, but a grudge like that doesn't go away."

"Nope, it would only fester over time."

"My aunt has been with him for ten years now, so before that. But depending on how severe her injuries were, she might have just healed enough to come after him now."

"Then she's conceivably had plenty of time to recover and get her strength back. Clearly, we need to find her. We could search for home fires involving burn victims, but we can't be sure this fire happened within Prince William County or the surrounding area. Has Don always lived round here?"

"No clue. And I'm not sure we'd find any news article about it anyway. She didn't die. The media thrives on *fatal*."

"Sad but true." She'd never advocate for journalism whether written or televised. Her viewpoint was tainted by one specific reporter for the local paper, though, who had gotten her into trouble more than once with his exaggerated and false allegations. The credo of the press that "the public has the right to know" was waved about as an excuse to tromp past boundaries and infringe on an individual's rights.

"Now, Bernie mentioned that Don got the insurance payout. That tells us the place must have been in his name."

"It's also likely this woman was living with him at the time."

"Then we search Don's previous addresses and see if any link us to this woman."

"Let's do it."

THIRTY

Amanda and Trent left the bar and went right to Central to dig further into Don Lambert's residential history. He had four addresses on file in the last fifteen years. All of them were in Woodbridge except for the oldest which was in Manassas. The two most recent were places Don had lived with Gertrude, leaving them to look closer at the oldest ones.

They did a system search to see if either address was also noted for another person. Luck must have finally been on their side because they had a hit fairly quickly. It was linked to Don's address from fifteen years ago.

"This has to be her. Marian Shepherd, fifty-five," Amanda said. "I'm quite sure that Mary, one of the names Bernie suggested, is a pet name for Marian."

"I think it is. So you said she's fifty-five now? That's eight years younger than Don, whatever that means, if anything. Where is she now?"

Amanda looked closer at her background. "Huh. The address she shared with Don is the last one showing on file, and she was there starting thirteen years ago. She's also not deceased, or the record would say, but it's like she's disappeared."

"Thirteen years ago probably makes her Don's last serious relationship before my aunt." Trent's tone was dark and sullen, and she could understand why. They didn't know exactly when things had ended with Marian, but on paper it seemed that Don had hopped from attempted murder right into bed with his aunt. "Where was she before the address in Manassas? That might help us."

"Looks like it was in Washington. But I'm still not sure how this helps." She tried to squeeze out the fear Marian was dead somewhere, her body never found. What if Don had caught up with her and finished what he'd started? He wouldn't admit to actual murder, would he? "I think Marian Shepherd has become our prime suspect. We can't ignore how closely Don's murder mirrors what he tried to do to her. She's probably been living under the radar, possibly with an assumed identity."

"Which makes it impossible for us to find her," Trent grumbled.

There must be some way... Her mind was a whirling mess, and it felt like a struggle to latch on to a single thought.

Trent snapped his fingers. "Check with the Department of Motor Vehicles, see if she has any vehicles registered to her."

Amanda did the quick search and shook her head. "Nothing active in the last eleven years, but there wouldn't be if she's going under another name."

"Okay, what about family? Do any show in the system? We could start there."

She smiled. At least her partner was thinking clearly. "Thank you. My mind's a mess right now. There's a lot going on up there."

"When isn't there?"

"True enough," she said offhandedly. If only he knew that part of her mental turmoil was due to her feelings for him. She read down the relationship section for Marian Shepherd. "Her mother's name is listed, but she's deceased. I'll go see if there are any other birth records under her name." Amanda worked as fast as her fingers would allow. "All right, jackpot. Marian has a brother, Darwin Shepherd..." She brought up his information. "Darwin lives right here in Woodbridge. Should we go pay him a visit?"

Trent looked at the clock on the wall, and it directed her attention there. "It's almost eleven. Want to leave this until the morning?"

Amanda was somewhat torn, but she wasn't ready to go home and face Logan. "Why wait? Darwin could be the key to solving Don's murder and putting this investigation to bed."

THIRTY-ONE

A man had answered the door. Late forties, brown hair, with a cleanly shaved face. "A little late for a house call, isn't it?"

Despite his complaint, Amanda thought he looked rather alert for the hour. After confirming they were police and he was Darwin Shepherd, she said, "We're sorry to disturb you, but it's an urgent matter. We are trying to find your sister."

"Mary, why? Is she in trouble?"

He referred to Marian by the nickname Bernie had, probably as he'd heard it from Don. "Could we come inside and talk a moment?"

"Sure." He took them to his living room, where they all got comfortable.

Amanda began, "Can you tell us where we might find your sister?"

"I have no idea. I haven't seen her in years or spoken to her since that bastard tried to kill her. You know about that, right? Is Don Lambert finally being investigated for what he did?" He studied their faces. "You know what he did, but I'm not getting the feeling you're here to build a case against him."

Amanda wasn't getting into Don's murder yet. "When did

he try to kill her?" All they had at this point was Marian had started living with Don thirteen years ago.

"Probably eleven years ago now."

Don and Marian had been a couple for two years before he decided to try to kill her. She also recalled eleven years ago was the last time Marian had a vehicle registered to her. She must have been keeping a low profile. That's if Amanda's other flitting theory about her being dead somewhere wasn't true.

"And you haven't spoken to your sister in all that time?" Trent asked, skepticism dripping from each syllable.

"Nope, but I don't blame her. She's probably doing all she can to remain invisible. I wouldn't put it past him to finish the job if he ever finds her. It's just the kind of guy he is. Why are you asking about Mary anyhow? Is she in danger from Don?"

"Not even possible," Trent said. "Don's dead, murdered Wednesday morning, found behind Patriot Plaza. Do you know anything about that?"

"No, I mean, why would I?"

Trent shrugged. "I dunno. Maybe you wanted to get back at the man who tried to kill your sister?"

"Why would I waste my life on him, and after all this time? That makes no sense."

"People have killed for less, and deep hurts tend to stay with a person." Long-lasting grudges led to murder more often than one might think.

"Well, as I said, I haven't even spoken with my sister since the fire. Before that, Don had a way of isolating her from her family and friends. It only took meeting the guy the once to figure out he was bad news. I tried to warn Mary, said that I had a bad feeling about the guy. She defended him with a slew of excuses. I still find it hard to believe that he broke my sister's spirit. She was so strong and had such an amazing sense of humor." His eyes glazed over.

Despite the passage of time, it seemed Darwin still loved his sister deeply, even if from a distance. But there was one slight discrepancy in what he said that Amanda wanted to revisit. "If you fell out of touch, how did you find out about the fire?"

"Believe it or not, Mary had me listed as an emergency contact. It came as a shock, but she was my sister, and I wanted to be there for her. The only thing was, I was out of the country when the call came. I should have caught the first flight back... But I didn't, and by the time I showed up at the hospital, she was gone. I'm not proud of myself for missing her." He cleared his throat. "The nurses and her doctor told me I missed her by a day, and they reiterated several times that she left against their advice."

"Was she injured badly?" They still didn't know the extent of Marian's suffering.

"Yeah. She had third-degree burns on much of her body and face. The hospital staff was mostly worried about infection setting in. Her face needed skin grafts, but the doctor still antici-pated permanent scarring. Honestly, I gathered they were surprised she had even survived for treatment. They were only 'cautiously optimistic' about her full recovery."

Marian had become the prime suspect in Amanda's mind, but what if her earlier theory was right? Had she died after leaving the hospital and refusing further treatment? "Can you tell us anything more about the fire? How she came to be rescued in the first place?" Until they knew for a fact Marian was dead, they had to explore her as a suspect in Don's murder. That meant learning as much as they could about her.

"I heard the entire house was pretty much engulfed in flames when the fire department showed up. I guess it was a neighbor from down the road who saw smoke and called it in. By the grace of God. They found my sister curled up and unconscious in the bedroom."

Darwin was sharing the details of his sister's horrible night without any show of emotion. Probably out of self-preservation.

It likely still hurt that he hadn't been in contact with her for years. Amanda could relate having had years apart from her siblings and her parents after losing Kevin and Lindsey. It was her decision to pull away, as if not seeing them would ease her grief. She was wrong.

"Did you find out what caused the fire?" Trent asked.

Darwin nodded. "A faulty space heater in the upstairs office. Apparently, it was a couple doors down from the main bedroom."

Not gasoline and a lit match, but it still boiled down to fire. "That doesn't sound intentional."

"You'd have to know Don to understand. He was physically abusive to my sister."

"She told you this?" Amanda volleyed back.

"Nope, but I saw the bruises right at the onset of their relationship."

"Did you ever go after Don to confront him?" Trent asked. "At any point?"

"Nope. And after the fire, since I'd been out of my sister's life for so long already, I didn't know where to find him."

"Did you ever take your suspicions to the police?" Amanda asked.

"I did and was turned away for my troubles. That's why when I saw you at my door, I thought maybe the police were finally taking my complaint seriously. I'm sorry to hear that's not the case. But thinking of Mary being free from that bastard has helped me find peace."

Amanda was curious if that thinking would have been enough. After all, in Darwin's mind, Don had tried to murder his sister and got away with it. While they had come with suspicions against the sister, Darwin would possess motive despite his protests to the contrary. "Could you tell us where you were Tuesday at eleven thirty PM until three AM Wednesday morning?"

"This to do with Don's murder? Are you considering me a suspect? As I told you, I've moved on and he's not worth going to prison over. Then or now."

"We're just doing our jobs here, Mr. Shepherd," she told him firmly.

"Easy enough. I would have been at work. You can call my boss and verify."

"Do you normally work the night shift?" If so, he should be there now unless it was his day off.

"I do, but today and tomorrow are my weekend this week."

"And where is work?" Trent asked.

"Roadrunner Solutions. The complete other side of town from Patriot Plaza."

Amanda was familiar with Roadrunner. They were a warehouse for third-party sellers and shipped globally. The fact Darwin was aware of where his work was in relation to Patriot Plaza didn't flag. Anyone familiar with the area would know that. "The name of your supervisor?"

"Antoine Adkins."

"All right. We'll give Mr. Adkins a call," she told him and slipped him her card. "If your sister turns up or you hear from her, call me immediately."

"Same goes for you too, eh? But wait, you never did actually say why you're interested in Mary."

She and Trent had already gotten outside and halfway down his front steps, but she turned around. "We just need to have a chat with her."

"Ah, so cop code for she's a suspect too."

"Good night, Mr. Shepherd." She pivoted again and waved a hand over her head.

"Neither confirm nor deny. I like it." Trent smiled as they got into the car.

She had her phone out and was searching for the number for Darwin's workplace. It was easy to find. She called and got through to Antoine Adkins without much effort. A few moments later she was hanging up. "Well, it seems the brother was telling the truth. Darwin's boss just confirmed he was at work during the time of Don's murder."

"Seems he's in the clear then. And while we might have learned more about Marian Shepherd and the fire, we don't have a lead on her whereabouts."

"I say we run all this past Malone and see if he backs issuing an APB for her." An all-points bulletin would alert all officers of the PWCPD to keep a lookout for Marian. The license photo on file with the DMV was out of date, but it would have to do.

"I'll let you make that call. I wouldn't want to pull him from bed."

"I'll handle him." Amanda talked confidently, but she didn't relish waking the sergeant up either. Long-time family friend or not, he needed his beauty sleep more than some.

THIRTY-TWO

Trent hadn't slept much last night. He was just eager to get the Lambert investigation wrapped up with a neat bow to relieve his aunt from all suspicion. She could get on with living her life and, ideally, be reunited with her family. That's if she could forgive him for dragging her down to Central twice and placing her in a holding cell.

It was 8:15 AM when he'd sat at his desk, beating Amanda in. He'd even gone a bit out of his way to stop at Hannah's Diner in Dumfries to get them both a coffee. He lived in Woodbridge, but Amanda swore they had the best coffee around and Trent couldn't argue with that.

Malone had approved the APB for Marian Shepherd last night before he and Amanda had gone home. Still no hits. No update from Digital Forensics on Don's laptop either. But the warrants for Seth Dodger's and Reid Sherman's phone records and financials were approved, and he forwarded them to the service providers and the banks.

While he worked, though, his mind was fixed on Marian. How did a person just disappear? He knew the logical answer involved procuring fake identification and living off the grid, but most people didn't have those resources within reach. The money or the contacts. Marian's brother's house was in a middle-income neighborhood, nothing grand, and he'd told them they weren't in touch. Marian had lived under Don's roof and rented in Washington, DC. Neither of which suggested she had disposable cash, possibly not even solid credit. Yet she had clearly been living off the grid and sustaining that existence somehow. But why come out now and risk her anonymity by killing Don? Though she might have figured the end justified the means.

Trent searched her employment record and found Marian's last listed job was with the Department of Public Works in Washington thirteen years ago. That timeline fit with when her address changed to Don's house in Manassas. He must have convinced her to leave her job for him. Just one step Don had taken to isolate her.

"Good morning," Amanda said, entering her cubicle, with a Hannah's coffee in hand.

He noticed she didn't bring in one for him, and that stung a bit. They often traded off buying for the other one. It didn't seem she'd given him any thought this morning.

"Oh. You got me a coffee?" She looked at him over the partition, eyes wide as if that was the most random and unexpected thing he could have done. "Thank you, but you didn't have to do that."

"You're welcome?"

"Well, I can never have enough coffee." She drank from the cup she'd come in with. "Tell me we have something."

He informed her of Marian's last job and where everything else stood. He'd just finished when the phone on his desk rang. "Detective Stenson," he answered and then he did the listening. He could hardly believe what his caller was telling him. He hung up, his gaze hanging in space.

"Hey, Trent. You all right?"

"Uh-huh, but you're not going to believe this. We just got a hit on the APB for Marian Shepherd, though apparently, it's Paula Dunn now."

"Great news. Where can we find her?"

"In her Woodbridge home. Murdered."

THIRTY-THREE

Police cruisers cordoned off the block surrounding the house of Marian Shepherd aka Paula Dunn. Neighbors were on their front lawns watching what was unfolding, and uniformed officers were encouraging them to go inside their homes or stand behind the established perimeter. No sign of the medical examiner or crime scene investigators yet, but they were undoubtably on the way. Sadly, the press wouldn't be far behind either. It would be impossible to keep this scene quiet from them for long.

Amanda polished off the coffee she had picked up and found herself wishing she'd taken the one Trent had gotten her along too. But she had to enforce boundaries between them, and she'd start small. There was no need for them to buy coffees for each other. They were more than capable of taking care of themselves. If Trent found this to be standoffish, oh well, she had to draw a line if she wanted to make things work with Logan. Though as he had said, love shouldn't take work. She shook the personal thoughts aside. She was at a murder scene, and that deserved her focus.

As she and Trent made their way toward the house, they

passed a brown courier truck parked at the curb out front. It struck her as out of place, so it or its driver must have factored in somehow.

Officer Leo Brandt was posted next to the front door of the house, and he shook his head when they approached. "It's a horror scene in there. Definitely not for the squeamish. The RO puked in the hedges."

Responding officer... The vomit explained the stench wafting up her nose. "Trent told me you were the one to call him. What else can you tell us?"

"Just to lay the foundation, as I told Trent, the victim's print came up in the system as Marian Shepherd. This was in conflict to photo ID found in her purse for a Paula Dunn."

Amanda took shallow breaths. Even still, she kept catching undercurrents of decomposition and blood, mingled with puke. She'd be pulling on her strong constitution for this one. If it was this bad outside, inside would be much worse. "Why were her prints in the system?"

"No criminal record, but the vic used to be an employee with the Department of Public Works in Washington. Government jobs often require that employees are fingerprinted."

Amanda nodded. Marian's old place of employment wasn't news. Trent had passed that on along with his suspicion that Don had likely convinced Marian to quit in an attempt to isolate and control her.

"Who found her?" Trent asked.

She had a feeling it was linked to the courier truck but remained quiet.

"The delivery guy, just doing his job. He came to drop off a package for the victim and saw a cat sitting on that table there." Leo nudged his head toward an expansive bay window. Just behind the glass was a table with a decorative bowl on its top. "It was sunning and licking blood from its front paws. Blood was caked to its face. The thing is a Persian. It used to be white. Now it's mostly, well..."

Red... Amanda's stomach tossed, her mind filling in what Leo had left unsaid and the reason. The cat had snacked on its owner.

"That's why you get dogs," Trent said.

Leo nodded. "Uh-huh. That right there. Cats are okay, but I'm more a dog man myself. But back on point, the driver called nine-one-one."

"Where's the cat now?" she asked, figuring she knew the answer.

"Animal control was called and came to collect it. I'm sure the CSIs will look at it, process what they can that might aid the investigation. Once they are finished with that though..."

Amanda nodded. The cat's fate was about as dark as its owner's. "Where's the driver now?"

"Officer Cochran is taking his statement in her cruiser."

Traci Cochran was a great officer, and in Amanda's opinion had a bright future with the PWCPD. Typically a first responding officer spoke to the person on scene. Traci might have been the one to puke in the hedge, letting the responsibility of contacting Trent fall to Officer Brandt.

Amanda and Trent got plastic booties, Tyvek suits, and masks from Officer Brandt and put them all on.

"The body's in the kitchen, at the back of the house. Everyone has been cleared out waiting for you guys and the rest of the party to show up."

The ME and CSIs...

Stepping inside, the masks did barely anything to suppress the odors. The pungent smells of decomp and blood hit like smacking into a wall. They would have found Marian Shepherd without Leo's directions simply by following their noses. And, boy, was it ripe. Add to the stench of death, there was a dirty litterbox somewhere nearby. Tears sprung to Amanda's eyes.

Bloody cat prints marked the hallway in both directions. The cat had returned and left its meal repeatedly. *Its meal...* Amanda wished that lingo and its imagery hadn't come to mind.

Normally, she and Trent would talk a lot at a scene, but if he was like her, he was keeping quiet out of self-preservation. The second they opened their mouths the odors would wick through the masks and coat their tongues. As it was, the suits likely did little to protect their hair, skin, and clothing.

They entered the kitchen, and Amanda stopped short in the doorway. Trent ran into her back.

"Oh, sor—"

She faced him, and his eyes were full of tears.

Amanda turned to look at what remained of Marian Shepherd. Much of her face was missing, having been eaten by her cat. There was a lot of blood, made to appear worse by the cat's activities. They also made it trickier to distinguish the source of the injury.

Amanda dared a few steps closer. Her stomach heaved, but thankfully her breakfast and coffee stayed down.

Then she spotted what was likely the fatal injury. A hole in Marian's chest. She pointed this out to Trent, and he nodded.

There was no weapon in the wound. The killer may have taken it with them.

She danced her gaze along the kitchen counters to a knife block next to the fridge. The slot for the chopping one was empty. Had it been used to kill Marian? Then again, it could be in the sink. She couldn't see inside it from here. The knife could have also gone missing a long time ago. It was too soon to jump to any conclusions.

Dwelling on the scene itself, nothing aside from the dead body indicated an altercation in the kitchen. It appeared as if Marian had been stabbed without fighting back. If so, that could suggest she'd known her killer. Had she let them inside, or did they catch her by surprise?

Amanda couldn't stop the flow of questions coming at her, nor did she want them to cease. An inquiring mind was the basis of any successful homicide investigation.

The blood was a dark burgundy, mostly congealed or dry, except for some wet prints left by the cat. That suggested Marian had been dead a while, possibly days, but Amanda would leave that determination to the medical examiner. While Marian's body had been feasted on, she was sure cats would eat their dead owners within a day. Dogs would rarely, if ever. They'd starve to death at their master's side.

As she continued to take in the scene, she worked to untangle how Marian Shepherd went from suspect to victim. Was her death somehow linked to Don's murder? Their past connection made it seem too coincidental to consider otherwise.

But she'd seen enough, and it was a sight that wouldn't leave her any time soon. She backed out of the room and gestured toward the front door.

Trent didn't waste a second before making the retreat himself.

Once outside, Amanda lifted her mask and let out a long exhale. She counted to five in her head before drawing in a breath. It still didn't do any good. They were inside for maybe five or ten minutes, and the damage was done. The smell would be lodged in their nostrils for hours to come. As for their clothes, they might best burn them.

She and Trent removed the Tyvek suits and booties and handed them over to Officer Brandt.

He blanched as he took them back. "I didn't exaggerate things an iota, did I?"

"No, you did not," Trent replied.

She and Trent moved to the front walkway and talked about what they had just seen.

"She's been dead a while," Amanda said, starting things off.

"I'd say so, but man that was a sight..." Trent winced.

"That's why we make the big bucks." She smiled at him, and he laughed. Light banter was the only way to survive such a grotesque crime scene. It somehow unburdened the mind and helped it process what it saw.

Trent pinched the shoulder of his jacket and sniffed it gingerly and quickly drew back, his complexion pale.

"Why on earth would you do that?"

"I'm an idiot. Obviously." He grinned.

"We were convinced Marian Shepherd killed Don. Now she's a victim. What do you make of that?" She was open to his ideas.

"I wonder if Don got to her. Bernie did say that Don talked about finishing the job if he ever caught up with her again. What if he did? As you said, she's been dead a while. Likely before Don."

"Which would still leave us with the mystery of who killed Don." That was one riddle that, for the life of her, Amanda couldn't figure out.

THIRTY-FOUR

Amanda and Trent caught up with Officer Traci Cochran just as the vehicle from the Office of the Chief Medical Examiner arrived. Not far behind them was the van from Crime Scene.

Traci popped out of the squad car to come over to them, leaving the courier driver in the front passenger seat. "He's an absolute mess," she told them.

"I'd be more worried about him if he wasn't," Trent said.

Amanda agreed. They hadn't seen the cat, but they saw the scene inside. "What's the driver's name and what's he saying?"

"Ward Church. Pardon me if I repeat anything you know, but he showed up with a delivery for Paula Dunn— Or would you prefer we call her Marian Shepherd?"

"Either is fine for our conversation," Amanda said quickly, hoping it would encourage Traci to continue her briefing.

"Church rang her doorbell, and that's when he spotted the —" She blanched and covered her mouth. Tears sprung to her eyes. A few seconds later, she lowered her arm. "Phew. I was going to say, 'not again.' But you should have seen that thing."

Mystery solved about who had vomited in the bushes. No

judgment on Amanda's part. She had hardly kept her breakfast and coffee down.

Traci went on. "Church has a clean record, and I feel quite confident in saying he had no involvement in what took place in that house. There was a package, verified that myself."

"And where is it now?" Trent asked.

"The trunk of my cruiser."

Amanda nodded. "I'd like to look at the contents." They might not have a bearing on the investigation, but Amanda's father, former police chief for the PWCPD, stressed the importance of leaving 'no stone unturned' in an investigation. He cautioned it was always the one you foolishly overlooked that would provide the key to solving a case.

"Want to do that now or..."

"Nah, we'll chat with him first," Amanda said. "Then, I don't see why he wouldn't be free to leave."

Traci dipped her head and returned to her car. This time she had Amanda and Trent at her heels. The officer tapped the front passenger-side window, then opened the door.

"Mr. Church," Traci said, "these are Detectives Steele, and Stenson. They have a few questions for you."

Ward Church regarded them with widened eyes. "Ah, sure." He unfolded himself from the car. He was at least six foot two.

"I'll be just over there if you need me." Officer Cochran pointed at Shepherd's driveway.

"Mr. Church," Amanda said, "what time did you arrive at the residence of Paula Dunn this morning?" She'd stick with the name on the package, so as not to confuse him.

"Eight on the mark. She was my first delivery. I just had to ring the bell and leave it on her step. But then I saw the... *the*..." Ward rubbed his brow and shook his head, clearly in shock and denial.

"If it's easier for you, we can return to the squad car, where you can take a seat," she told him.

"No, I'll... I'll get through it. Just ask me whatever you need to."

Amanda felt for the guy. The graphic image of a cat licking its bloody paws would be fodder for his nightmares for months to come. "What was the origin of the package?"

"You'd have to check the label. I don't know."

She nodded. "Do you make deliveries to Paula Dunn often?"

"Maybe once a month."

"Okay, thank you for being so cooperative." Amanda handed him her card and one for Victim Services.

"Does this mean that I can go?"

"It does, but if you feel you'd like to speak with someone about what you saw here today, contact Victim Services. One of the cards I gave you is for them. They are an extension of the Prince William County PD, free to use, and offer skilled counselors."

"I think I'll be fine. But can I call if I change my mind in the coming days?"

"Absolutely," she responded.

"Thank you." He left then, and she watched him walk away until Officer Cochran cut in front of her view.

The officer popped the lid of her trunk, and sitting inside was a cube-shaped box about twenty inches square. The shipping label was conveniently staring up at them.

Amanda leaned over to read it. "Some company out of California."

"Well, whatever it is, it's got some heft," Cochran told them.

Trent stepped up beside Amanda. "If it's all right with you...?" He gestured to the box, and she moved out of the way. He was already gloved up, and he had his keys out to slit the tape. He opened the flaps and revealed another one.

"Gurr. This drives me crazy," Cochran said. "I mean I get why this happens sometimes, but not this time. It's like when companies ship a bottle of nail polish in a box big enough to house a few hardcover books."

"I can't relate. Well, to the nail polish thing anyhow." Amanda checked out the officer's nails, which were a pale pink.

The officer pulled her hand back as if in a self-conscious reaction. "I find doing my nails relaxing. If that makes me a freak..." She gave a shoulder shrug like she didn't care what anyone thought.

Amanda smiled at her before focusing back on Trent and the boxes. In the time she'd talked with Cochran, he was into the second package.

"It's just a set of pasta bowls." Trent had one in his hand. It was a blue Mediterranean design. Pretty, but on the surface, irrelevant to the case. Except...

"Is there anything to tell us when it was bought or how it was paid for? Just by chance?" To order a product online, a person needed a credit card. Presumably Paula Dunn wouldn't have one as she was a fabrication. But the driver said he delivered to her house about once a month. Maybe she was making a larger deal out of this than was warranted.

"Let me see." Trent set the interior box beside the shipping one. "Ah-ha. A packing slip from the manufacturer. Looks like it was ordered directly from the seller. It's made out to Paula Dunn, ordered last Friday, and paid with credit card."

"All right, well, that tells me Marian's identity as Paula Dunn must be convincing enough to get her credit. Unless she borrowed someone else's."

"Excuse me! Officer!" A man in his sixties was yelling from the tape line at Officer Cochran. His cheeks were bright red as was the tip of his nose. He wore a cable-knit cardigan and pressed pants as if it were autumn weather, but this morning was rather mild.

"Here we go," Cochran mumbled before heading over. "Sir, I'm going to have to ask that you please keep your voice down and stay behind the line."

The man did the opposite, making endeavors to duck beneath the barricade. Officer Wyatt, who had been standing down the line, went over to assist Cochran in getting the man under control.

"Wait, don't— Are they detectives? What happened? Please, I need to speak with them."

The man's adamant persistence had Amanda's attention. She walked over with Trent. "What is it I can do for you, Mr...?"

"Bruce Butler. I'm Paula's landlord. Did something happen to her?"

Cochran and Wyatt looked at Amanda. She nodded for them to let the man through.

On this side of the barricade, he shivered and rubbed his arms as a subtle gust rustled past. "Please, just tell me what's going on."

She and Trent led him away from the straining ears of the growing crowd and stopped in front of Officer Cochran's squad car.

Amanda turned to the man. "Mr. Butler, Paula Dunn was murdered."

"She was—" He covered his mouth, and his knees buckled.

Trent buoyed him and corralled him to the front passenger seat. "Just have a seat. We can appreciate this news must come as quite a shock."

Bruce remained silent, blinking slowly, his eyelashes loaded with unshed tears. If he was this upset already, things were about to get much worse for him.

THIRTY-FIVE

"I don't understand this. It just makes no sense to me. She was murdered?" Bruce was rubbing his head, and regarding Amanda and Trent with wet eyes. "Why? Who would do such a thing?"

"How well did you know... Paula Dunn?" Amanda had almost slipped and said Marian Shepherd.

"Not well, really. She just rented my property."

"For how long?" Trent had his tablet out and appeared ready to make notes.

"Since this past December."

Heading into six months, but where had Marian Shepherd been before that? After the fire, had she returned to Washington? Though even if she had, it didn't explain why she had recently resurfaced in Woodbridge. Had that decision proved to be a fatal mistake? Maybe Don had found her and finished what he'd tried to do all those years ago? Though he stabbed her instead of using fire. Before she or Trent said anything, Bruce spoke again.

"But she already gave her notice."

"I take it there was no term commitment in the lease?" Most

landlords asked for a year, but more on Amanda's mind was what had Marian living here for so brief a time. Though she may have been planning to move somewhere else in town.

"I don't ask for that."

She nodded. "Do you know where she was moving?"

"I don't. She never offered, and I never asked."

"What about before she rented from you? Do you know where she lived prior? I assume you checked references." Amanda was trying to piece together Marian's life.

Bruce rubbed his forehead. "I wish I had, but it looked like she'd been through a lot in her life. She had scars on her face, like she'd been burned, but she had honest eyes. She had rent to cover first and last, so I was happy enough."

"And where did she move from?" Trent asked, with a glance at Amanda, acknowledging that the question had initially been hers and had gone unanswered.

"I'm quite sure it was Washington."

It was probably easier to hide in a large city. "Did she say what brought her to Woodbridge?"

Bruce shook his head. "Nah. That would have been poking my nose too far into her business. She was a rather private person, and I wanted to rent the place. I didn't need to scare her off."

"You said she had first and last, but what about employment? Do you know where she worked? I assume that was on her application." It was also possible Marian supported herself these last eleven years working cash jobs. Again, Amanda's father's words about looking under every rock came to mind. And they needed to find out as much about her as they could. It wasn't like they could look up the employment record of a fabrication.

"I should come up to this century, protect myself, but I'm old-school, and made a verbal arrangement with her."

"You might want to start having tenants fill out an application and put the rental agreement in writing. As you said, to protect yourself." Amanda, in good conscience, couldn't remain silent on the matter.

"I know. We did have a conversation once about her work though. I'm quite sure it involved animals."

That was better than nothing, but she asked, "Can you offer us any more specifics than that?"

"Oh, I remember now. Paws for a Cause. Yeah, that's it."

Paws for a Cause was a medium-size shelter that took in abused and neglected cats and dogs, nursed them back to health, and adopted them out. "Okay, thank you. We'll speak with them there. Did Paula have any boyfriends?"

"No idea. As I said, I didn't nose into her personal affairs."

"How did you find out something was going on here today?" Amanda hadn't seen the news trucks pull up, so either Bruce lived nearby and had seen the commotion outside his window, or someone had alerted him.

"I live there." Bruce pointed to a brick bungalow a few houses past the barricade. "I just got back from breakfast out when I saw what was going on down here. Speaking of..." He rubbed his stomach and paled.

Amanda looked at Trent, seriously hoping that Bruce kept his food down. Her constitution drew the line at watching someone vomit. She was likely to join in. Time to use what they just found out to their advantage though. "Living that close, you ever see anyone come around her place? Men or women?"

"Ah..." More rubbing of his forehead. "I do remember seeing a man at her door last Friday."

"Can you describe him?" Trent rushed out.

"Don't think he was quite six feet. He had dark hair and was a little stocky. I only saw him from behind. Couldn't tell you his age."

Tingles spread over her arms. The vague description could

fit Don Lambert. It all came down to timing. "What time was this?"

"I was getting home from dinner out with friends, so around five or six o'clock."

Early meal aside, it was possible Don had been at Marian's door. This was hours before that man accosted him at JJ's between nine and ten. It would come down to when Don got off work, and what Gertrude might add. Presumably he ate dinner at home. "Does the name Don Lambert sound familiar to you?"

"Nope."

"Detective Stenson, would you happen to have a photo of Mr. Lambert that you can show Mr. Butler?" He hadn't seen the man's face last Friday, but that didn't mean he hadn't spotted Don hanging around on another occasion.

Trent worked his finger around the tablet's screen and, within seconds, he produced the requested photo and held it for Bruce to see. "Recognize him?"

"No, sorry."

"No need to apologize," Amanda assured him. "You've been a huge help. Did you notice what the man from last Friday was driving?"

"I wasn't paying close attention. I just saw him because I glanced out my front window. Was more a passing observation."

"All good. Thank you for taking the time to answer our questions." She extended her business card to him.

"What's going to happen from here?" He exited the car with a groan and a rub of his left knee. He put her card in his sweater pocket. "I have people who are supposed to move in next month."

Amanda made eye contact with Trent. That was unlikely to remain on schedule. The stench of decomposition would have seeped through the drywall into the studs of the home. The inside would need to be gutted and redone. Even then, the prospective tenants might not want to live where a murder had taken place.

"Detectives?" He raised his eyebrows, prompting them for a response.

"The house will require some renovations, Mr. Butler," she said, putting it mildly. "You would be best to notify the next tenants there will be a delay to their moving in."

"Why? How long of a delay are we talking about here? I need the rental income from that place to live."

She hadn't wanted to be the one to tell him this, but it seemed there was no way around it. And he would find out sooner or later. Informing him now would be a kindness. "Due to the circumstances of Ms. Dunn's demise, you will need to call in a company that specializes in forensic cleanup. They will likely suggest an entire gut and renovation to the premises."

"What?" Bruce's mouth fell open. "That will cost a fortune. I can't afford to..." He stumbled back against the cruiser, using it to support himself.

"Your insurance may cover it. I suggest you start the process by reaching out to them." Amanda felt for him. It really wasn't the type of thing anyone could predict.

"Okay, okay..." Bruce was muttering as he walked back toward the tape, in the direction of his home.

"Poor guy," Trent said.

"I was thinking the same. I was also thinking it's very possible that Don Lambert killed Marian. He was confronted by that man at the bar on Friday, but that was later at night."

Trent nodded. "Butler's description for Marian's visitor could fit Don. He was likely finished his workday by five or six. I could call his boss, confirm when he left on Friday."

"I think we should. Actually... The CSIs found blood in Don's Buick from an unknown donor. Could it be...?" She met Trent's gaze.

"You think it might belong to Marian Shepherd?"

"It could. Transfer from the murder scene."

"All right, but how does that get on the front passenger-side floormat?"

Her eyes widened as the answer hit. "It's from the murder weapon," she spat.

"Pretend I'm lost..." He smiled at her.

"You saw the stab wound in Marian's chest?" Once he nodded, she continued. "I noticed a knife was missing from the block on her counter. I may be getting ahead of myself, but I have this burning feeling in my gut that Don killed Marian. What if he transported the knife on the floormat and the blood transferred from that?" It all sounded so plausible as she laid it out to Trent that goosebumps laced her arms.

THIRTY-SIX

Amanda didn't have any plans to go back inside Marian's house, but it also wasn't necessary. What she'd seen was etched into her brain, and the CSIs would capture it in photographs and video should she wish to revisit it. Rideout and his assistant, Liam, wheeled Marian's remains, zipped up inside a black body bag, out the front door.

She and Trent followed them to their van and waited while they loaded Marian into the back. Then the four of them tucked around the side of the van to shelter themselves from the gawkers.

"I could have lived without ever seeing that," Liam said. It was a sad reflection of their work when a burned-out human husk and a body eaten by a cat competed for the most grotesque scene. And that was just this week.

Amanda refused to conjure the imagery of either in any clarity. "I take it CSIs Blair and Donnelly are still inside?" They nodded, and she asked, "What can you tell us?"

"The vic's cat got a little munchy," Rideout said.

So much for not seeing everything again. "Maybe we could forego morgue humor this once."

Rideout smirked. "I never took you for the queasy type."

"Even the tough have their limits. Time of death? Cause of death?" She rushed out the questions to ensure the medical examiner would move the conversation forward. Given the wound in Marian's chest, the *manner* of death was obviously murder.

"Death was at least a week ago," Rideout said. "I'll be able to confirm with more accuracy once I've run tests back at the morgue."

A week ago would have been Friday. The same day a man similar to Don Lambert's description was seen at Marian's door. Could that be a coincidence? In the realm of possibilities, sure, but she wasn't buying it. She was quite certain Don had killed Marian but was trying not to pigeon-hole the investigation either. "And cause?"

"Preliminary, I suspect it's connected to the stab wound in her chest. I'll confirm once I've finished the autopsy. For now, I can confidently say the edges of the cut appear clean, so I'd wager something non-serrated was used. But that's as much as I dare presume."

"Like a chopping knife?" she asked.

"Could be. The CSIs pointed out a missing one from the kitchen's knife block, but I don't want to be influenced and run on an assumption."

His response didn't surprise her, and his resistance to jumping to conclusions was one thing she respected about him. "So as far as you know, the knife still hasn't been found?"

Rideout shook his head. "It wasn't while we were in there."

Amanda glanced at Trent, who nodded. Had the knife, or murder weapon, at one time been on the floormat of Don's Buick?

The *PWC News* truck pulled up and parked. Diana Wesson hopped out with her cameraman in tow. She was leading the race toward the tape in heels. Impressive if the woman didn't irk Amanda so much.

Rideout pointed at the reporter, turned, and headed toward the driver's seat. "That's my cue. Time to go."

If only I was so lucky...

"The autopsy should happen later today. I'll text you," Liam told them before leaving to join Rideout in the van.

"And there you have it." Amanda put her hands on her hips, for the moment forgetting about Diana, as she absorbed what Rideout told them. "Time of death tells us it could have been Don."

"Just one more thing he got away with? Guy couldn't even stay alive to go to prison."

"He might not have gotten away with anything, and it could be argued he received worse," she tossed back, thinking of his remains in some freezer in the morgue.

"Are you suggesting someone killed Don for killing Marian?"

It was an unsavory thought because it suggested Don's killer was aware Marian was dead and left her body for her cat to feast on. But how could anyone who cared about Marian enough to avenge her murder be so callous about her death? The two points were in complete conflict. "All I know is anything's possible until we rule it out."

Rideout pulled away, leaving her and Trent in the open.

Diana's piercing voice rose above all else. "Yoo-hoo! Detective Steele. Is it true? Was a woman murdered in her home?"

Amanda shut her eyes briefly and took some deep breaths, trying to curb her rising fiery temper. The myth about redheads was fact. But this specific reporter possessed a special talent for burrowing under her skin like a tick.

The crowd was giving the reporter and cameraman space to get to the cordon line, and all eyes were on Amanda and Trent.

Diana was waving wildly. "Detective? Just one minute of your time?"

"I'll take care of her." Trent stomped off before Amanda could stop him. "If you don't get back from the line, you'll be arrested for interfering with a police investigation."

Undeterred, Diana leaned forward, stretching her arm over the tape and putting her microphone in Trent's face. "Detective Stenson, tell the people of Prince William County what happened here today. The public has a right to know."

Amanda rolled her eyes, grateful Trent was taking lead on this.

"Three words for you," he said.

"Yes?" Diana cooed.

"Public Information Office." He saluted her and returned to Amanda.

She turned her back and snickered. "That was good. Thank you, my friend." The PIO was responsible for handling media statements for the police department.

"Anytime." He smiled, but the expression faded quickly. "Let me make that call to Don's work, see when he left work on Friday."

"Just ask for all of last week, in case she died before Friday."

"You got it."

Amanda saw CSI Blair waving her over to Marian's front step. Her spirit was willing, but her feet didn't want to move. That would put her right up-close to the rank smells again. But her curiosity won out. If the lead CSI was signaling for her, it had to be good.

"I thought you'd want to see this." CSI Blair extended a phone.

Amanda gloved up and took the device from her.

"This belonged to the vic. I already got in. Check out her photo gallery."

Tingles ran over Amanda's shoulders as she opened the app.

Her eyes popped at what she saw there. Photo upon photo of the same subject, in different places, at different times. "That's Don Lambert."

"Yep, and lots of him. I'd say the vic was stalking him. You think the two cases are connected?"

"I think this erases any doubts." How it all fit together yet, though, she wasn't sure. She scrolled through the pictures. Don at his work, in his driveway, at JJ's, and at the Java Stop.

"So, I spoke to Don's boss. Guess Don was quite religious about checking out at five on the dot every day." Trent's voice cut through her thoughts. She'd been so absorbed in Marian's phone she hadn't heard him or sensed he'd come over. When she didn't respond, he said, "Am I missing something?"

"Oh yeah." Amanda held the phone's screen toward him.

Trent leaned in to look, squinted, and pulled back. "Why does she have pictures of Don?"

"That might rise to question of the day," Amanda said. "There must be... Do you know how many?"

Blair smiled. "One hundred and ten to be precise."

"Dating back how far?" Trent asked.

"To the middle of December."

Amanda looked at Trent. "She moved in here at the start of December and starts tracking Don within a couple of weeks. That makes it seem like she came to Woodbridge to do just that. But to what end?"

"To learn his movements, figure out a place to target him, to get revenge," Trent suggested.

"If so, her plan backfired spectacularly," CSI Blair weighed in. "But why would she seek revenge?"

"Don and Marian Shepherd aka Paula Dunn have a history going back thirteen years." Amanda told Blair about their relationship, how Don had tried to kill her eleven years ago, and that the landlord mentioned a male visitor last Friday that loosely fit Don's description.

"Oh," Blair said.

"Exactly," Amanda agreed. "But we're still left with the question of who killed Don, whether or not he killed Marian."

"May I?" Trent held out gloved hands to take the phone from Amanda. He moved his finger around the screen. A few seconds later, he said, "There doesn't seem to be any call history or texts on here."

"Or contacts, which is even more strange," Blair added. "Maybe Digital Forensics can get somewhere and resurrect deleted messages or contacts. Regardless, I suggest reaching out to the service provider for her records."

"We'll be doing that for sure," Amanda said.

CSI Blair took the phone back and zipped it in a plastic evidence bag. "Other things you might benefit from knowing. To start, there's no sign of forced entry."

"She let her killer inside..." Amanda chewed on how that would reconcile with Don Lambert. Surely, seeing the man who tried to kill her eleven years ago on her doorstep would have had her calling 911. But she hadn't. Maybe Trent was heading somewhere when he'd mentioned Marian seeking revenge. And it did coincide with their initial interest in Marian. Had she let Don into her home, thinking she'd have the upper hand? "Your phrasing made it sound like you had a few things to share...?"

Blair nodded. "Just one more for now. Suitcases were pulled out in a second bedroom. It looked like the vic had been packing for a trip. There was also a passport there in the name of Marian Shepherd."

Amanda worked to untangle that knot. "Let me get this straight. She had other ID stating she was Paula Dunn. It was also how the landlord knew her, how she ordered those bowls..."

"Bowls?" Blair interjected, confusion manifesting in her wrinkled brow.

"The package the courier was trying to deliver. If she was planning a trip, why order china in the days leading up to the getaway? It might not mean anything, but the timing seems odd."

"I find the fact she bought it when she was supposed to be moving out more noteworthy," Trent began. "I'd think the time to nest would be once she was in the new place. Whatever she acquired now she'd just have to lug with her."

"True," Amanda said. "Along the lines of what Trent brought up, was there any sign she was packing house?"

"None."

"Which makes no sense," Amanda said.

"Unless she planned on making a run for it," Trent suggested. "Take her revenge and skip town?"

"Then the suitcase would indicate she'd planned to do that soon. Don, or whoever her killer was, got to her before she had a chance." Amanda felt there was something groundbreaking in what she and Trent were discussing, but couldn't quite piece it all together yet.

"Well, that's it for now," Blair said. "But if Donnelly or I find anything else of note, you'll be the next to know."

"Thanks. But just before you get back to work in there... Once you get a chance, can you see if the blood sample taken from Don Lambert's Buick is a match for the vic?" If Amanda was a betting woman, she'd wager the results would confirm.

"You got it." Blair returned inside the house.

Amanda turned to Trent. "I'm not a fan of things not lining up."

"Me either, but on the upside? Poking around the anomalies is usually how we get to the truth."

"Yes, there is that."

"I'm fixed on the fact Marian had obvious plans to leave. The suitcase, the notice... Had she planned to kill Don, but he just beat her to it?"

"Exactly where I arrived. And if it was Don at her door on Friday night, she might have seen it as an opportunity."

"*If?* I thought we figured he was."

"We speculated the possibility," she corrected. "The only thing that is a slight niggle for me is no sign of forced entry. If a man who tried to kill you turned up at your door, would you just let them inside your home?" A moment ago, she speculated Marian may have been confident she'd turn the tables on Don, but would she have taken that chance? It was her life on the line.

"He could have forced his way past her."

"I can get behind that theory. So, Marian moves back six months ago, pretty much starts stalking Don immediately, familiarizing herself with his habits and routines. Only somewhere along the way, Don spotted her. He came here to confront her. One way or another he winds up inside. Marian might have thought she could kill him. After all, the guy shows up at her door, essentially presenting himself to her. She could decide it was as good a time as any."

"But it didn't work out that way. Instead, Don kills her," Trent finished.

"Bingo."

"All well and good, but even if it is true, we still have Don's murder to solve."

His direct statement had her mind returning to anyone who might want revenge for Marian's murder. Like before though, she dismissed that theory. Besides, it was possible Don's murder wasn't related to Marian's. This still left them with the suspects they were considering before Marian's dead body turned up. The bookie, an employee of the enforcer, the jealous lover, and Gertrude.

"Detectives?" Officer McRoy was hurrying over to them. Jerrod was a rather recent transfer to the PWCPD. "I thought you'd like to hear this right away. I'm one of the officers canvassing the area, and more than one neighbor has mentioned a red Kia in the area in the last couple of weeks. I guess before then, they'd never seen it."

Amanda's heart sank, and she looked over at Trent. Color splashed his cheeks.

"It could belong to someone new living in the neighborhood," Trent quickly countered.

She could appreciate he'd want a speedy explanation because this implicated his aunt again. "When was it last spotted?"

"Last Friday, but the homeowner seems foggy on the time."

"Thanks, Jerrod."

"Glad to be of help, ma'am." He dipped his head to them and left.

"Don't even say it, Amanda. There must be hundreds of red Kias out there." It didn't take a second for Trent to go on the defensive. "And how are we going to twist this? My aunt killed Don and Marian now? And days apart?" He shook his head. "There's no way."

"I don't know, and neither do you. We have to speak with her again." He might have stumbled on the *days apart* bit, but she didn't. It would insert some separation and muddy the investigations.

"Fine. Let's get it over with. The car knows its way to her house by now."

Knows its way to her house... If that red Kia was Gertrude's, why was she in Marian's neighborhood? How did she even know where she lived? Had Gertrude followed Don here and thought Marian was one of his mistresses? Maybe she had done more than watch. Did she kill both her husband and his presumed lover?

THIRTY-SEVEN

The day was slipping away, but Amanda and Trent both opted to pop home for a quick shower and change of clothes. No way she could have forged ahead smelling like decomp. And the scene had taken any appetite they might have had. It was three o'clock by the time they arrived at Gertrude's house.

Amanda's phone rang on the way up the front walk. She stopped to answer, and Trent stood next to her.

"It's Hudson," her caller told her. "It turns out that tip Reid Sherman gave you panned out. We retrieved the backup drive from the locker. Seth Dodger ordered the hits for the bodies we pulled from the ground. There's even a recording where he commissioned Sherman to scare and rough up Gertrude Lambert."

Not that he'd ever denied that. But if Seth ordered hits, it was unlikely he'd change his MO and suddenly do the dirty work and kill Don himself. "Sounds like you've got them both then," she told him.

"That we do. Just thought you'd like to know."

"Appreciate—" And Hudson was gone. "*It.*" Amanda

pushed out the last word to finish her thought and filled Trent in.

"I'd love to see the smug look on the bookie's face vanish when he realizes there's no deal."

"He won't be too impressed, that's for sure. He'll be going away for life, along with Sherman." Under law a person who commissions murder could be charged along with the person who physically committed the crime. But her mind turned over something else. It strongly seemed that the murders of Marian and Don were linked, but the bookie didn't really fit into that picture. At least, they hadn't uncovered any reason Seth Dodger would want Marian dead. From the sounds of it, he hadn't ordered a hit on Don, either. Also, Seth didn't match the physical description of Marian's visitor on Friday evening. It was possible he turned up another time, but Amanda didn't think he killed Marian. But did he kill Don? She really wasn't so sure anymore. As she'd just thought, he paid people to handle those things.

"Trent? You're back again?" Gertrude held the door open as they approached, letting them enter the house without any resistance this time. "What have I supposedly done now?"

The woman looked a decade older since the first time they saw her a few days ago. She'd no doubt been through a lot but was the stress made worse due to guilt? Amanda was determined to keep an open mind.

"We just need to ask you some questions," Trent told her.

"Should I put on some tea?"

Trent looked at Amanda, wide-eyed, clearly surprised by the kind gesture. "I would love one," he said. "Amanda?"

"Sounds lovely." Not a fan of tea, she was being nice. Trent knew she'd prefer a black coffee, but why rock this particular boat? Gertrude seemed to be in a cooperative mood so there was no sense in jeopardizing that.

"Okay. I'll be right back. Have a seat in the living room."

Gertrude headed for the kitchen while Amanda and Trent did as she'd said.

"Tea?" Trent said in a whisper to Amanda. "I know it's not your favorite and appreciate you going along with it."

"No problem." She smiled at him.

"She offered tea," he reiterated as if he needed to repeat this for his aunt's hospitality to sink in.

"It seems you might be breaking down her defenses."

"Or giving her a breakdown, more like it. I hate this, Amanda."

"I get that, but we're just doing our jobs. Right? Let's focus on that."

He locked his gaze with hers. "What I keep reminding myself."

Gertrude entered the room and sat on the couch. "You said you had questions, so should I relax? You haven't carted me off in handcuffs yet."

Trent turned away from his aunt, and Amanda felt the nudge to step in.

"We've never cuffed you, Mrs. Lambert," Amanda said. "I can appreciate the last few days have been trying, but you're not the only one who has suffered."

Gertrude's face pinched in on itself, and her chin quivered. She looked at Trent, but he wasn't returning eye contact.

Amanda went on. "We've never once mistreated or mishandled you. In fact, if you were anyone other than Trent's aunt, things may have gone a lot differently for you." The admission served as a magnifying glass for self-scrutiny. They had afforded Gertrude leniencies they wouldn't have other suspects. "We've uncovered some evidence that led us here again today."

"*Evidence?*" Gertrude's voice sounded strained.

"Have you heard of Marian Shepherd?" she asked.

Gertrude pinched the collar of her shirt and slowly nodded.

"How do you know her?" It seemed like a no-brainer, but it was good to have her answer on record.

"She was Don's ex. He was with her before me."

Amanda imagined that Don held back the fact he'd tried to burn Marian alive. It wasn't exactly a working pickup line. "Did you ever meet her?"

"I hadn't. He just told me about her."

Amanda latched on to Gertrude's phrasing. There was something so precise about it that it didn't settle. She felt close to figuring out why when the kettle clicked and scattered her thoughts. No one moved to attend to it, as the energy in the room became dark.

"He told me what he did to her. Not at the start obviously. I assume you know?"

Amanda and Trent nodded.

"He, ah, said if I didn't watch my mouth, he'd do the same to me. And to my family if I didn't get them to back off." Gertrude hunched forward and sobbed into her hands.

A few more beats of tense silence before Trent got up and sat next to her on the couch. He put an arm around her and took one of her hands. "Is that why you cut us from your life?"

"Yes." She sniffled.

The unfolding scene chipped at Amanda's heart, threatening to topple her logic. But her cop brain saw Gertrude's admission as solid motive for killing Don. Maybe Gertrude snapped, sick of Don's threats, and killed him the same way he'd held over her head. "Then you've never been to Marian's house? Not even recently?"

"No, I..."

Trent petitioned Amanda with a quick look as he stood and walked to the kitchen, presumably to make the tea. His timing could have been better, but she took it as deliberate. He was buying his aunt a respite from the questioning, a move initiated by a nephew not a detective. From an investigative standpoint, Amanda had Gertrude where she wanted her. That was emotionally compromised and invested. With this imposed break in the conversation, Gertrude might retreat into her shell.

Trent returned with a tray holding three steaming cups, teabag strings hanging over the lips, sugar and milk on the side. He nodded at Amanda. At least he hadn't waited for the tea to finish steeping before returning. But still...

"Mrs. Lambert, you just told us you've never met Marian or been to her house..." Amanda's mind pieced together Gertrude's earlier phrasing. It was her response to Amanda's question about whether she'd ever met Marian. She'd said, *I hadn't.* In the context of the conversation the past tense could be overlooked, but examined in another light it might be telling. Had Gertrude met Marian? Maybe not at the onset of her relationship with Don, but more recently? Her evasiveness suggested it was possible. Why she might want to hide this sank in Amanda's gut. "Why was your Kia spotted in Marian's neighborhood?" She wasn't even questioning that it was hers anymore and ignored the side-glance Trent shot her.

"I can't answer that. I mean, I don't even know where she lives."

Gertrude made direct eye contact, which Amanda found unsettling. She was lying. "You suspected Don was cheating on you and followed him for that purpose. Did you find out he was seeing Marian again?" She presented that scenario as reality to gauge Gertrude's reaction.

"Really? She took him back after...? And that bastard." Her face bunched in a grimace.

It wasn't a pretty picture, rather the expression was of betrayal and anger. Amanda sat back in her chair. "I take it that is news to you?"

"Shocking."

Amanda found Gertrude's responses to this hypothetical

curious. Typically when speaking of Don and his affairs, she seemed rather docile, bordering on accepting. Something about the thought of Marian with Don had Gertrude reacting as if it were a more personal slight. Was it just Don and Marian's personal history or was there more to it? "It's best that you be fully honest with us, Mrs. Lambert. If there's—"

"Please stop calling me that," she snapped.

Trent's timer on his phone beeped, and he took the teabags out.

"It's just Gertrude. Call me that. Or Miss Shaw, my maiden name."

"Very well, Gertrude," Amanda said. "I'll do as you request. So you never followed Don to Marian's house?" Amanda added the name of the street this time.

"No."

"People have said they saw you in the area." Amanda was guilty of stretching the truth, not a crime, but she was deploying it as an interview tactic. Like she would on any other suspect.

"Amanda, could I have a minute?" Trent was on his feet and pointing toward the doorway.

"Ah, sure."

In the hallway, he spun on her. "Why are you attacking her?"

"Attacking her? You can't be serious, Trent. I'm going easy on her."

"You're baiting her and lying. We haven't proven it was her Kia. No one came forward to identify my aunt in the neighborhood. We came here to talk to her and feel her out, not accuse her. What happened to building a case?"

Amanda hurt for him, appreciated his compromised position, but they also had their jobs to do. "This is the job, whether you like it or not. We put things out there and gauge the reaction."

"No, I'm not on board with this," he said firmly. "And even

if this wasn't my aunt, this isn't how we normally work. We need to see if we can get CCTV to confirm it was even her Kia. We wouldn't continue to run on assumptions."

She angled her head. "She's toying with us. Even you must see things are not adding up here."

"I do. With you too. It's like you're overcompensating. You're so concerned with not being seen as extending liberties, you're taking the extreme opposite stance. Please, I ask as a friend, let's stop questioning her for now. We'll wait until we get the CCTV footage and check doorbell cams from the area and go from there."

The desperate peal in his voice resonated, and he might have been spot on with his accusation. "Fine. For you."

"Good. The videos might help us see if Don was at Marian's house on Friday too. Thank you."

"You're welcome." She watched as he returned to the living room and listened as nephew and aunt started a heartfelt conversation. Amanda gave them some time and overheard Gertrude ask about Trent's mom, her sister, then Trent's sisters, and finally his dad. After several minutes, Amanda popped back into the room. "Trent, we should probably..." She jacked a thumb toward the front door.

"You never even drank your tea," Gertrude said to her.

"Another time, but thank you." Amanda let herself outside where she'd wait for Trent next to the car.

When he came out of the house a few moments later, he said, "Thank you for allowing me some time with her."

"You're welcome again." She nudged her shoulder into his. *Boundaries, Steele!* "Sorry, I shouldn't have done that... the shoulder bump thing."

"It's okay."

They were still touching, as it started becoming painfully obvious to her. She was the first to move and walked to the passenger side. "We should notify Marian's brother and have a talk with Marian's coworkers at the animal shelter. One of them might know about her personal life." If all else failed to focus her mind, directing it to work was usually effective.

THIRTY-EIGHT

Marian's brother, Darwin, took the news of his sister's death about as well as Amanda had expected. Shock, denial, and anger all rolled over him. He remained adamant he hadn't seen or heard from his sister in years. It seemed that she had been living in Woodbridge for the last six months without reaching out. He'd paled when they told him about the pictures on Marian's phone and their conclusion she'd been stalking Don. Tears had fallen when his mind led him to conclude Don found out and killed her. He was a mess when they'd left him, telling them he'd need a lot of time to process all of this.

She and Trent left Darwin with their sympathies and drove to the animal shelter. For once they weren't in a fight against the clock. The place was open until six, and they pulled in at four thirty.

Several dogs were running in a kenneled area off the back, most barking or howling, as Amanda and Trent walked through the lot toward the shelter's front door. A young woman in the yard waved at them as they passed.

A twentysomething woman at the front desk greeted them with a toothy grin. "Are you looking to adopt?"

Amanda saw that Trent passed her a side-glance, but she didn't meet his gaze. It was clear the clerk had mistaken them for a couple.

She pulled her badge. "Detectives Steele, and Stenson," she added, gesturing to Trent.

"Oh." Her grin faltered, then regained power. "You can still adopt though, right? Maybe one for each of you?"

"No time for a dog, unfortunately," Trent said.

Lucky for Amanda that Zoe wasn't here, or she'd be leaving with one. "What he said. Listen, we'd like to speak with the manager if we could."

"Trisha? Sure. May I ask what it's about?"

Amanda smiled at the clerk's poor attempt to conceal her curiosity, but told her, "It's about an employee, Paula Dunn." At least she'd said the right name and not Marian Shepherd.

"Ah, well, Paula wasn't an employee. She was a volunteer, but she's gone now. She just started the second week in December but gave her notice a couple of weeks ago. She wasn't even here six months."

There was a lot of information packed into that response. One, Marian would have started here just after assuming rental of Butler's property. Two, if she volunteered, they still didn't know how Marian had supported herself. Hopefully her financials would shed light on that. Three, it seemed that six months might have been worth stressing. "Why did she leave?"

"You'd have to talk to Trisha about that. I'll get her but, say, is Paula all right?"

"It's a police matter," Amanda said, "but if you could get your manager, Trisha...?"

"Uh-huh. Trisha Mosley. I'll get her." She smiled and entered an office behind the desk. Soon after, she returned with a woman in her forties, long frizzy blond hair worn down without any defined shape or style. No makeup either, but a pleasant resting expression.

"I was told you want to speak about Paula Dunn?"

"That's right," Amanda said. "Would we be able to do that in an office or meeting room? Somewhere that might offer more privacy?"

"Follow me."

Trisha took them to the adoption room. While it might smell like a wet dog, it was neat and organized. There was a desk and three chairs, and a window that looked over kennels in the back. Papers were squared and tidy in several trays. Posters on the wall laid out what to expect when adopting. Amanda didn't give them a lot of time but one said something about the 3-3-3 rule, whatever that was.

"We haven't introduced ourselves yet," Amanda began and told Trisha their names.

"Sit, please." Trisha sat behind the desk and gestured to the chairs across from it. "You wanted to talk about Paula Dunn?" A few rows of lines formed across her brow. "Is she okay?"

"Unfortunately, she was found murdered in her home this morning," Amanda said. "When was the last time you saw her?"

"Oh." Trisha sat back in her chair, visibly shocked. "Hmm, Wednesday last week was her last day. She wasn't even here six months. I'm guessing something must have happened in her personal life for her to..." Trisha rubbed her neck. "Do you have any idea who did this to her?"

Amanda shook her head. "That's why we're here asking questions. The clerk at the front flagged six months too. Is there some meaning to that?"

"Oh, we request volunteers make a minimum six-month commitment. It takes time to train someone on how everything works here, so putting that stipulation in a volunteer application only makes sense. I just can't believe that she's dead."

Amanda imagined the word *murdered* rolling through the woman's eyes on tickertape.

"Were you close?" Trent crossed his leg in a T-bar across his knee and rested his tablet there.

"Not really. We got along fine but never socialized outside of here. She never shared about her personal life, but she seemed to be that way with everyone. I just took it that she was a private person."

Marian's landlord had said the same thing, and Amanda understood why. For one, the man she likely last trusted had tried to kill her. Two, if she was stalking Don with a sinister intention, she'd want to keep a low profile. Not that Amanda was certain how that applied to volunteering here. She wasn't even getting a paycheck. It must have just been a love for animals moving her to do more with her life. "I still need to ask, are you aware of anyone who had an issue with her?"

"No one I can think of. Paula was kindhearted, and she was great with the animals that came in here. She especially gravitated to the worst cases of abuse and neglect. She said they needed more love than the others."

Marian had probably empathized with them after what she'd been through with Don.

Trisha added, "She also expressed that what she admired most about animals was their natural ability to love unconditionally, unlike humans. But she probably experienced, well..." Trisha touched her face. "I'm guessing she was in a fire at one time. She wore a facial covering most of the time. A hijab, I believe they're called."

"Was she Muslim?" Trent asked.

Trisha shrugged. "I can't speak to her religious convictions. But she had one rather large scar on her cheek, and one time I saw her with the scarf off, and the line ran down her neck." As she spoke, Trisha pointed out the area on herself. "People can be quite cruel. But she's right that animals don't judge."

"No, they don't." Amanda recalled Darwin mentioning the

doctors told him that Marian's face had been badly burned. The landlord had brought up the scars too. She and Trent hadn't been able to make out much detail at the scene given the horror show the cat had created. Having the disfigurement raised again provided additional motive for Marian to want revenge. But had Don beat her to it? Or were they looking for someone else entirely? Due diligence required they dig. This steered her thoughts to the unidentified male visitor from last Friday. "Was Paula seeing anyone?"

"I'm not sure if it was anything serious, but a good-looking guy picked her up for lunch the other day."

"Can you be more specific?" Trent asked.

"It was the start of last week. Monday or Tuesday? I couldn't tell you his name, but he would have been late thirties, early forties."

The landlord couldn't peg an age on Marian's visitor last Friday, but she had been fifty-five, placing the man ten years her junior. "Can you describe his looks?"

"Brown hair, brown eyes, a little thickset... under six feet."

That was pretty much a perfect replica of the description they received from the landlord about Marian's visitor. Hearing this again, Amanda's heart picked up speed as pieces clicked together. The man's build could also apply to the mystery figure who had set Don Lambert on fire. They'd been busy thinking about Don as Marian's killer, which he still might be, but this thinking opened a possibility in the Lambert case. Had Marian hired someone to kill Don? Then again, the evidence hadn't given them anything to suspect that. "Do you think someone else here might be able to tell us more about this man?"

"You could ask around, but I wouldn't waste my breath. I never got the impression she opened up to anyone here."

It was frustrating being potentially close to the killer yet so far away. "Do you know where they had lunch?" If Trisha did, she and Trent could try the restaurant and see what their surveillance video or payment record might tell them.

"Again, no. Sorry."

It had been a long shot... "I realize she just volunteered here, but did she leave anything behind or have a workspace that hasn't been cleared out?"

"No."

Amanda got up and gave the woman her card.

"Actually, what's going to happen to Cleopatra now that Paula's... dead?"

A queen of ancient Egypt... "Who...?" But the second Amanda asked, a bad feeling washed over her.

"Paula's Persian. Is a friend going to take her in?"

Amanda and Trent glanced at each other. If he was thinking what she was, putting the cat's fate delicately was going to be challenging. "She's being taken care of. Not to worry," she said, settling on neutral territory, not a lie and generic enough not to invite further inquiries.

"That's good to hear. Before you leave, is there any chance either of you would be interested in adopting a dog? We've got a full house."

Amanda waved off the invitation as did Trent. Her mind was tossing around all they'd learned in there. Stepping outside, everything was quiet. Outdoor playtime for the dogs must be over.

"So what are we looking at here?" Trent unlocked the car, and they got in. "Did Trisha just describe the same man as Marian's landlord? Though how could we begin to know when both are rather vague."

"Except the landlord never mentioned age. Trisha said that Marian's lunch date was in his late thirties or early forties."

"Right, and that's not a fit for Don."

"Not that we suspected they were seeing each other and sharing meals. But this person sounds the right size for Don's killer. It clicked for me hearing build and height a second time. Did the same person kill Marian and Don?"

"If so, where does that leave us?"

"Paula Dunn might have found herself a love interest, but that doesn't gel with no call history or contacts. So in answer to your question. I have no idea, Trent, but we better figure it out."

THIRTY-NINE

Amanda and Trent looked through the phone records and financials for Seth Dodger and Reid Sherman, but nothing flagged. No suspicious communications and no abnormal money transfers or deposits. And if they were looking at the same man for the murders of Marian and Don, neither of them were a fit. "Maybe it's time we release the bookie and his enforcer from suspicion, Trent."

"And put our focus on who?"

His question held a challenge. She could practically hear his anticipation that she was going to counter with his aunt. The truth was she had more interest in this unknown man who had taken Marian for lunch, possibly paid her a visit, and was a fit for the mystery figure who murdered Don. She couldn't dismiss that Gertrude had plausible motive to kill Marian and Don either, though. On that angle, CCTV footage from Marian's neighborhood had been requested. Warrants had also been approved and forwarded for Paula Dunn's phone records and her financials. From all these perspectives, the investigation was in a holding pattern. The clock on the wall told her it was close to five o'clock, and she just didn't have the energy or bandwidth to start anything. "I'd say the mystery man, but without a place to start there, I say we call it a week, pick up on Monday morning."

"You mean take the entire weekend off?"

"Why not? We're due." Stepping away might provide her and Trent a fresh perspective. But she couldn't wait to see the shock on Logan's and Zoe's faces when she turned up in time for Friday dinner and announced she was home until Monday.

"I'm not going to argue." Trent packed up his desk and was on the move faster than she was.

On the way home, she couldn't stop smiling. She hadn't given Logan a heads-up for two reasons. One, she was going for the surprise factor. Two, cautious optimism. She didn't want to risk disappointing them if something came up in the case between Central and home that curtailed her plans. She rarely gave herself over to taking time off, as if it were some sort of beacon to the universe to busy her again. More times than she could count, she and Trent were called in for a development in a case when they had allowed themselves to step back for a day or two.

Her phone rang over the Bluetooth system in her car, and she cussed under her breath. *I should have known...* But when Becky's name came up on the screen, she smiled. This call wasn't likely to be bringing more dead bodies or leads to follow. While Becky Tulson was her best friend from kindergarten, and an officer with the Dumfries PD, she probably wasn't calling about the Lambert case.

Amanda answered before it rang a second time. "Hey, lady!"

"Hey, it's feels like it's been forever since I've heard your voice."

"Too long, that's for sure." They both had busy schedules, and it had been at least a few months since Amanda had more than a quick chat with Becky. "How have you been? How are you?" She made a turn, the car guiding her home by memory. One more right, and she'd be on her street. She pulled to the curb to continue this conversation with her friend. She didn't want to turn up in her driveway on the phone. She wanted to be present with Logan and Zoe from the moment she parked.

"Good, good. You?"

"It's a little nuts these days."

"When isn't it? That seems to be your life though."

"Jeez, thanks."

"Well, am I wrong?"

"No." Amanda laughed, and Becky followed suit.

"I heard about the case involving Trent's uncle. Pass on my condolences."

"They won't be necessary. He hated the man, but long story."

"Oh. Still, though, that must make things sticky."

"You know it." Amanda had set her mind to the weekend, releasing the case and its complications, and had no desire to be sucked back in.

After a few beats of silence, Becky said, "So the reason I'm calling, besides to hear your lovely voice, is to ask if you wanted to go out tonight? We haven't had a girls' night in forever. What do you say?"

Becky's offer would be tempting if she didn't need some quality time with her family. *Family...* Yes, that's what Logan had become. Why did she even entertain romantic thoughts about Trent? She swallowed roughly. "I can't tonight."

Becky moaned in protest, never one to take rejection well.

"I have plans with Logan and Zoe." She put it out there, and her voice softly cracked. It was going to feel so amazing to surprise them. Logan had asked her pointblank about her priority in life, and she was going to prove it was him and Zoe.

"Are you sure everything is okay?"

She should advance to Detective... She considered confessing her attraction to Trent and her fantasies of being a couple. But just the thought of verbalizing this felt like she'd be betraying Logan. So too did bringing up the fact things felt unsettled between her and Logan at the moment. "Yeah, it's all good. But raincheck, okay? Something soon."

"You bet. Squeeze Zoe and Logan for me. Love ya."

"Back at ya."

Amanda resumed her drive home, quick to swipe a rogue tear away. She'd been wavering so much these past few months, weighing whether her relationship with Logan was the real deal. Every time she flipped it around to examine, she landed on the fact they were only at this crossroads because of her. It was her slip, her transgression. And while she couldn't undo the past, she could make it up to him as they moved forward. A good place to start might be forgiving herself. Then she'd push it completely from her mind. If only it were that easy. But in her logical mind, she and Logan made sense. While they may not relate when it came to her job, the fact he wasn't a cop was a good thing. It gave them things to talk about other than murder and killers. Like a regular couple, they were left with real, everyday life.

She pulled into her driveway, and Zoe ran out to greet her before she turned the car off. The girl's long blond hair was fanned out behind her, and her arms were flailing. The sight had Amanda's heart galloping. It would seem she was forgiven.

"Mandy!" Zoe wrapped her arms around Amanda's legs.

She hunched down to get an honest hug. And it felt so damn good. Nothing quite compared to being embraced by a child. But this one also seemed to embody forgiveness.

"Logan said we're going to get pizza. It's not even Tuesday. But we're not making it. We're ordering delivery." Zoe said *delivery* like the heavens themselves had opened and shone its approval.

Amanda laughed at the girl's enthusiasm. She and Zoe had a ritual of Pizza Tuesdays in rebellion to Taco Tuesdays since she took Zoe in. But they crafted their creations from scratch. "We just had pizza on Tuesday. You want it again?" she teased.

"I'd eat it every day!" Zoe grinned.

Amanda noticed something red around Zoe's mouth and tried to wipe it off. Zoe resisted with a squeal of delight and ran back into the house. Logan must have given her some drink with red food dye. If it contained sugar, she was going to be up late. At least tomorrow wasn't a school day.

"Hey, beautiful." Logan greeted her at the door with a kiss and hug.

She sank into the embrace, refusing to let him go when he first tried to back out. She put her head to his chest and listened to his heartbeat.

"Ick," Zoe groaned.

She moved back, and Zoe was standing next to them, her arms dangling at her sides like a primate. "Why you little brat." Amanda mussed Zoe's hair and playfully roared.

Zoe took off screaming through the house, down the hall, headed toward her room.

Amanda would have gone after her if she wasn't out of breath from laughing hysterically. Logan was laughing too.

"It's so great to have you home."

"I'll do you one better. I'm here *all* weekend."

"Really? Wow, that's incredible."

She held up a hand. "That's the plan, but we'll hold off promising this to Zoe. Just in case."

"I can live with that." He pulled her to him again and kissed her temple, then grabbed her sides and wriggled his fingers.

Amanda took off running like Zoe had and sought shelter in the girl's room. The reprieve was short-lived when Logan came in a few seconds later. She and Zoe ganged up on Logan, making it two against one. It was Logan's turn to play scared and run off.

Zoe led the pursuit, with Amanda right behind her. At times like this, thoughts of ever being with Trent slipped away. Trent was a good partner and friend, but this right here with Logan and Zoe was the real deal.

FORTY

Amanda felt refreshed and rejuvenated walking into Central on Monday morning. The weekend with Logan and Zoe was exactly what she had needed. The time gave her the clarity to see that she was sabotaging things with Logan out of guilt about finding love again. She opted to bring in coffee from Hannah's Diner for herself and Trent. She'd been making too much of it on Friday. Friends bought each other coffee. No big deal. She set his cup on his desk, and it would be there when he got in.

She went into her cubicle, and the first thing she did was check her email. Blair must have been up with the roosters. A message from her, with the evidence list from the Shepherd/Dunn case, was waiting in Amanda's inbox. She clicked on it just as Trent stepped into his cubicle, armed with a single coffee.

"Good morning," he said to her.

"Morning."

"We actually took the entire weekend, right? I wasn't dreaming?" He smiled at her.

"That we did." She returned the expression. "We weren't called in for any more dead bodies..."

He laughed. "Miracle of miracles. Oh, you got me a coffee?" Trent lifted the one she'd placed on his desk.

"I did."

"And I got you nothing."

She shrugged. "Consider us even."

He nodded, seeming to catch that she was referring to Friday when she'd turned up her nose at the one he'd brought her. "Any word about Shepherd's phone records or financials?" Trent dropped onto his chair and eyed her over the partition.

"No, but we have the evidence list from the Shepherd case. Oh, and I heard from Detective Briggs about Don's laptop." That was one business call she did receive over the weekend, but it wasn't enough to derail her.

"He contacted you about that? I had my name on the submission."

"I'm not sure why he called me instead."

"Not a big deal really. What did he say? Does it get us any closer to finding a killer?"

Malone stepped into the opening of her cubicle. "We're getting close?"

"Unfortunately not." Amanda passed Trent a glance. "Digital Forensics didn't find anything noteworthy on Lambert's laptop."

"Nowhere there. Tell me you've got something." Malone looked at her and Trent, eyes full of expectation. She wasn't sure why he'd anticipate anything. They took the weekend off, and he'd been briefed before they headed home.

"A renewed zeal for the case," she put out with a smile, thinking he'd pick up on the implication.

"I forgot. You actually took time off," Malone said. "Any epiphanies hit?"

"Not for me," she admitted.

"Me either."

Malone groaned.

"But," she rushed out, "we have the evidence list from the Shepherd/Dunn case. It might give us a jumping point."

"Keep me posted." With that, Malone was off, mumbling something.

"He sounds thrilled," Trent said, sarcasm alive and well.

"Wasn't missed on you, eh? Well, you didn't get struck with some grand epiphany this weekend, did you?"

"Nope, but would you think less of me if I said I didn't really give the case much thought?"

"Not at all. I was the same."

"Good for us, then. Our minds needed a break."

"Well, the break's over. I've got the list up over here. Wanna join?"

Trent rolled his chair into her cubicle and settled close to her. His cologne hit her nose, and thankfully didn't elicit the same impact it often did. Hopefully that meant she'd finally released her stupid crush on him.

She read down the screen and slowed when she got to the contents of Shepherd's kitchen garbage. In an investigation, what a person threw away often proved to be law enforcement's treasure, providing insight into the victim's last movements.

Amanda pointed out one line that got her attention. "There was an ATM receipt dated from Friday afternoon two weeks ago."

"The day we believe she was killed."

"Yep. Blair said it was for two grand, probably the withdrawal limit. So what was she planning?"

"And where did she get the money in the first place?"

"Yet another mystery to solve."

"Look what else Blair noted." Trent's turn to gesture at the screen. "This withdrawal pretty much emptied out the account."

"Worth noting for sure. And she was packing a suitcase, had

her passport out. Where was she planning to go? There was no mention of any airline tickets."

"Maybe she was jetting off with her mystery date? He could have been handling the travel arrangements."

"Possible, I suppose. It's just all the pieces don't fit. She was planning to move but bought pasta bowls, just so she'd have to lug them with her? She's getting ready for a vacation and not packing house? Between the purchase and the timing, taking a vacation just seems odd to me." Her gaze drifted back to her monitor. "Blair noted the money wasn't recovered in the house."

"Huh. I mean, why would it be? That might make it too easy for us. Instead, we have another question. Where the hell did it go?"

"Her killer could have taken it. If it was Don, he could have used it to pay a bigger installment to his bookie."

"It's possible. That with the advance from his credit card and withdrawal from his bank account would total forty-five hundred."

"We need to confirm how much he gave Seth Dodger."

"I doubt he's going to talk to us."

"Suppose you're right. We're not his favorite people on the planet." She returned her focus to the list. There were receipts found in the garbage too. It didn't take a mathematician to see they didn't tally two grand. One was interesting, nonetheless. It was from Luigi's, a pizzeria in Woodbridge, from two Tuesdays ago at one thirty in the afternoon. "Where Marian went with her mystery date?" Amanda pressed a finger to her screen and raised her eyebrows.

"Let's go find out."

"I'm with you. And I'm quite sure I remember seeing cameras in their dining room. If we get lucky, we get a look at this mystery man for ourselves."

"Real luck would be an ID."

FORTY-ONE

Luigi's Pizzeria wasn't due to open until eleven, but the lights were on inside. Undeterred, Amanda knocked on the rear door. The restaurant boasted freshly made ingredients, which implied someone would need to get an early start on the day. And, sure enough, a man responded and said to hold on a minute. One had stretched to two or three by the time the door was swung open.

A man in a stained white apron stood there. "I appreciate your enthusiasm, but we don't open for a—" He stopped at the sight of their badges. "Cops? Really? What is it now?"

An interesting reaction that suggested the police were here often. "We're hoping that you'll let us see whatever security footage you might have from two Tuesdays ago between noon and two." She padded the time on the receipt. While she was aware cameras were posted in the dining room, it might prove helpful if they had ones on the parking lot too. She had searched for them when they were out there but hadn't seen any.

"And I need a million dollars, lady."

"It's *Detective*," Trent interjected. "Detective Stenson, and she's Detective Steele."

"And I'm Santa Claus."

"Good, then hopefully you'll gift us what we asked for," Trent said, tacking on a fake smile.

"Dry humor. I like it." The man's previously sour expression gave way to a brilliant grin. "Come in, and I'll see what I can do for you, funny guy." The man led the way inside, and Trent turned to Amanda and shook his head.

Amanda smiled, and it was curbed only by the delightful smells of the kitchen as they passed through. The tantalizing aromas of simmering tomatoes and freshly chopped garlic and onion had her stomach rumbling. She'd even had breakfast that morning with Logan and Zoe before heading out.

The man stirred the sauce on the stove with a wooden spoon on scale with something from a fairy tale to be used in a witch's cauldron. Once finished, he set it on the stainless-steel stovetop adding a dollop of sauce to what was already there. In front of them was proof that the restaurant used homemade pizza sauce.

"So I'm not really Santa Claus," the man said, turning around. "Though I doubt you believed that. Real name is Charlie Crowe, with an *e* like that Russell guy."

Amanda liked Charlie's spunk, but resisted the urge to smile at his reference to the award-winning actor.

Charlie continued. "You said you're looking for surveillance footage, but I'm going to need you to be a bit more specific. See, I have cameras on the parking lot, dining room, and on the cash register."

"That's a lot of cameras," Trent said.

"Before I came to the food industry, I worked in security. I don't like leaving anything to chance and holes in coverage is a huge pet peeve."

"Let's start with the dining room," Amanda said.

"Which part?"

This guy was certainly thorough with his surveillance. She considered them fortunate when they netted footage from *a* camera. She was about to respond when Charlie spoke again.

"Actually... I assume you're interested in a specific customer. If you have a receipt, it will show the table number. That will point me to the camera to focus on."

"We do have that. One minute." Trent worked his finger over the screen of his tablet. A moment later, he held it toward Charlie and asked, "Where can I find the table number?"

Charlie stepped beside Trent and pointed. "Table seven. That's on the right side of the dining room about midway. That would be camera three." He said no more and stayed put.

"So, can we watch its footage?" Amanda prompted. "And the one on the parking lot?"

"Here's the thing. There are two things that need to be addressed first."

"Okay," she dragged out.

"One, I don't just hand over my footage to anyone. And two, there was a technical glitch that rendered the camera from the parking lot useless for that Tuesday you're interested in."

With that, any hope of getting a license plate on Marian's lunch date was gone.

Trent squared his shoulders. "Well, *one*, we're not anyone. We're Prince William County PD."

"Douse it down just a bit there." Charlie held out his hand, palm flat to the floor, and motioned as if he were tamping something.

Trent became rigid at the reprimand. "That camera footage may very well aid a homicide investigation. I can't imagine you'd want to be seen as interfering with a—"

Charlie's mouth slowly turned into a smile, knowing and cocky. "Oh, I never said I wouldn't hand it over. But I would like to see a warrant before I do. Get me that, and Bob's your uncle. Heck, I'll even forward you a digital copy so that you can review it to your heart's content."

Amanda never took to the phrase. Really, what did Bob being anyone's uncle truly mean? "Mr. Crowe," she began. "Detective Stenson made a strong point. That footage may go a long way to helping us with our investigation."

"If you think it's that pertinent, you shouldn't have a problem securing a warrant." With that, Charlie returned to his pot of simmering sauce.

"Give us five minutes." Trent left the kitchen through the back door, his phone to his ear.

She told Charlie they'd be right back and followed Trent outside. He was already deep in conversation with an on-call judge to get a verbal warrant. If they got that, which she didn't foresee a problem with, they'd have to eventually file paperwork to support it. But things would keep moving forward in the meantime.

"We believe this person might be crucial to the investigation... One of the last people to see her alive... Yes, we're talking about Tuesday two weeks ago, and it seems she was killed three days later on Friday. This person knew the victim. We haven't been able to uncover any friends or boyfriends... Thank you." Trent gave her a thumbs up and, soon after, put his phone away. "We've got the greenlight from Judge Anderson, but he made me work for it."

"So I heard."

They returned to inform Charlie they had authorization to view and collect his video footage from two Tuesdays ago.

"All right, I'll make the request."

"Make the request?" she stammered.

"Yeah. All the security is managed off-site. I'll have to contact the company and get the footage sent over." He repeated the day and time she'd requested. "That right?"

"It is. As soon as you get it, forward it." Amanda gave him her business card, and she and Trent left through the back door.

"Unbelievable. He doesn't bother to mention the security is done off-site until the last minute," Trent seethed.

"Frustrating to be sure." Her phone rang, and the caller identity told her it was CSI Blair. Amanda answered with, "Just let me put you on speak—"

"Actually," Blair said, stopping Amanda. "Please don't."

"What is it?" A sick feeling washed over Amanda. Had something happened to Trent's aunt?

Trent raised an eyebrow at Amanda as if to ask who it was. She subtly shook her head, her stomach unsettled as she waited for Blair to answer.

"Donnelly and I have been in since early this morning. You received my email with the evidence list?"

"I did, but I haven't had a chance to review it all." The suspense was boiling the acid in her gut. The delay was utter torture.

"Good. At least you received it. I'm calling about the blood sample found in Don's Buick. It is a match to Marian Shepherd."

"Great news. We can tie him to her." Though Amanda's enthusiasm was doused when she realized that could circumvent their thinking one man had killed Don and Marian. But she failed to see why Trent couldn't have been privy to this update.

A brief silence on Blair's end, then, "There is something else... It's the reason that I didn't want to be put on speaker. I'm hoping you will handle this one with Trent."

Amanda's stomach became lead. "What is it?"

"We lifted some prints from Shepherd's kitchen. There was a cup in the dishwasher. Amanda, it had Gertrude Lambert's fingerprints on it."

Amanda's world began to spin. She could feel Trent watching her, but she refused him eye contact. Gertrude had told them she'd never met Marian. Or had the truth slipped out? How had she put it when asked if she knew Marian? Something along the lines of she *hadn't* met her. Truth from the perspective of one point in time, just not the present. "You're absolutely sure?"

"I'm certain you don't need to ask that," Blair said gently.

"Yeah, you're right. I'm sorry. Ah, thanks for the update." Amanda ended the call and slowly lowered her arm. Gertrude was proven a liar again, but did that make her a killer? And how did she break this update to Trent?

FORTY-TWO

Trent wasn't sure how to react when Amanda told him his aunt's prints were inside Marian Shepherd's house. And he was still reeling several hours after finding out. There were too many emotions to pin down. Shock, anger, and denial all battled for precedence. And just when he'd started to believe their relationship could be rebuilt. But the most shocking response of all was he still found himself wanting to defend his aunt. Despite the fact she'd lied to him. Again. To make things worse, his aunt hadn't just met Marian but, in all probability, was in her home not long before she was killed. After all, the dishwasher hadn't been run.

Search warrants were in place for his aunt's residence and vehicle. They covered anything that could connect her to the murders of Don Lambert and Marian Shepherd. Rideout's autopsy findings concluded Shepherd had been stabbed with a chopping knife, and it could be the one missing from the block on Marian's counter. He cringed to think they might find it in his aunt's house.

Trent also had another warrant in hand for the arrest of

Gertrude Lambert. That piece of paper made him sick to his stomach. He'd only pull it out if there was no other recourse.

His aunt answered the door before he or Amanda rang the bell. She poked her head out, and looked past them to the curb. Parked there was an officer in a police cruiser. Coming up behind them was the van from Crime Scene.

"What's going on, Trent?" she asked, eyes wide.

The bruises from earlier in the week were greenish-brown and fading. "Crime scene investigators will be searching the property and your car. If I could get the keys for your Kia and the house..." He held out his palm.

"Trent?" His name, one word, strangled by trepidation.

"The faster you are to cooperate, the sooner we can put this behind us," he said firmly, as he concentrated on keeping his hand out and steady. He couldn't allow himself to be swayed by her emotions or his own. While Amanda had offered to take lead, it was something he felt the need to do himself. If only to prove he could. He was determined to approach this objectively with a detached point of view as he would with a stranger. The woman in front of him had been in the home of a murder victim, possibly the last person to see her alive. Worse yet, the one who may have taken her life.

"Okay." One word, and Trent tried to pretend he didn't see how her hand trembled as she retrieved her key ring from a hook inside the door. "Both keys are there."

Trent passed them to Amanda, who walked down the driveway to give them to CSI Donnelly.

"Am I under arrest?" His aunt rubbed her neck, turning the skin blotchy and red.

"We'll start with a conversation down at Central."

"I don't understand."

"You told us that you never met Marian Shepherd," Trent said, a bit of hurt slipping into his voice against his best efforts to keep it at bay.

"I..."

"What I thought. You lied to us again. Now, Officer Brandt is going to take you to the station where we'll continue our conversation."

"I'm going in a police car... like a..." His aunt's eyes filled with tears, and it stabbed Trent's heart, but what could he do about it? She'd brought this on herself by lying to them.

He stuck out his chin. "It's just procedure."

"But I'm *not* under arrest?" She seemed to be struggling to understand.

He remained silent, weighed down by the paper in his pocket. It pained him to think that reality may not be far off. "We just have some questions. Please, put on your shoes, and grab a jacket or sweater if you'd like."

"Ah, all right." She slipped into shoes and put on a light jacket.

"Gertrude Lambert, you can come with me." Officer Brandt had come up behind Trent.

His aunt gave him a passing glance as Leo escorted her to the police cruiser. A few tears hit her cheek, and the sight was a stab to Trent's chest. But he reminded himself none of this was his fault. In fact he'd done everything he could to help his aunt.

Amanda stepped inside again. "How are you doing?"

Past her, he watched Officer Brandt pull away, Aunt Gertrude loaded in the back like a criminal. "Honestly? I've been better, but I've got a job to do, and I'm doing it."

"That you are. I wish I could say it gets easier..."

Trent just nodded. He was starting to get a solid idea how hard Amanda truly had it when she had to bring in a loved one on murder charges. As the saying goes, until you walk in someone else's shoes, you can't appreciate what they're going through. He took a few deep breaths as he stepped outside and shut the front door. He and Amanda joined the CSIs who were both at work on his aunt's Kia.

"Anything thus far?" Amanda asked them.

"No blood trace, but we lifted several prints from the steering wheel. They still need to be processed, but they're all likely to belong to your aunt, Trent," CSI Blair said.

He had no desire to look at the investigator. It bothered him that she'd made Amanda shoulder the responsibility of passing along the news about his aunt's prints. She had been through enough in her life without adding that. And was her ad-lib supposed to help? If anything, it put his aunt more in the frame. Her Kia in Marian's neighborhood, with proof only his aunt was ever behind the wheel wasn't helpful in the least. "Just lock up the car and house when you're finished," he said. "The house key should be on that key ring too." He headed toward the department car.

"Will do." Blair's response hit his back.

His mind was a mess. His aunt, a killer? Was it really possible? It was hard to refute that the evidence kept pointing at her. He might do better to surrender and accept what it was telling him. If only it were that easy. But he had this niggling feeling that he and Amanda were missing something. It was triggered by Blair's comment about his aunt's prints likely being the only ones on the steering wheel of her Kia. "Shepherd's blood was in Don's vehicle. Wouldn't that suggest he killed Marian?"

"It could, but..." Amanda's voice trailed off but came back stronger. "Is it possible your aunt sometimes drove his vehicle?"

He'd been confident he'd found a loophole, something to draw the attention back to Don. So much for that. "She might have." He sighed and massaged his temple. A headache of epic proportions was moving in.

"Then... Well, you might not want to hear what I thought."

"It doesn't matter what I want. Just be straight with me. What are you thinking?" He could tell from the downward curve of her lips that her theory was going to implicate his aunt.

"Don could have reignited things with Marian, or it may

just have appeared that way... to your aunt. What's to say she didn't reach her limit and drive over to Marian's house in Don's Buick?"

"And have a nice spot of tea with the woman before stabbing her in the chest?"

"I need to be able to talk freely, and I've been watching every word coming from my mouth. That stops now. The way I see it, Gertrude could have wanted to talk things out, get a true feel for what was going on. But she might not have liked what she heard. She then decided to kill Marian. Unless she had something to hide, why lie to us about meeting Marian?"

He threw his arms up. "I'm not a mind reader."

"And you don't have to be. You do need to keep an open mind though."

"Trust me, I'm doing my best. Sadly, I see how things look." He met her gaze and nodded. "She appears guilty as hell." Admitting this out loud came as a blow, but if he were being honest, that didn't matter if it was the truth.

FORTY-THREE

Amanda saw this case taking a toll on Trent, but she had no way of easing his pain. In fact, she had made it worse when she passed on CSI Blair's finding. The light had drained from his eyes, and it hadn't yet returned. If anything, his gaze had become darker, shadowed. The enchanted nephew had been devoured by the seasoned detective. Despite this, Amanda insisted on taking the lead on the interview with Gertrude back at Central. It might save him some future regrets.

The three of them were in Interview Room One. Gertrude had adamantly rejected a lawyer despite Trent suggesting she get one. She was holding a water bottle with both hands. Her chin was trembling, and she was shivering despite the jacket she had on. She also seemed to be refusing eye contact with Trent.

Amanda settled into her chair, relaxed her posture some. "Ms. Shaw, we asked you before if you ever met Marian Shepherd in person. Do you remember what you told us?"

"That I hadn't."

This confirmed her wording had been intentional and deceitful, but to what end? "When did you see her last?"

"Two Fridays ago."

Amanda stiffened at her quick recall. "You're sure it was then?"

"Positive." Gertrude nudged out her chin.

"Where was this?"

"At her house."

"What time were you there?"

"I'd say midafternoon. Around three."

The landlord had said he saw a man at her door, not that he saw Marian answer. Amanda stiffened at Gertrude's admission. She put herself at the scene of a murder. "Have you been in touch over the years, or were you more recently acquainted?"

Gertrude wet her lips with her tongue, then ended up taking a drink of her water. "More recently."

"And how did you come to meet?"

"I told you that I followed Don on the night of his death?"

Amanda could have been a stickler and corrected her. Night of his *murder*. She could also point out that she only admitted as much once they had her on camera. "Yes."

"That wasn't the only time. I followed him once in his SUV, keeping at a good distance, to a neighborhood in the east end."

"If you were in his vehicle, was he driving your Kia?" Trent piped in.

"Uh-huh."

Amanda couldn't blame her partner for latching on to that loophole. And that was fair. She'd thought of Gertrude driving the Buick, so why couldn't it work the other way? If it was Gertrude's Kia the neighbor had seen, Don could have been behind the wheel. They needed that CCTV footage to come through. "Did Don often drive your Kia?"

"Enough, I guess. He probably wanted to snoop around inside to see if he could catch me doing anything he didn't approve of."

"All right, please continue with what you were saying," Amanda told her. "He drove to the east end…"

"Uh-huh. He turned around in a driveway. I didn't think anything of it until I noticed the blue sedan there."

This struck as proof Don knew where Marian had lived. "Why did the car stand out to you?"

"One just like it drove by our house several times. I suspected it belonged to Don's mistress, so I started tailing her."

Marian Shepherd didn't have any vehicles registered to her name. It's possible Paula Dunn had under her alias, but not likely, so where had the blue sedan come from? And where was it now? She scribbled this note on a piece of paper inside the folder she'd brought into the room. "Can you tell us the make and model of the car?"

Gertrude shook her head.

"What did you find out from following her?"

"At first, just that she volunteered at Paws for a Cause. I chatted with her, pretending to be interested in adopting. Suddenly, seeing the scars on her face and neck, like she'd been in a fire, clicked for me. That and seeing Don turn in her driveway out of all the driveways on the street. I asked her if her name was Marian Shepherd. She quickly hushed me and took me aside. She told me that everyone there knew her as Paula Dunn."

"Did she say why?"

"I didn't ask at the time but found out later that she assumed a new identity to hide from Don. Obviously, she didn't do a good job of that. He must have found out where she lived. Why are you so interested in my knowing Marian anyway? Why drag me in here?" Gertrude rubbed her arms. "Is she okay? Did something happen to her?"

"Marian Shepherd was found murdered, and we believe she was killed the Friday you two had tea at her house." Amanda let those details stand on their own, allowing Gertrude time for the implication to sink in.

It took a few seconds, but then Gertrude gasped, and her eyes widened. "You think that I... that *I*— No. That's not possible. She was alive when I left. Could it be that Don... that he did this? He was still alive then." She folded over herself, crying.

Amanda let some time pass but asked, "Why were you at Marian's house in the first place?"

"We were just having a tea and a chat."

"About what?"

Now, Gertrude looked at Trent. "I really was going to leave him. Meeting Marian gave me the courage. I finally found my own strength. I wanted to learn how she escaped him."

Amanda felt Trent's energy lighten. What Gertrude said supported her earlier admission of attempting to hack into Don's laptop. Further, if what she told them was true, Don would have strong motive to kill Marian. There was his expressed desire to finish what he'd started *and* a fresh trigger. He stood to lose Gertrude. Apparently, he had found out where Marian lived. Had he discovered that she was stalking him and followed her home? "Do you think Don figured out you were talking with Marian and planning to leave him?"

"I tried to cover my tracks, but... well, she's dead. Now I wonder if he did find out."

"How often did you meet with Marian?"

"Just the two times I told you about. At the shelter and tea at her house."

"Did she ever mention a boyfriend?" Amanda was now curious how Marian's lunch date factored into her life.

Gertrude shook her head.

Amanda couldn't foresee a reason to lie about this, but the truth was often obscured in the mind of the liar. Had she slipped by confessing she drove Don's SUV? Was it her fault that Marian's blood ended up on the floormat? A transfer from transporting the murder weapon? Gertrude had presented a believable story, but was that all it was? Fiction? "Did you drive your car or Don's over to her place that Friday?"

"My car. Don had his at work."

If that was fact, it put Don firmly in the frame for killing Marian. But while they couldn't get answers from the dead, Gertrude may be able to help further. "Did Marian give you any indication she still feared Don?"

"Not really. I told her I'd followed him to her place once though. She dismissed the news with a wave of her hand. Now, I think she should have taken it seriously. At the time, I was busy admiring her courage. She had a wild spark about her. I wanted that for myself."

From the sounds of it, Marian was finished with playing victim and had her mind set on revenge, as she and Trent had theorized before. "Marian moved from Washington in December. Did she ever tell you why she moved here?"

"No."

Amanda nodded. "What time did you leave Marian's house after your chat?"

"I was gone by four. I needed to get home to cook Don dinner."

"And when did he get home?"

"Would have been six. After he ate, he left and stayed out until about midnight."

That afforded Don time to swing past Marian's house after work and kill her. The timing also lined up for him to be who Marian's landlord had seen at her door. It was nauseating to think that if Don had killed her, he was beyond the reach of the justice system. Violent death aside. But this thought daisy chained and linked to another. It was a possibility she and Trent had discussed before. Had Don's killer been getting even for Marian's murder? And, if so, how did that work when Marian's body had been left to rot and be eaten by her cat?

Amanda's phone rang, and Blair's name was on the screen. "Trent, join me, please."

They went next door to the observation room, where Amanda answered on speaker.

"Trent and I are both here," she said.

"We found the knife we believe was used to kill Marian Shepherd. It is a match to the set from her home." Blair's delivery was somber.

Trent cleared his throat. "Where was it?"

"Tucked into the back corner of a cabinet in the laundry room, wrapped in a woman's scarf. I'm so sorry, Trent. I can't imagine how you must be feeling right now."

"No, you can't." Trent pulled out a chair and sat down. Elbows to knees, he leaned forward and gripped his head.

"Thanks for letting us know." Amanda hung up and sat next to Trent. She didn't say a word, but just held space for him.

He didn't speak until several minutes later. "I can't believe my aunt did this. I just can't accept it. There are two people who lived in that house."

"There were."

"Yet, you don't sound convinced Don killed Marian. You think my aunt took out her and Don?"

"I'm just trying to make sense of the evidence."

"I get that, but I don't believe it's all in."

Before Blair's call, Amanda was convinced Don had killed Marian. With one update, she was uncertain again. After all, Gertrude had motive, means, and opportunity for both Marian and Don.

Trent looked through the one-way mirror, and it had Amanda following suit. Gertrude appeared small and frail, like she was much older than her sixty-seven years. But no one who had been subjected to psychological and physical abuse could walk away completely unscathed. Had it altered her personality? Turned her homicidal? Adrenaline also empowered a person beyond their normal capabilities.

"What do you think we're missing?" Amanda eventually asked.

"We haven't tracked down Marian's friend. We can't just ignore he's the right build to be who killed Don and who was on Marian's doorstep."

"You make a good point. Your aunt also mentioned a blue sedan in Marian's driveway. No vehicles were registered to her real name, and none were there when we went to the crime scene."

"Right, so maybe it belongs to her lunch companion. Not that we can narrow down ownership on color alone. And we're in a holding pattern until we get that video from Luigi's. I'm not sure how else we could even start to go about finding this guy."

"The video should be here soon. But there's something else that's bugging me. Your aunt said Marian didn't even seem concerned that Don might have found her. Were we right that Marian had returned to town with murder on her mind? Say he did show up at her door that Friday night, and instead of being afraid she saw an opportunity to kill him then and there."

"Only, he got the upper hand. Now, just hear me out, Amanda. Aunt Gertrude told us she was at Marian's house looking for advice on how to leave Don. What if he figured that out? Not just that Marian was stalking him?"

"I had the same thought," she admitted.

"All right, well this is where I might veer off. All the evidence against my aunt is either circumstantial or neat. What if Don saw an opportunity himself? One, finish the job with Marian, and two, frame his current wife for the murder." Trent held up a hand to stop her from interrupting and went on. "Don wasn't going to be bested by a woman, let alone two of them. I wonder if he didn't manipulate things to frame my aunt. It would present like a classic case of a spurned wife killing her husband's mistress."

Amanda chewed on what he said, then nodded. "I can give you that."

"He just didn't expect all his scheming would end up with him in a body bag. But even that ends up, inadvertently, making my aunt look even more like the spurned wife. It reads as if she had motive for killing them both."

Amanda looked in on Gertrude again, and she was crying into her hands. It was hard to imagine that woman as a violent killer, someone capable of pouring gasoline on a man and lighting him on fire. But appearances were deceiving. "I don't know, Trent. I mean it is possible."

Trent snapped his fingers. "Exactly. And as long as doubt exists, we can't lock up my aunt."

"All right, let's say we find this friend of Marian's, what exactly do you expect this to do for the case? For your aunt?"

"To start, someone else killed Don. If this lunch date of Marian's was a close friend, what's to say he wasn't more than that?"

"Like a hit man?" She registered her skepticism ringing back to her own ears.

"Could be. We haven't looked at her financials, but I was thinking more along the lines of a partner in crime."

"I don't know... That seems a leap."

"Sure, and we've made bigger ones and been right before. Let's say Marian and her friend were both after Don. The reason for him, I don't know. It could just be as simple as him loving Marian and working with her to get retribution."

"Sure. But then we'd circle back to another point. Did this person know Marian was murdered and left her in her home? It sounds quite callous for someone with an ounce of affection for her."

"Unless this person was fixed on the bigger picture. Their original plan to take out Don."

"This all sounds..." She searched her mind for the right word, somewhere along the lines of imaginative, a desperate theory by a nephew wanting to help his aunt. The chime notification of a new text message served as a useful distraction to save her from responding. She checked her phone and informed Trent, "It's Charlie Crowe from Luigi's. He says the video footage we've been waiting for should be in my inbox."

FORTY-FOUR

Amanda spoke with Gertrude about the knife before she and Trent watched the surveillance video from the pizzeria. When they told her the weapon used to kill Marian Shepherd was found in a cabinet in her laundry room, she'd been speechless. Her mouth had opened and shut, gaping like a fish out of water. Her eyes were wet and wide, and she kept laying a hand over her chest. Thankfully, she didn't start hyperventilating, but she did cry.

"I swear that I have no idea how that got there."

Gertrude's claim was still ringing in Amanda's ears when they left her with an officer who would take her to a jail cell.

"I believe my aunt, Amanda," Trent said to her as they walked back to their cubicles. "Even if that makes me crazy. But I owe it to her to explore the other angles we talked about."

"Like Don framing her for murder?"

"Yep. And the knife was found in the laundry room. My aunt's territory. What's to say Don didn't put it there to make my aunt look guilty? That would make sense to me."

Amanda admired Trent's faith and loyalty to his aunt, but

unless something drastic happened to shift the direction of the case, Gertrude would be going to prison.

It was four thirty in the afternoon by the time she and Trent sat in front of her computer, coffees in hand, to watch the pizzeria footage.

She hit the play button. Around noon, a man with brown hair and a woman wearing a hijab were shown to a table. With one direct look at the camera, Marian Shepherd was staring back at them.

"Trisha told us she wore one," Trent said.

Amanda focused on the man. He was about four or five inches taller than Marian, so about five eleven, with the right build to be the man who murdered Don and showed up at Marian's door. Unfortunately, he was seated with his back to the camera and there wasn't a shot of his face. It was hard to know if he avoided it intentionally or if it was coincidental.

"It would be nice to get a look at this guy, but one thing is clear. It's not Don," she offered. "So who was he to Marian? A friend? A lover?"

"A partner in crime?" Trent volleyed back, drawing attention to his earlier theory that Marian was working with someone to get revenge on Don.

And we're back to that... Amanda didn't respond but kept watching the video play out.

The man left the table, still faceless. But when he returned a few minutes later, they had him.

Amanda paused the video and looked over at Trent. "Brother," she affirmed. "But I clearly remember that Darwin Shepherd told us he hasn't seen his sister in many years."

"People lie."

Not that he needed to point that out to her, but she had it coming in response to her comment. "He probably never thought we'd see this video. What if the siblings were conspiring to murder Don?"

Trent smiled. "Giving my theory credit, I see. To start, this would clear my aunt."

"Only if we could prove it. Do you think Darwin knew his sister was dead?" Her stomach soured at the thought he could leave her there, but her mind niggled on something else.

"Then we're back to why he wouldn't call it in."

Amanda tried to unravel that mystery and landed on an idea. "Maybe he couldn't afford to."

"Now, I'm lost."

"Your turn to hear me out. Let's say the siblings planned to kill Don together. The brother discovers his sister and believes Don got to her. If he calls it in, he won't have the freedom to kill Don."

"So he lets her be found in due course," Trent said slowly, his mind clearly at work in the background. "But why wait until days later to kill Don? And didn't we verify Darwin's alibi?"

"Uh-huh. He was working the night of Don's murder, but maybe he stepped out during his shift and his boss didn't know. It is possible."

"It is. We need to pay a visit to Darwin's boss and have a chat."

"Oh, we will, but there's something else. That jealous boyfriend or husband who confronted Don at JJ's, what if it wasn't either? What if it was Darwin Shepherd?" Amanda imagined him finding his sister, how flooded with rage he'd be. Would he be able to talk himself down if he was face to face with his sister's killer?

Trent's face pinched in uncertainty. "His way of letting Don know he would be coming for him?"

"Could be. All we know is he told Don to stay away from her. But what if it was, he *should have* stayed away?"

"Possible, but if he was wanting to keep a low profile, doing that would kiss it goodbye."

"He likely wasn't thinking entirely straight. He'd have been compromised mentally and emotionally. Clearly not in his right mind. I'd like to show Darwin's pic to Don's friends, just to see if they recognize him."

"Okay, one thing I am failing to grasp. If the guy up in Don's face was Darwin, why retreat? And why wait for days to kill him? I guess I'm back to that."

"If I'm right about any of this, only Darwin could answer that. One hypothetical is the original plan with his sister had been to torch Don behind Patriot Plaza in the early morning of Wednesday. Then Darwin stuck to that plan, to see it through, in her memory."

"It's still chilling that he'd leave his sister's dead body in her house without calling it in."

"He became consumed by living up to his promise to his sister. If he wanted to carry that out, he couldn't come forward. Oh, the bowls..."

Trent scrunched up his face. "I'll need more than that."

"Marian might not have ordered them. It could have been Darwin using Marian's, or should I say Paula's, credit card information. Even his own for that matter." The financials weren't available yet, and she hadn't heard if Marian had a credit card in her wallet. Amanda continued. "He'd have known the bowls would arrive after he killed Don and—"

"Lead to the discovery of his sister," Trent finished.

Amanda nodded. "This theory is starting to take shape. Marian's moving back to the county, stalking Don to find out his haunts, emptying her bank account, giving notice at her job, the luggage, and passport. It even explains the reason for the pasta bowls when she was supposed to be moving."

"They must have pieced together from Marian's stalking that Don was in the area of Patriot Plaza on the first and fifteenth of the month. Maybe even on other occasions, as he wasn't killed on either of those days. But they might have figured it was as good a place as any. Only for all this to work, if

Darwin was the man who confronted Don, he must not have known he was Marian's brother."

"Assuming Darwin was honest about that part, he'd only met Don once about thirteen years ago. If he had confronted Don at JJ's, Don might not have known who he was."

"Well, if we're right about any of this we better get moving," Trent said. "Darwin no longer has any reason to stick around."

"He might already be gone. I'm driving." Amanda had a heavier foot than her partner.

Amanda and Trent filled Malone in on their theory, and an unmarked car was dispatched to sit outside Darwin's house while they hit Darwin's place of employment. Given the day of the week and the time, if Darwin hadn't left town, he could be there.

They had to flash their badges a few times to get past security at Roadrunner Solutions and gain an audience with Antoine Adkins, Darwin's boss. They had further questions for the manager about the night of Don's murder and figured he'd also be able to summon Darwin from the warehouse floor. They were in Antoine's office now. The man was perched behind his desk while Amanda and Trent were seated in chairs across from him.

"I'd like to help, but Darwin's not here tonight," Antoine told them.

"Not scheduled to work or...?" Amanda had a bad feeling creeping in.

"He called in sick."

Tingles ran through Amanda. Was Darwin legitimately ill? Or was he on the run? But if the latter, why call in with some pretense? Had he seen it as a way to buy himself more time? Though if Darwin had plans to leave town, why stick around this long? Don had been murdered the middle of last week. Did he want to ensure his sister was found? "Does he call in sick often?"

"Second time in ten years, both in the last couple of weeks."

Trent angled his head. "When was the other time?"

"Two Fridays ago. Something about a family emergency."

Finding his sister's body would qualify. If Darwin wasn't working, he also could have been the man to confront Don at JJ's. "No specifics beyond that?"

Antoine shook his head.

"When we spoke on the phone the other day," Amanda said, "you confirmed that Darwin Shepherd was here between eleven PM Tuesday and three AM Wednesday. Are you sure he was here for his entire shift? He didn't leave the premises for a meal or a break?"

"Huh, well, I'm not sure I can vouch for that." Antoine rubbed his face, his hands running over his whiskers and making the sound of abrading sandpaper.

The skin tightened on the back of her neck. His failure to check may have delayed the investigation. "So he does get breaks?"

"Two fifteen-minute and an hour for lunch. Or whatever you want to call a meal in the middle of the night."

Amanda didn't care about giving it any label. "Who could tell us if he stepped out?"

"That might be tricky. The warehouse is automated and employees are rather spread out."

Amanda thought back to the security they had to go through to get onto the property. Also the high fence. It was more likely they had video surveillance than not. "What about cameras? Do any capture the parking lot? One might have got Darwin leaving or returning."

"We have cameras, but you'd need to speak to the security department about the details. I'm sure they'd let you take a look as long as what you're after in no way implicates Roadrunner...?"

"I don't see how it would," she said. "We're just interested in Darwin's movements that night."

"Okay. I'd ask why, but I have a feeling you're not going to satisfy my curiosity."

Amanda gave him a tight smile. "I can't. Open investigation."

"I figured that would be your response. Come with me, and I'll introduce you to Bob."

Antoine took them through a warren of hallways to an office with several monitors mounted on one wall. In front of them was a curved desk with three stations but only two employees. A man and a woman. It was the man who stood and approached them.

"Bob, these are detectives with the Prince William County PD," Antoine said. "They need your assistance, if you'd be so kind."

The female employee glanced over but was quick about getting back to her work.

"It all depends on what you need, but I'll do my best," Bob told them. "I'm the head of security here at Roadrunner."

"We need to have a look at the video footage of the parking lot from Tuesday evening into Wednesday morning of last week, say any time from— What time would he take his meal break?" Amanda asked, directing this question to Antoine.

"Between eleven and midnight."

Right in the sweet spot of the time she originally inquired about. But she and Trent could have jumped things by coming here. The mystery figure near Don's Buick Encore was captured at eleven forty-five. If it had been Darwin, he'd need to be on his way back to work to clock in for midnight. That's if employees here clocked in, which she'd ask about in a minute. "Then let's say eleven until one AM," she told Bob.

He looked at Antoine, who added, "They're interested in the employee lot."

"You got it. Just give me a few minutes," Bob said.

"One question for you, Mr. Adkins, while Bob loads the video." She made a point to dip her head in silent appreciation to the security guy. "You mentioned automation. Do employees punch in and out?"

"You bet."

She was trying to ignore her rising anger. Would Antoine have seen Darwin clocked out if he'd actually looked? Though even if he had, that alone wouldn't tell him he left the premises. That loophole was the only thing stopping her from lashing out at the manager. "Is this something that's ever reviewed?"

"Every two weeks ahead of payroll. Each department head is responsible for making sure their employees are working their hours and showing up on time."

"Did you look at Mr. Shepherd's from last week yet?" she asked. "Maybe when I called?"

"The system is locked for the current week to avoid potential for tampering. I would be doing that this week. The report is on my desk, as we speak."

That explanation doused her temper some, and a flush of adrenaline coursed through her. She could feel in her bones that they were getting close to stitching up the investigation. "Can you see what times Mr. Shepherd checked in and out last Tuesday?"

"You bet. I'll be right back." With that Antoine left, and Amanda and Trent walked over to Bob.

"I've already got it loaded," Bob told them and nudged his head to a monitor labeled *Three*. "I'll play it there." He started it at ten fifty-five and forwarded until a pickup was approaching to leave the lot. The timestamp read eleven-oh-five.

"That's Darwin Shepherd's truck," the female security officer said.

So, Darwin had left work, but did he go to Patriot Plaza and murder Don? She also realized how all thoughts of the blue sedan had slipped her mind. If Darwin was in contact with his sister as they suspected, the car might be in his name. He could have given it to his sister to use, while he managed the payments and insurance with her living off the grid. If they could cement that, it would go a long way to building the case against him too. "Is that the only vehicle he has?"

"As far as I know," the woman said.

Amanda nodded. No harm in asking, but they'd still check to see if a blue sedan was registered to Darwin.

On the screen, Darwin left the lot.

"Please forward slowly until his return," Trent said to Bob.

Vehicles went in and out, but it wasn't until one thirty AM that Darwin came back.

Amanda looked at Trent. "I'll be damned."

"Uh-huh. Someone took a long lunch," Trent said.

More than that... Darwin had plenty enough time to murder Don, get himself together and get back to work.

Antoine returned and stood in the doorway, holding a thick printout, which she assumed was the timesheet report. "Darwin was late back from meal break on Tuesday night." He pointed at a line on the page, showing he'd clocked in at one forty.

"That's what we're seeing." Amanda nudged her head to the paused video and timestamp. Darwin Shepherd had a lot of explaining to do.

"I guess you didn't need this after all. But I must say my curiosity is getting the best of me. What is his late return telling you?" Antoine asked, and the two security employees were also watching Amanda and Trent, interested in the answer.

"As you assumed before, the reason for our interest is privileged police information. But if you hear from or see Darwin Shepherd, you are to call me immediately." She gave her card to him and Bob and requested that the security manager send a copy of the video to her email. Then she and Trent left Road-runner Solutions.

"So Darwin clocked out to go kill Don Lambert and returned to work like nothing happened," Trent said.

"That's sure what it looks like to me." She pointed to the onboard computer in the car. "We never got around to this yet, but bring up the DMV. Does Darwin have any blue sedans registered to him?"

"One second." Trent's fingers flew over the keyboard, stopped. "Uh-huh. A blue Prius."

"How much do you want to bet that's the blue sedan your aunt mentioned seeing in Marian's driveway?"

"Darwin got it for his sister to use and probably took care of the insurance too. But that raises another question."

"Where is it now?" they voiced in unison.

FORTY-FIVE

Amanda called Malone to inform him about what they found out at Roadrunner Solutions. She declined the offer of further backup from SWAT, arguing a quiet approach might work best. It helped her case with Malone that Darwin Shepherd didn't have any guns registered to him. She also called Logan, and he had handled the news she'd be home late quite well. The time she'd spent with him this weekend had gone a long way to smoothing things out between them. Their relationship finally felt like it was picking up from where it had been before she'd kissed Trent in December.

Darwin Shepherd's pickup was in his driveway, but there was no sign of the blue Prius. He could have left town in the sedan.

Amanda told the officer parked a few houses down to remain on standby while she and Trent went to Darwin's door.

As they approached Darwin's house, she turned to Trent. "As I told Malone, I think it's best we approach Darwin calm, collected, and with an open mind. We might not have it all figured out just right."

"Though the chances are slim we're wrong," Trent muttered.

"I agree. Just be careful, ever aware."

"You bet."

Amanda rang Darwin's doorbell. The curtain on the side-light twitched and was quickly followed by pounding footsteps headed away from them.

A tremor ran through her, a knowing in her gut. "He's making a run for it."

Trent was already ahead of her. He'd jumped from the front stoop and was tearing around the corner of the house. She followed while yelling for the officer to call for more backup.

She ran, catching up with Trent, who was tucked against the side of the house near the back.

The rear screen door rattled in its frame as it was slammed open and hit the siding.

Trent popped around the corner with Amanda, and both had their Glocks at the ready.

"Prince William County PD! Stop!" Amanda called out.

Darwin lifted a gun and immediately fired, sending them scurrying around the corner for cover.

Trent peeked out a moment later. "He's on the move."

She and Trent followed Darwin as he ran toward the back of the lot, which spilled onto a ravine. They kept a distance and juked behind whatever they could for cover or concealment as they huffed it through the yard.

Branches were snapping and breaking underfoot as Darwin made his way down the hillside. Amanda and Trent reached the top, and Darwin stopped, turned, and fired on them again. They both ducked down.

"Good news for us is he has bad aim," she said.

"Finding a bright side in this?"

She shrugged. "I take what I can."

"Personally, I want to strangle that son of a bitch," Trent grumbled.

"After me." She hadn't put off dinner with her family to get a bullet in the head. "We should probably hold back. Wait for more backup."

"No way. We're here. We have to move now, or we could lose him."

"Where's he going to go? He's got no vehicle."

"He has a gun, Amanda. He can hijack one."

The thought of other people being placed in danger put her back in motion. There was a road at the base of the ravine that could be accessed through a small patch of woods. They started down the hill, which had a steep incline. The placement of their steps had to be watched closely. One misstep and—

The ground gave way beneath Amanda's feet. Her gun dropped from her hand as she free-fell, her arms reaching out trying to grab hold of anything she could. Her fingers scrambled, grazing over rock, stones, plants, and tree roots.

Just when she thought this was it, the way she was going to die, she jolted to a stop. Nothing but air beneath her feet, and looking down... *Don't look down!*

"Hold on!" Trent yelled at her.

He'd caught the hood on her jacket, and she was hanging there.

"Try to grab on to something."

Sound advice but easier said than done. She eyed the precipice wall. Nothing that would support her weight. There weren't even any solid-looking footholds. But she just couldn't give up. She had too much to live for. Zoe.

Her fight reignited, she reached out and grabbed hold of a root. But it snapped and fell. She dared to watch it spiral down. The bottom of the ravine must have been a few stories below her. The ground was uneven and rocky. A fall would undoubtedly prove fatal.

"Eyes on me," Trent told her. He was lying down now, his shoulders hanging over the ledge.

"I can't grab anything." Panic seized her chest, and tears burned her eyes. In this contest against gravity, it was the sure winner.

"We're getting you out of this. You hear me? Now, I'm going to take one of my hands off your hood. You need to reach out and grab it. Hear me?"

"I can't."

"You *can*."

Mere seconds likely ticked off, but time was stretched out. She met Trent's gaze.

"On the count of three. One. Two. *Three!*" He let go of her hood, and she thrust out her hand to take his. Their palms latched together in a solid grip. "Now, we're going to do it again," Trent said. "Then I'll have you by both hands."

She wanted to protest that they got lucky once, why press it, but she was infused with adrenaline. "Got it."

He released her hood, and cried out, holding her weight for a fraction of time by one arm. But then their other hands connected. Gravel from the ledge rained on her face, and she looked away to shield her eyes.

"We've got this, okay. Just trust me. Put your feet against the wall and walk up."

Her entire body was trembling, but this was a matter of life and death. She had to overcome her fear if she was going to survive. *We've got this*, she mentally coached herself, while relying on Trent's strength and letting it buoy her. Suddenly, gravity's pull didn't feel as strong. Hope moved in. He pulled, and she did her best to dig the toes of her shoes into the dirt wall and find some purchase points.

"Just a few more inches." Strain was in his voice, but she trusted him to pull her to safety. He moved back as she climbed.

A few more moments of effort, and her elbows were on solid ground. She hoisted the rest of her body up with Trent's help.

She rolled onto her back, looking up at the sky, but her vision was filled with Trent's face looking down at her. He had his upper body leaned over hers. Her heart was beating wildly, but it was no longer from fear of dying. It was from fear of daring to live, to make the choice her heart wanted. "I thought I was going to die," she said, the words leaving her lips in a whisper.

Just when she thought he was going to lean down and kiss her, he stepped back and held out a hand to help her to her feet. "You'll be fine. You're okay?"

"Yeah, I'm..." She brushed dirt and grass off her clothing, anything to distract her from what she was feeling. "Are you?"

He nodded without saying a word. He was holding intense eye contact with her though, and she read that he was feeling the same draw as she was. But there was also a cool edge to his gaze, a wall. Then it edged in and took over. "Shepherd," he pushed out.

"Yeah, we better, ah, get moving."

They made their way around the broken ground, even more careful of their footing than before. Thankfully, they made it to the bottom without any more incidents.

She walked over to where her gun had fallen and searched the area. She found it next to a clump of long grass and lifted it to show Trent. He nodded, and they stood still and listened.

Silence, but for a flock of chirping sparrows that flew up into the sky. Amanda pointed from them to where they had taken flight. Darwin had possibly spooked the birds, and sure enough, he stepped into view and started running away.

"Prince William County PD! Stop!" she yelled as loud as she could.

Darwin looked over his shoulder and fired. The round entered a tree a mere five feet from them.

"His aim seems to be improving," Trent said.

"We need to figure out a way to loop around, surprise him from the front. How about you keep following him and work to flush him out? I'll turn a sharp left and circle back."

"Trap him in the middle? Let's do it."

They both set out, and Amanda was confident this plan was the best and fastest way to bring this little nature outing to a close. She reached the edge of the woods and traced back around. The sound of crunching twigs told her Darwin was coming toward her, though she couldn't see him. Then he stepped into a clearing.

Her heart hammered in her chest as they stood face to face. He had his gun on her, but she had hers trained on him. "PWCPD! Gun down, or I will shoot you!"

Darwin didn't respond and kept walking slowly toward her.

"Stop!"

He continued to advance. If he came one more step closer, she'd have no choice.

And he did.

She squeezed her trigger, and the round met with Darwin's right shoulder. It pushed him backward, and the gun fell from his hand. She rushed over to stop him from retrieving his weapon. "Darwin Shepherd, you're under arrest for—"

He straightened out, the back of his hand catching her unprepared as he struck her across her face. She staggered to keep her balance, as her vision flashed white, and she bit down on her tongue. Blood filled her mouth.

"Stop right there!" Trent yelled.

Darwin almost had his gun in hand when Amanda hip-checked him, and he toppled, falling over. She wasted no time assuming a stance in front of him, her gun leveled at him.

Even then, he reached for his weapon. She stomped on his hand, and he let out a loud howl.

Trent moved in and dragged Darwin to his feet and cuffed him.

A bit too late to the party, the cracking of branches and call-outs notified them of advancing officers.

"Darwin Shepherd, you're under arrest for the murder of Don Lambert," she said and proceeded to prattle off his Miranda rights.

Then she caught her breath.

FORTY-SIX

It was ten thirty the next morning by the time Amanda and Trent were able to question Darwin Shepherd. The round from her gun had hit a tendon in his shoulder, and it had required rather extensive surgery. It was a justified shooting, and she'd face no disciplinary action whatsoever. She even had her regular service weapon back already. Trent finally got his back too from firing it last week.

"Just keep it short," the nurse told Amanda when she and Trent signed in at the desk.

She entered Darwin's room first, and he groaned at the sight of her.

"How did you figure out I killed Don?" he asked as they moved closer toward the bed. "I was careful."

Amanda smiled. "You messed up, like most criminals eventually do. To start, you lied to us. You said you hadn't seen your sister in years, not since she got together with Don."

"What's to say I wasn't telling the truth?"

"Luigi's Pizzeria for lunch two Tuesdays ago ring any bells for you? They got you on video." Trent inserted this gem.

His jaw tightened, and he shook his head. "I told Marian it was too risky being in public together."

"Yet you picked her up for lunch at the animal shelter," Amanda pointed out. "That's what started us looking for you. Of course, we didn't know who her mysterious lunch date was until we found a receipt at your sister's house from Luigi's and saw the video footage. But speaking of your sister, she was stabbed, found in her home." She didn't even bother trying to lessen the blow. After all, if they were completely right about him, he left her dead body there to decompose.

"I had nothing to do with that." He clamped his mouth shut, and tears welled in his eyes.

"We didn't figure you did, but your lack of shock at this news makes me suspect you knew she was dead. When did you find out?" It was possible he'd seen the news on TV or read about the murder, but Amanda was certain their suspicion was correct, and he knew firsthand.

"Two Fridays ago... in the evening. I was going to send her out of town, save her from him. I was too late." Darwin started sobbing, and they gave him a few minutes to compose himself.

It had obviously destroyed him to leave her there, but the point was he still had. His anguish reminded her of an earlier idea she and Trent had talked about though. "It was you who ordered the pasta bowls wasn't it? You were hoping that she'd be found by the delivery guy."

"I hated to think of her just lying there..." A loud gasp.

"Why not take her cat?" Trent asked, and Amanda hoped for some mercy and that he wouldn't reveal everything from the murder scene.

"Cleopatra? That cat hated me. She'd hiss at me from ten feet away."

Silence spread for a few moments. If Darwin knew that cats would eat their dead owners, he didn't go there. Neither did she nor Trent.

"Do you think Don killed her?" Amanda asked.

"Who else would it be?" he volleyed back.

"Did you confront Don at JJ's bar?" They had already shown his picture to Don's friends and Bernie. All of them ID'd Darwin, but she wanted to hear this from him directly.

"What of it?"

"Risky move," she said.

"Yeah, well no one knows me there. That bastard didn't even recognize me."

"You and Marian were planning to burn Don alive for some time, weren't you?" Trent asked.

Darwin remained quiet.

She'd take that as confirmation, and it also explained why he'd left Don at the bar without much fight. His mind was on a larger objective. "When you found out your sister was dead, you decided to go ahead on your own, stick to your original plan," she said, laying out the likely scenario.

"Damn right I did. In her memory. He deserved to suffer for what he'd put her through. She was conscious when the flames started eating her flesh. He needed to feel that same pain, but he still got off easy. My poor sister's suffering continued for the eleven years since the fire. She was left disfigured. People treated her differently. If it wasn't with disdain, it was with pity. Men weren't attracted to her. But, just for the record, all of what I told you wasn't a complete lie. I hadn't seen Marian for years until she reached out last summer. She told me she was tired of hiding and needed to be free of Don once and for all. Asked if I'd help."

The registration on Darwin's Prius showed he'd purchased it back in September. "You bought her a car to use?"

"Yeah."

The Prius had been found in Darwin's garage. "Then she moved into town back in December."

"That's right."

"Why didn't you just let her live with you?" Trent asked.

"Deniability."

Amanda had to admit that had briefly worked.

Darwin winced as he shifted his position on the bed. "I couldn't let my sister take care of it alone. I finally had a chance to get her back in my life. I thought that I could keep her safe but..." His voice turned gravelly, and his eyes became wet. He cleared his throat, and added, "Volunteering at the shelter part-time was her idea. She said being around animals gave her peace. I worked longer hours, but she had time to study Don's movements. Which you've probably deduced by now. She insisted on taking pictures. I warned her not to but..."

"We found the photographs." They'd also received Marian's phone records from the service provider which confirmed the siblings had been in touch. Marian must have simply deleted the call history from the physical device. "How did she know where to start to find Don?"

"He's worked at the same place all these years. It wasn't hard. She followed him from there."

It was almost scary how easy it was to track people down. "Only Don found out she was following him..."

"Yeah, and he started stalking her. She was terrified, but she chose the plaza as where she wanted to strike. From her stalking, she found out about his trips to the plaza twice a month. We missed the first, and there was no way I was waiting until the fifteenth after what he did to Mary. I left work on Tuesday for my meal break and went to his house. I wasn't there long when he went out. I followed, already prepared to do what needed to be done. I had the jerry can of gasoline in the bed of my truck. And, as if it were poetic justice, he ended up near Patriot Plaza. It was as if Mary's ghost were leading him there. The method was an easy choice. Eye for an eye."

Amanda was somewhat surprised by how forthcoming Darwin was being about everything, but it would seem he needed to clear his conscience. Maybe he also viewed owning up to his crime as punishment for not protecting his sister from Don. In the past and recently. "But you were there for your sister. And it was before last summer. Not long after the house fire?"

"No foolin' you."

She recognized Darwin's lie immediately, but she had Marian's bank records to thank for that. Her account was opened ten years ago, and regular monthly deposits traced back to Darwin. "You've been nothing but helpful to your sister. Did you help her form her new identity as Paula Dunn way back then?"

"Yes."

Amanda nodded, her inkling spot on. "So you got her a new ID, homes along the way, vehicles...?"

"Yes."

"And you helped her financially," she said.

"She ran out of money. What was I supposed to do? She was my sister." Fresh tears fell, and he wiped them away.

Amanda couldn't help but think of the old saying about revenge and the need to dig two graves. In this case the casualty tally was three, only Darwin's would be in a metaphorical sense. He'd spend the rest of his life behind bars. But with the focus on money, Amanda wanted to discuss something else. "We found an ATM slip that showed Marian withdrew two thousand dollars the day she was murdered, but we've never recovered it. Can you tell us what happened to the money?"

Darwin licked his lips and briefly glanced away. "I took it. I'm not proud of that fact, but it wasn't going to do her good anymore."

"Just like the Prius. You reclaimed it?"

He nodded. "Took a couple trips back and forth because I had driven to her house in my truck. My poor, sweet sister. I'm not sorry about what I did, and I'd do it again in a heartbeat. That shit deserved what he got." He reiterated the sentiment he'd made earlier, meeting Amanda's eye with a defiant and cold gaze.

"Are you willing to put all that you told us in writing?" she asked.

"Sure. There's nothing else left for me. Mary was all I had. I don't have money socked away for lawyers, and it's obviously too late to run."

Trent gave Darwin a notepad and a pen.

It wasn't often they obtained a written confession, but it was refreshing when it happened. Not that the road to here had been easy. They'd been shot at, and she'd almost fallen to her death. She swallowed hard on that, tried to focus on Darwin writing his confession. Otherwise, she'd dwell on the fact that when she thought her time was up, Logan hadn't come to mind. And it might not mean any more than her focus being on Zoe, the little girl, who truly needed her. Logan would move on much easier.

As she and Trent left the hospital with Darwin's signed confession, Amanda's phone rang. It was CSI Blair, and she put her on speaker.

"I've got news that will make your day," she said.

Amanda smiled at Trent, but he didn't return the expression. His mouth was tense. No doubt his mind was on the fact that while they had solved Don Lambert's murder, they only had a strong suspicion that Don had killed Marian Shepherd. Gertrude was still a suspect in that case. "Let us have it," Amanda replied.

"CCTV footage from Marian Shepherd's aka Paula Dunn's neighborhood came back. It shows Don in his Buick Encore driving into Marian's neighborhood just after five o'clock Friday evening and leaving about five forty."

Trent was smiling now. "And, as we thought, Marian's

blood found on his front passenger mat was likely transfer from the knife."

"I'd say more than likely," Blair said. "It also explains why there was such a small amount. The knife was wrapped in a woman's scarf too. Though more accurately, not just any scarf, but a hijab."

"A hijab." Amanda latched on to that. "Can you tell me what it looks like, the color or pattern?"

"A dark teal."

"Sounds like the one Marian wore to Luigi's," Amanda said, mostly to Trent.

"I also have a confession," Blair started. "Don's SUV was dripping oil. I noticed this on Ingrid Street, but I couldn't be sure it was from his vehicle or one that had parked in that spot previously. But I also found oil in Marian Shepherd's driveway, and in your aunt's, Trent. These samples all match. I didn't want to mention this until I ran the tests. The last thing I wanted was to get your hopes up and it not pan out. I'm sorry if my holding this back until now upsets you."

"No need to apologize," Trent said. "This puts Don's vehicle at the scene of Marian's murder and paired with the CCTV footage, this clears my aunt. I knew she couldn't kill anyone. My aunt is innocent."

"That she is. Don killed Marian Shepherd." Amanda smiled at Trent.

"Thank God this is finally over," he said and added, "Thank you, Emma."

"Hey, I just follow the evidence, but I'm glad it ended up working out in your aunt's favor." With that, Blair ended the call.

Trent was looking at Amanda, smiling. "I can't wait to tell her the good news. She's free to go."

He drove them toward Central, and Amanda's mind tossed

over how things had worked out. There was closure and justice, even if it came in different forms. While Don would never face a day in prison, he had paid the ultimate price. The one thing niggling for her was how Don had discovered Marian was back in town.

FORTY-SEVEN

Being able to release his aunt made Trent one happy man, but his nerves were frayed as he pulled into his parents' driveway that night. Aunt Gertrude was in the front passenger seat of his Jeep.

He looked over at her. "You're ready for this?"

"As ready as I'll ever be." She took his hand over the console and squeezed. "You're sure your mother is all right with my just showing up after all this time?"

"She's waited for this day to come. Trust me." He moved for his door, but his aunt stayed put. "What is it?"

"I'm so sorry for the way I've treated you. Not just since Don was murdered, but before that." A tear splashed her cheek, and she wiped it away. "I was just so afraid of Don, of what he might do. Not to me but to you. He said he'd shoot you if you showed up at the door one more time. That's why I was so cruel the last time. I couldn't risk you coming back."

Trent's heart softened. At the time he thought he could convince her to leave with him, that he'd protect her from Don. Meanwhile, she'd been that way to protect *him*. Her apology didn't wipe out all the pain she'd inflicted over the years, but it came awfully close. He was eager to leave the past behind and move forward. "Thank you for the apology and your explanation. At least now, you have nothing to fear."

"My head knows that. But it's hard to fully shake my fear of that man." She leaned forward and cried into her hands.

"I will do whatever I can to help."

She reached into her purse for a tissue and dabbed her nose. "I love you, Trent. You've always been a great kid, and you've become an incredible man. I see that you've made an excellent life for yourself."

"Thank you."

"You and Amanda, is it?" He nodded, and his aunt continued. "You make an excellent pair. Am I right to believe there's something between you?"

His aunt's astute observation cut through him, but it would have sliced even deeper if he hadn't resolved to set his feelings for Amanda aside. She had repeatedly made it clear that she was with Logan. To continue fantasizing about a future together, he'd be throwing away his life. "We're just partners, but we do care for each other."

"Oh, I thought I sensed more than that. A chemistry between you."

His aunt didn't need to tell him and, damn, after coming so close to losing her at the ravine, it had taken all his willpower not to kiss her. Though his thinking was flawed. Amanda wasn't his to lose. "Yeah, well... She's involved with someone, and so am I."

"You are? Tell me all about her." She smiled, and the expression thawed his soul. It had been such a terribly long time since he'd seen it.

"Her name is Kelsey, and she's great. We've been seeing each other for about five or six months now."

"Sounds serious."

He nodded. "It could be. You'll love her."

"I'd love to meet her, as I'm sure the rest of the family would." His aunt bobbed her eyebrows.

He'd forgotten about this aspect of his aunt's personality. The matchmaker. "One day maybe." The thought of making the introduction had crossed his mind, but he let some insecurities hold him back. Kelsey Pierce was ambitious and had a beautiful soul. She understood him to the extent she could, not being a cop, and she really listened when he spoke. What if his invitation struck her as moving their relationship along too fast and she bailed? But really, what was the worst she could say? And if she got spooked by this next step, then they weren't meant for each other. It was better to find out sooner than later. Being reunited with his aunt and witnessing how strong of a woman she was infused him with some confidence. "But for now we better get inside." He pointed to his parents' house.

"Just before we do, there's one more thing I need to tell you. It's been killing me to hold it back."

The atmosphere in the car changed. Whatever she was about to say was monumental.

"I saw it all." Her voice was small, a sliver above a whisper, and it sent shivers running down the back of his neck and arms.

"Saw what?"

"I haven't been fully truthful with you, or forthcoming. But technically you never asked if I saw Don's murder."

He swallowed roughly. "You saw it?" The question scraped from his throat, and she nodded.

"The whole thing."

"Why didn't you tell me or call the police at the time?"

"I didn't want to get involved, Trent. I just... I could see myself going to prison. And I almost did anyway. Thankfully you believed in me."

"I did." The words were barely audible. If his aunt had said something sooner, would the case have been wrapped up faster? Or would the outcome have been what his aunt had feared?

"I'm sorry I didn't tell you this before now, Trent, but I really was afraid."

Trent took a few moments to assimilate his aunt's admission but came to conclude it wouldn't have made a difference. Not a good one anyhow. It would have certainly pigeon-holed the investigation. "I understand."

"Oh, thank you for that and bless you. I wasn't sure how you'd take it, but I needed to tell you. I couldn't have that hanging between us as we move forward."

"I appreciate that." He gently tapped the back of his aunt's hand. "Don hurt you for ten years, but now you're free of him. No more being afraid, okay? You have your family by your side, now and always."

A few tears fell down his aunt's cheeks, but she was quick to smile. She pointed at the front window. "They're getting impatient." Trent's father and his sisters were standing there, and his mother was likely at the door.

"Then, let's not keep them waiting anymore." He left the Jeep and walked around to his aunt's side to help her get out.

His parents and two sisters were standing just inside the front door by the time Trent and his aunt got there. When his mother and aunt ran into each other's arms, there wasn't a dry eye in the place. Including Trent's.

He supposed if the last couple of weeks had taught him anything, it was that a person should seize every moment. He excused himself for a couple of minutes to call Kelsey. Any doubts he had about inviting her to meet his family washed away when he heard her voice. That brought a smile to his face.

Amanda could have gone home for the night, but she was determined to check off one final thing. Gratefully, Logan agreed to hold off dinner so the three of them could eat together.

She entered Java Stop. Unless Don caught on to Marian

outside his work, the coffee shop was a strong contender for where she was discovered. And maybe it didn't really matter in the grand scheme of things. The case was closed, but she liked answers to all the questions.

"You again?" Tanner groaned when she reached the counter.

"I shouldn't be too long." It was a caveat she didn't really have the right to offer, but if her hunch was right, she might make good on it.

"You need to see more video?"

She smiled at him. "You should be the detective."

Tanner told another server on shift they were on their own for a bit, and they walked to the back office.

"For when?" he asked.

"Let's say the first and fifteenth of each month starting with December, between eleven thirty and midnight." Darwin had confirmed he and his sister knew Don was in this area on those days. It wasn't a stretch to think they knew about the coffee shop and bookie either.

"You're kidding me."

"Nope."

"Okay. You'll need to handle this on your own." Tanner told her how to load the footage and returned to the front, leaving her to watch.

She watched those specific days in December and nada. On January first, she caught her first glimpse of a woman in a teal hijab. It concealed most of her face, revealing only her eyes. She was seated in the back corner of the shop, positioned within line of sight to where Don and Seth were seated and making an exchange.

As Amanda continued to watch the video, it didn't seem Don paid her any attention. Amanda brought up the video for January fifteenth and so on. Each time she spotted Marian.

It wasn't until April fifteenth that Don gave any inkling that he'd even noticed the woman. That night, he stopped next to her table before leaving. Marian turned away, but he smiled before he headed through the doors to the lot.

Amanda stopped the video. Her last curiosity was now satisfied. Don had first discovered he had a stalker at Java Stop about two weeks before her murder. This left him time to flip things around and follow her, find out where she lived and plan how he was going to finish her off. Maybe he thought that trapping her in another house fire would quickly point back to him, and that's why he chose to stab her instead. Trent's theory about Don wanting to frame Gertrude also had merit. In true Don fashion, he must have used the time to torture her mentally. Gertrude had said she followed him once to Marian's where he just turned around in the driveway.

There was no way around it. Life was messy. It was affected by the people surrounding us. While some relationships lifted our spirits, others were toxic. Dwelling on this, Amanda was grateful for her circle. She had been blessed, but there was one thing she couldn't ignore any longer. It was either time to commit to her future with Logan or let him go. But would it be her head or her heart that would win out? It was something she gave deep thought to as she left the coffee shop and headed home.

A LETTER FROM CAROLYN

Dear reader,

I want to say a huge thank you for choosing to read *The Wildfire Girl*. If you enjoyed it and would like to hear about new releases in the Amanda Steele series, just sign up at the following link. Your email address will never be shared, and you can unsubscribe at any time.

www.bookouture.com/carolyn-arnold

If you loved *The Wildfire Girl*, I would be incredibly grateful if you would write a brief, honest review. This book highlighted a personal gratitude of mine. I've been so blessed by being surrounded with good men in my life. All of them respect and admire that I am a strong, independent, and ambitious woman. But, sadly, not all men are of the same mind. There are some who, like Don Lambert in this book, treat women as less-than. Some are verbally abusive, while others also resort to their fists. It's sickening to think that in this day and age when society claims to be so advanced, domestic violence still exists.

In fact, statistics tell us that on average, every minute twenty people were physically assaulted by their partner in the United States in 2023! That number is unacceptable. Any number but zero shouldn't be tolerated.

My heart goes out to the women and men (because that happens too!) who find themselves in this situation. I hope that they will one day find their inner strength and a way to get out of these situations. There are organizations and people out there willing to help. Please, take their hands.

For the abusive partners, we can only hope that one day they will wake up and realize how their behavior is unacceptable. I realize all this may sound like a pipe dream, but it starts with one household, then two, then more. My wish is that one day we will see peace in all homes, that family will become a refuge for everyone, not just those who are "lucky" enough. We all deserve to be loved and cared for as we, in turn, spread the same.

But as I was saying, I hope you loved *The Wildfire Girl*, and will be joining me for more Detective Amanda Steele in the future. You will know if you're familiar with Prince William County that that I've taken creative liberties and built it into a fictional world of my making.

Also, if you'd like to continue investigating murder, you'll be happy to know I also offer several other bestselling series for you to savor—everything from crime fiction, to cozy mysteries, to thrillers and action adventures. One of these series features Detective Madison Knight, another kick-ass female detective, who will risk her life, her badge—whatever it takes—to find justice for murder victims.

If you enjoy being in the Prince William County, Virginia, area, you might want to return in my Brandon Fisher FBI series. It takes part in the expanded world of Amanda Steele, as her best friend is dating Brandon. But these books are perfect for readers who love heart-pounding thrillers and are fascinated with the psychology of serial killers. Each installment is a new case with a fresh bloody trail to follow. Hunt with the FBI's Behavioral Analysis Unit and profile some of the most devious and darkest minds on the planet.

I would also like to thank my husband for his continued support.

Last but certainly not least, I love hearing from my readers! You can get in touch on my social media, or my website. This is also a good way to stay notified of my new releases. You can also reach out to me via email at Carolyn@CarolynArnold.net.

Wishing you a thrill a word!

Carolyn Arnold

www.carolynarnold.net

f facebook.com/AuthorCarolynArnold

X x.com/Carolyn_Arnold

g goodreads.com/carolyn_arnold

PUBLISHING TEAM

Turning a manuscript into a book requires the efforts of many people. The publishing team at Bookouture would like to acknowledge everyone who contributed to this publication.

Audio
Alba Proko
Sinead O'Connor
Melissa Tran

Commercial
Lauren Morrissette
Hannah Richmond
Imogen Allport

Cover design
Head Design Ltd

Data and analysis
Mark Alder
Mohamed Bussuri

Editorial
Claire Simmonds
Jen Shannon

Copyeditor
Fraser Crichton

Proofreader
Becca Allen

Marketing
Alex Crow
Melanie Price
Occy Carr
Ciara Rosney
Martyna Młynarska

Operations and distribution
Marina Valles
Stephanie Straub

Production
Hannah Snetsinger
Mandy Kullar
Jen Shannon

Publicity
Kim Nash
Noelle Holten
Jess Readett
Sarah Hardy

Rights and contracts
Peta Nightingale
Richard King
Saidah Graham

Printed in the USA
CPSIA information can be obtained
at www.ICGtesting.com
LVHW092119100824
787938LV00005B/109